Also by Ron Schwab

The Lockes

Last Will

Medicine Wheel

Hell's Fire

The Law Wranglers

Deal with the Devil

Mouth of Hell

The Last Hunt

Summer's Child

Adam's First Wife

Escape from El Gato

The Prince of Santa Fe

Peyote Spirits

The Coyote Saga

Night of the Coyote

Return of the Coyote

Twilight of the Coyote

The Blood Hounds

The Blood Hounds

No Man's Land

Looking for Trouble

Snapp vs. Snapp

Lucky Five

Old Dogs

Day of the Dog

Lockwood

The Accidental Sheriff

Beware a Pale Horse

Trouble

Sioux Sunrise

Paint the Hills Red

Grit

Cut Nose

The Long Walk

Coldsmith

Ghost of the Guadalupe

Bushwa

Unbroken

Dismal Trail

The Wolf's Mouth

Ron Schwab

Uplands Press
OMAHA, NEBRASKA

Uplands Press
512 S 51st Street
Omaha, NE 68106
www.uplandspress.com

Ordering Information:
Quantity sales. Special discounts are available on quantity purchases by corporations, associations, and others. For details, contact the "Special Sales Department" at the address above.

Uplands Press / Ron Schwab -- 1st ed.
ISBN 978-1-943421-81-7

The Wolf's Mouth

Chapter 1

GINNY HARWOOD WAS astride her blue roan mare, Artemis, in the rolling hills north of the Canadian River in the Texas panhandle, when she heard gunfire coming from the direction of the family trading post a mile to the southeast. It was a balmy late April morning, a sleepy day she had been savoring as the bright sun was just starting to bathe her neck and shoulders.

She had been checking the small cowherd for newborn calves and possible injuries or ailments that might need attention. If necessary, she could cut a cow from the herd, and with the help of her black and white shepherd dog, Skipper, drive the animal back to the farmstead's small barn for attention. But now the gunshots grabbed her attention, and she turned Artemis back south and rode to the top of a ridge calling to her dog to follow.

"Skipper, let's go, boy." Skipper had been more interested in a rabbit bouncing across the prairie, but he obeyed and wheeled and ran after her.

Now Ginny saw smoke rising from the farmstead, too black and thick to be coming from the woodstove, which was mostly for cooking since the passing of winter. She plucked the spyglass from her saddlebags and focused it on the farmstead where the log home with trading post attached and barn and corrals were located. The distance was too far to make out much detail, but she saw the flames engulfing the house and trading post and dancing along the barn roof.

Her heart raced, and she reined Artemis down the slope onto a deer and cattle trail that snaked through the hills that led to the farmstead. When she emerged onto the flatlands that edged the building site, her first instinct was to turn back and run for her life. Artemis could outrun most critters.

But then she saw her father. Pa was stretched out on the ground while an Indian carved on his scalp. She pulled her Winchester from its scabbard, levered a cartridge into the chamber, aimed, and squeezed the trigger. The warrior gloried for just an instant with the dark-haired scalp in one hand and knife in the other before the rifle cracked and a slug drove into his chest, dropping him next to his victim.

She could see a half dozen of the raiders scattered about and assumed there were others outside her line of vision. There were at least three other Indians, but one stocky man was Negro, and another full-bearded man was white. Judging from his wide-brimmed hat and boots, she thought the other might be Mexican. Strangely, none had noticed her yet, apparently because they were absorbed with collecting the horses and were accustomed to the sound of gunfire. She was also partially hidden by the smoke and dust that shrouded the melee.

She started to fire her rifle again when she was interrupted by her mother's screaming from the front of the burning house. Skipper started barking and shot past her, obviously headed for her mother. Ginny moved in closer now, so she could see around the corner where she spied Helen Harwood's naked form, a young white man with his britches dropped towering over her. Skipper tore into the man with fierce growling and teeth gnashing, fastening his jaw on the attacker's thigh. With his trousers tangled around his ankles, the attacker lost his balance and toppled over, landing on the stone walk that led from the hitching rail to the trading post. Skipper was on him instantly, tearing at his face and neck, but she could not get a clear shot at the man with the dog in the way.

She saw Ma trying to roll over and crawl away, but she barely moved, and then she saw the blood streaming down her abdomen and nearly gagged at the mutilation of her breasts. Ma was clearly bleeding out, dying. Rage overtook her fear now, and she barely felt the slug that ripped into her shoulder as she reined around the corner of the house to get to her mother's side. She heard the gunfire and saw Skipper drop limp over his enemy's chest, his furry body riddled with bullet holes. She was sobbing now, oblivious to the blood that soaked the neck and shoulder of her own shirt, and she dismounted and walked toward the son-of-a-bitch working his way out from beneath her old friend. She was going to put a slug in his brain before she died.

She stopped abruptly when she was yanked back by an arm that lifted her from her feet and pulled her back against the chest of some rancid-breathed animal that held her like a vice, forcing her to watch while a warrior split her mother's forehead with a war axe and then knelt beside her and began to take her scalp. "Sick bastard," Ginny screamed, pulling to escape and get to the warrior. Then she froze when she saw Ricky's body sprawled in the yard beyond the hitching rail. Her little brother was dead, too.

Suddenly, she began to retch, the pressure on her neck forcing most of the vomit back into her throat, choking her and triggering a coughing fit. Then she heard her sisters crying and screaming. She saw them now mounted on horses being led away by three of the warriors who were departing. They were alive, but to what end? What would these bastards do to them?

The grip on her neck relaxed and a hand closed on her wrist and yanked her around to face her captor. He was the black-bearded man she had seen earlier. He was a bearish man, tall and beefy with a few stubs of rotted teeth in his smug grin. "Okay, bitch. You and me's gonna have us a good time before you take that last breath."

She was ready to die, but she would be damned if this ugly beast would get his poke without a fight. Then she glimpsed the sheathed skinning knife on his belt. She feigned trying to pull away before she stepped toward him, clutched the knife's hilt, pulled it free and drove the blade into his fleshy side just below the ribcage. He howled with pain and stumbled back, his hand cupped over the wound. He drew back his hand and for a moment appeared mesmerized by the blood, before he glared at her. She still clutched the knife, pointing the blade toward him, ready to take another swipe if she got a chance. This time she would strike for his male parts.

The man saw that she was not surrendering and drew his pistol from its holster and aimed it. She knew now that the end was coming.

"No," a voice came from off to her right.

She looked up and, some twenty feet distant, saw a mounted warrior holding a bow with a nocked arrow. The left side of his face was painted black and the right side white where a jagged scar ran from below this eye to the cheek bone. He was a ghostlike figure, the only warrior stripped to his waist, his arms and torso rippling with muscle. A gray wolf's skin was draped over his head and shoulders, falling down his back. It was anchored with a rawhide strip around his neck and part of the skin with vacant eyes and upper nose formed a cap on his head.

She clung to her knife and met his gaze challengingly as if daring him to approach. He seemed to be studying her as though pondering something.

Finally, he spoke. "Do not shoot her. Take no scalp. Warrior Woman will die like warrior." He raised the bow with the nocked arrow, pulled back the bowstring, and released the arrow, driving it so deeply into her abdomen that part of the arrowhead protruded from her back.

Ginny looked down at the arrow sticking out of her gut. She was going to die, but she didn't feel any pain, not yet anyhow. She saw her rifle lying on the ground not more than ten feet away. She was not finished. That damned Indian would die with her. Slowly, she staggered toward the rifle, but just before she bent over to pick it up, another arrow struck her between the shoulder blades. This time the pain was agonizing but brief, ending quickly when she plunged forward and collapsed on the ground facedown, and blackness descended and bestowed relief.

Chapter 2

CONGRAVE CLINTON CALLAWAY cinched the saddle on his buckskin gelding and anchored the bedroll and saddlebags, then double-checked Chester the white mule's load to confirm it was secured. Satisfied, he led his mount and pack mule from the stable to the front of the headquarters house of the Triple C Ranch where his older brother Clifford Caesar Callaway III waited with a scowl on his face and arms folded across his chest. Congrave, or "Con" as most called him, had dreaded the final confrontation, but it would be a relief to get past it.

Clifford glared at Con as he approached, his steel-gray eyes peering from beneath thick black eyebrows, his sneer not hidden by the handlebar mustache that dominated his face. Con's brother, at age thirty-five, was slightly more than ten years older than his only sibling and was an imposing figure standing at three inches over six feet, barrel-chested and thick-waisted. Con, only a few inches shorter, was not dwarfed by his brother but was lean and sinewy and certainly far less vocal than Clifford, who tended to be a loud and bullying sort. Truth was that Con from early childhood had been half afraid of his older sibling, always walking on eggshells to escape Clifford's taunts and outright wrath triggered by some usually imagined misdeed.

"So you're really going to pull out, desert the family ranch."

"It's not the family ranch. Pa left it all to you, and that's fine with me. But I've got no reason to stay. Pa's been gone five years, and I never knew our mother. Besides, I never spent much time here growing up. I just think it's time for me to move on."

"I had in mind for you being foreman here someday. If you hadn't gone off and joined the Army, you would have been well on your way by now. You'll be slinking back here within a year with your tail between your legs, and I won't give you that chance then."

"Time will tell, I guess."

"I'd still up my offer on the five hundred acres Pa left you down by the Canadian River to ten dollars an acre.

That's five thousand dollars. You wouldn't earn that much in five or six years punching cattle."

"Like I told you, Clifford, it's not for sale."

"There ain't no other buyers for that hill country."

"I suppose not." He mounted his buckskin, Quanah, named for the Comanche chief he purchased the horse from at Fort Sill during the last days of his enlistment.

Clifford said, "Are you going to tell me where the hell you're headed?"

"I'm going south to look at my place on the Canadian. After that I'll be heading east, west, or farther south."

"That ain't telling me a damn thing."

"I've told you all I know." He reined Quanah away and rode down the wagon trail leading south from the ranch, Chester hitched to a lead rope following behind. Several miles later, he passed the Triple C's south boundary. The ranch consisted of about twelve thousand acres of grassland owned by Clifford Callaway and another ten thousand acres of public lands grazed by Triple C cattle rent-free till some bureaucrat objected. Con suspected that somebody at the United States Department of Interior was taking bribes to close his eyes. Clifford seemed confident he would purchase the land soon, likely with assistance from the same bureaucrat who would be paid well for his services.

The ranch claimed a spot in the northeast corner of the Texas panhandle with Indian Territory as the east boundary and butting up against an area identified on maps as "Public Land Strip" on the north. This tract consisted of a strip of land about thirty-five miles wide running east and west and slightly over 160 miles long, and it was commonly called "No Man's Land" because it was not apportioned to any state or territory and had no laws or authorized lawmen. Accordingly, it was a hideaway for lawbreakers and sinners of every sort. It also tended to make the Triple C an easy target for rustlers, forcing Clifford to hire his own gunslingers to protect his herds.

In addition to Texas on the south, No Man's Land stopped at the border of New Mexico Territory on the west and parts of Colorado and Kansas on the north. At this time, in the spring of 1878, Clifford aspired to own a chunk of the strip after Congress got the chaotic area untangled and assigned a home.

The Triple C's name represented the initials of Con's father, Clifford Caesar Callaway II. He knew nothing about his grandfather who first carried the name, other than his claimed link to English nobility of some sort. Con had not expected any inheritance from his father, so the will's provision that gave him the Canadian parcel was a surprise. His father had always made it clear that the Triple C spread and its herds would pass to his eldest son, a European tradition that many in the new country still followed.

Con saw a rider leading a pack horse nearly a half mile to the west moving across the prairie toward him. As the figure neared, he recognized the distinctive black and white spotted mount owned by Ezra Stumpf and the sorrel horse that was doing pack animal duty this day. Then, as he got a better look at the rider, he saw the coonskin cap, not so common these days. He reined in Quanah and waited. Ezra rode up to him with a grin, absent two front teeth, appearing from a full white beard past due for trimming.

"Howdy, Con. I heard you was pulling out, and I'd already decided to take leave of that butt-headed brother of yours, so I figured I might ride with you for a spell, if y'all don't mind."

"Well, you'd be welcome company," Con said with some reservation. He tended to be satisfied with his own company most of the time, and Ezra was inclined to talk a steady stream. "I don't know where I'm headed, but I'll know when I get there."

"Hell, that's the way I've lived my whole life since my mountain man days in the thirties and forties right up to now. Never stayed more than two years anyplace, excepting three with the Comanche. My two years at the Triple C was up a few weeks back by my count."

"Let's ride then. I want to visit some land along the Canadian River I'm supposed to own. I've never been there and want to see if I can locate it before I move on."

"How you gonna find it if you ain't never seen it?"

"I've got landmarks written down, but I've got doubts that the ownership is even recorded anyplace. Still, my brother wanted to buy the place. That made me think it's not worthless."

"You don't trust the son-of-a-bitch either, do you?"

That night they camped in a small canyon that Con judged to be no more than a half day's ride to the Canadian River. The canyon was less than fifty feet deep but offered fresh water that trickled from the sandstone wall into a natural basin at the base, which overflowed to form a stream that provided water for the critters.

Con did not mind when Ezra volunteered to fix supper, if he would take care of laying and starting a fire. The old codger limped slowly about the campsite but scavenged the supplies they had unloaded from both the pack animals till he found what he wanted, while Con searched out fallen branches from the scattering of trees in the canyon. Cottonwood and cedar did not make good firewood, but he could not collect oak or ash if none existed in the canyon.

He got a smoky fire started, and by the time Ezra was ready to put the Dutch oven on some coals, he was able to scrape out enough for a baking bed. Ezra took a little hand scoop from his supplies and spread some coals on the oven lid to furnish top heat. It wasn't long before Con could smell biscuits baking and beans and bacon slices heating in the frying pan, and he found himself suddenly starving.

As dusk settled over the rugged prairie lands, the men sat by the fire eating from their tin plates. Con said, "Good grub, Ezra. The biscuits are perfect, and it appears there will be plenty for breakfast."

"That was the idea. Likely, it will be biscuits and coffee."

"Suits me fine. Triple C is going to miss its chuck house cook. What did Clifford say about you leaving?"

"Nothing. I didn't tell him. Got up to date on pay last week and decided it was time to move on. I suppose he'll be madder than a rattler on a hot skillet by now."

"It won't put him in a good mood, that's for dang sure."

"That man's only got one mood—sour."

Con shrugged. "You might be right."

"You ain't never been too tight with your brother, have you? I noticed you sort of stayed away from him when you could, and you always ate at the chuck house with the hands instead of with the family in the ranch house."

"I'm more than ten years younger than Clifford. My mother died giving birth to me. My ma's sister, my aunt Kate Moore, was there to care for me, and after six months my father agreed that she could take me back to Fort Larned in Kansas where she had been teaching school. I was raised at the fort, and that's where I got the notion I belonged in the Army."

"And you was in the Army near five years as I recollect?"

"Yes. I loved life at the fort, but we moved to Dodge City when I was thirteen, and Aunt Kate continued as a schoolteacher there. I realized later that Aunt Kate had made the move because Fort Larned did not offer high school, and she was determined I get an education. We shared a house owned by Aunt Kate's friend, a lady I came to call Aunt Judy, who was also a schoolteacher." He was not about to tell the old codger that he later figured out that Aunt Kate and Aunt Judy, neither of whom was yet fifty years old, had been more than friends since their own school days in Kansas City.

"Y'all didn't see your pa and brother all them years?"

"After I was six or so, Aunt Kate took me to visit every summer for a month, sometimes two, but she always went with me, riding horseback with a rifle in her scabbard. I think she feared my father would try to keep me because there were some loud fusses starting a few days before we were going to leave. After I was fourteen, it became my choice, and she didn't stay on during the summer visits. I always went back to Dodge City, though. My father and Clifford yelled at me over leaving the ranch, but by then I had my own horse and rifle, and there was no way they could hold me. I think Clifford resented my being there even though he was a grown man by then, but he put on an act for my father."

"So you're an educated man?"

"Finished high school. I suppose that qualifies in this part of the country. I know I disappointed Aunt Kate some by enlisting in the Army and not going on to college, but she accepted it. I write from wherever I'm at, and she always answered when I was in the Army, but her letters wouldn't catch up with me for months. I hope to settle someplace soon, and then we can stay in touch better. I'll go visit, too, and with the railroad growing like it is, maybe she and Aunt Judy can come visit me."

"Never writ a letter to nobody. Never learned the reading and writing stuff but like to think I learnt me some other things along the way."

"Aunt Kate said that if we pay attention, everything we do is an education. I heard you talking about your years with the Comanches. You even learned some of the language, I think you said."

"Good enough to get by."

"I rode with General Ranald Slidell Mackenzie. I chased and fought the Comanche all over the Southwest for almost five years, but I never learned a word of the language. It would have sure come in handy, though."

"One of the fellers said you was a sergeant."

"First sergeant. I was offered a second lieutenant's commission if I would reenlist for three years. It took me about a minute to say 'no thanks.' I'd had my fill of Army life by then. Not sorry I did it—part of my education—but I knew by then I didn't want to make that my life."

"But y'all don't know where you're going or what you're going to do?"

Con shrugged. "I'll know when I stumble across it."

"Well, I found it early on. I learned quick that I like wandering. I lost count, but I'm several years past seventy now, and I ain't sure what happens if I can't get around no more. Hoping I just drop off my horse and die someday or that some kind soul puts a lead slug in my head."

"You never wanted a family, I take it?"

He did not answer directly. "Had one once when I was with the Comanches. Had me a woman and two kids, a boy and a girl. This was long before the whites started hogging all the space. Some Mexican traders came to the village and brung the smallpox with them. That kilt my family but lots slower than bullets. I'd planned to move on after the next buffalo hunt and take them with me into the mountains up north of Santa Fe. I waited too long."

"I'm sorry. I never knew."

"Hardly ever talk about it. I look to make folks laugh with most of my stories. Just a reminder that we never know what's over the next dang hill."

It never took much to kill Con's mood for talking. He got to his feet. "I'll tend to clean up. I'd like to hit the trail not long after sunrise, so we'll probably want to grab our shuteye soon."

Chapter 3

CON AND EZRA rode at a leisurely pace this morning, taking time to view the countryside as they headed south. It was late morning, and Ezra, having passed through the area often over the years, estimated that the Canadian River should not be more than an hour distant. They figured they would have lunch and rest the mounts on the riverside before commencing their search for the property.

Con understood that the property he supposedly owned was along the north bank of the Canadian River and that the east boundary was Indian Territory, but he was not confident he and Ezra could even locate it. Five hundred acres comprised a laughably small tract in West Texas, especially when weighed against the ranch owned and operated by Charles Goodnight and John Adair. Several days' ride southwest in the Palo Duro Canyon area, that ranch approached 100,000 acres.

Clifford had only informed Con a month earlier of his inheritance along the Canadian River and provided him with a drawing showing boundary landmarks. Before that disclosure, Clifford had not even shared the contents of their father's will, although Clifford Caesar Callaway II had been dead for over five years. Con had never had an expectation of inheritance, his brother being the elder son and Con having had so little to do with the ranch over the years. But why had Clifford waited so long to make the disclosure and immediately started to press for purchase? He supposed that the place had been targeted as a strategic location for future ranch expansion.

Most land in the panhandle had not yet been legally surveyed, and property lines were frequently disputed, thus keeping the lawyers well-fed. The drawing showed the Canadian River as the south boundary of the tract and the line between Texas and Indian Territory as the east line. But even that line was defined by stones, presumably placed by the first claimant. The surveyed line might establish something entirely different. If he decided he cared about the land and had a purpose for it, he would likely need to seek the guidance of a law wrangler.

Con just had not wanted to sell Clifford a parcel of land he had not yet seen.

The prairie lands over which the riders traveled was an area of contrasts, stretches of rolling hills that suddenly gave way to flatlands and then to rocky ridges. There had been several big snows this winter and life-giving spring rains, so the hills and flatlands were carpeted with many shades of green today. He knew this country often turned dry, sucking the moisture from the earth and turning the greens quickly to dying browns, but still there was something about these open spaces and the remoteness that called to him.

He reined Quanah nearer to Mort, the sorrel gelding Ezra was riding today. "Ezra, are you smelling smoke?"

"Yep. I have been for a spell, and it ain't a grass fire. Too strong to be coming from a woodstove. It's said Injuns ain't been causing so much trouble in Texas these days, leastways this far north, but this kind of smoke always perked my eyes and ears up. Not a time for us to be dozing in the saddle."

The old coot spent half his saddle time sleeping, something Con had seen a fair number of soldiers do but a sometimes-helpful knack he had never acquired. With the possibilities of Comanche showing up when least expected, it was a talent he did not seek to acquire. "Wish we had a spyglass. I always carried one in the saddlebags when I was a soldier."

"We'll see what's going on in a quarter hour's time."

As Ezra predicted, they soon came up over a rise and saw what they had been smelling. Con could make out the smoldering remains of a house and barn in the distance. Even what appeared to be a chicken house or storage shed had collapsed and was near ashes. The privy, some distance behind the residence, remained undisturbed. The only other structure still standing stood back from the others. It was a three-sided loafing shed with the south side open and surrounded by perhaps twenty acres of pasture. Such structures were generally used to shelter horses or cattle kept near home for one reason or another.

The only sign of life on the place was a lonely, saddled horse standing in front of the house remains. Con could make out forms strewn about the yard and knew what they would find there. He had viewed this scene too many times during his Army years when he was chasing Comanche with Mackenzie. "Comanche," he said.

"Yep. Most likely. Apaches wouldn't venture this far north. These either jumped the reservation or never went in the first place."

"They're gone now and not likely to be back. They hit quick, did what they came to do and got out."

"Yeah, they likely got all the horses, maybe cleaned the house of anything useful to them."

Con sighed. "There won't be anybody alive to help, but we'd better ride in to see what we can do for the dead and see if we can get any information to report to the Army. Fort Elliott is south of here, maybe a hard day's ride, no more than two. I spent a few months there during my Army days. It was just a new post then, put there mostly to protect settlers from Indian raids."

"Didn't do no good here. Injuns—-especially Comanches—know where the soldiers are and just go where they ain't."

Con shrugged. He dreaded the task that lay in front of him. "We've got work to do. I guess that shovel I packed on old Chester's load is going to be busy."

The buzzards were already circling the farmstead when the two men rode into the yard. Con counted four bodies strewn about the area, one where a saddled blue roan mare stood, as if waiting for her rider to awaken. She moved away ten feet or so when the visitors appeared but did not spook and run. Then Con noticed she was limping slightly and figured she was not up to running just yet.

Ezra said, "Mare's got a slug in her hip. If that's her only problem, we can likely fix it and won't have to put her down. Purty critter."

They dismounted and tied their mounts and pack animals to one of the two hitching rails. Two were unusual, and from the looks of the building's remains, Con suspected part of the structure had been used for a business, likely a trading post.

They checked the victims to confirm that none were alive, although Con had no illusion that anyone survived the slaughter. The woman's naked body was a gory sight, her breasts sliced away, and her head split open with an axe, probably only after she had been raped multiple times. A scalping knife had claimed a trophy of what would have included a strip of long, auburn hair.

Ezra was on his knees next to the man, probably the woman's husband. He yelled at Con who was walking toward what looked to be the body of a boy. "This feller's dead for sure. Scalped and his privates cut off." He got up and limped over to the body near where the horse had stood. "I'll check the other man near the house."

Con knelt beside the boy. He'd been shot multiple times but not otherwise mutilated. His wheat-straw colored hair had not been touched, his scalp likely spared because there was no honor in killing an eleven or twelve-year old boy.

Ezra called to him again. "Con, you better get over here. This ain't no man. I got me a young lady here, and she ain't dead. Not yet anyhow."

Chapter 4

CON MOVED TO Ezra's side and began to cough as he neared the house where the smoke was thicker. The prone figure on the ground was motionless, and he saw no sign of life until her upper back, where the fletched shaft of an arrow protruded, rose and fell. Then he saw the arrowpoint jutting out off to the left side of her lower back, and hope died. She appeared to have a left shoulder wound as well, but that was nothing compared to the horror of the lower wound where the arrow had nearly passed through her body.

Con said, "We've got to get her away from the smoke. That's not helping her breathe, and we can't see what problems she's got with this smoke eating our eyes out."

"Biggest problem will be digging another grave. All we can do is be with her, try to make her comfortable while she dies. I don't like saying it, but it will be over for this young lady within a day."

"You take her feet, and I'll hook under her arms and pray we don't make things worse. We'll lay her out on the grass under that big cottonwood tree for now, and then I'll take my bedroll apart, and we can move her onto a blanket."

Gently, they turned her over and carried her across the wagon trail in front of the smoldering building toward the ancient tree. The blue roan mare followed, favoring the wounded leg some, but Con figured she would be fine with a little time after they got the slug out. The horse obviously belonged to the young woman and sensed the strangers would do neither any harm.

Soon they had the woman stretched out on her right side on a blanket. Ezra said, "Do you know anything about doctoring?"

"I've tended to a lot of battle wounds. We didn't often have a doctor or medical assistant with us in the field during Comanche chases, and somehow I generally got assigned to the patchwork after a fight."

"Well, them's Comanche arrows stuck in this gal."

"Yeah, but right now we don't care whose they are. The shaft that entered below the ribs must have broken when she fell. That's the devil that's most likely to do her in. The back arrow didn't sink so deep."

"Ain't much to be done for her with that dang arrow through her guts."

"Do you suppose you could get some water boiling in one of our kettles? There's a pump in front of the house, and you shouldn't have trouble digging out some hot coals someplace. I'm going to prop her up against the tree trunk some, so the arrows don't do more damage. Then I'll get my straight razor from the saddlebags, and I've got a sharp pocketknife, too."

"You ain't fixing to cut on her?"

"I don't know how I'm going to go about this, but we can't get her anyplace for help soon enough to do any good. A travois would slow us down, so a trip to Fort Elliott would take us at least three days, and that bouncing around on the contraption would likely make her worse."

Con maneuvered the woman up against the tree trunk and was startled when he heard a moan. When he looked down, he saw a pair of expressionless brownish-green eyes looking up at him. Then they closed. This was the first time that she seemed a genuine living creature. He waited a bit to be certain she was not going to revive again and then went to retrieve some things from the saddlebags.

He returned with the straight edge, several kerchiefs, and a small, leather draw-string bag where he stashed supplies for treating simple cuts that were inevitable when working at a ranch. He also brought one of his two extra shirts. He dropped to the ground and moved his patient back to her left side for the moment.

While he waited for Ezra to bring the water, he studied the young woman stretched out on the blanket. Only at first glance would she pass as a man or boy. The boots and faded denim britches might fool a stranger for a minute, but her body had gentle curves in places where a man did not. She was long-legged and slender, just short of skinny. He judged her to be an inch or two less than five and a half feet tall. Her auburn hair was cropped short, not nearly reaching her shoulders, and her features appeared delicately carved beneath the dirt covered face.

He had not paid much attention to the shoulder wound because the blood was browning, signaling that the bleeding had slowed or stopped. The arrow wounds were not bleeding profusely either, but that meant nothing for he had no notion of what might be happening internally where the shaft had passed through her abdomen.

Con sliced the bloody shirt and the half-chemise beneath it from her upper body, taking care not to disturb the fabric clinging to the protruding arrows for the moment. He examined the shoulder wound and was encouraged to find that, as he suspected, the slug had passed through flesh, and that his task would be to keep the bleeding staunched, perhaps stitch it enough to assist healing and reduce scarring. That would come later. This young woman who could not be much past twenty had challenge enough to live another day. He had never seen a soldier hit this badly live long enough to talk about it.

When Ezra returned and set a pot of boiling water down beside Con, he said, "Found a burying place about fifty paces behind the house on some higher ground. Two wood crosses there, I can't read letters good, but there's something carved there. Plenty of space for the poor folks laying in the yard and the dog, too. Digging don't look to be too hard there."

"We've got this young lady to look after first."

"Don't mean no disrespect, Con, but I don't think we'll be looking after her very long. She's in the worst of a bad way."

"I need your help here for just about fifteen minutes, and then I'd like to have you head over to the river. From the tree line to the south, I'm guessing that the Canadian isn't more than fifty yards from here."

"Yeah, I seen that strip of woods winding like a dang snake down that way."

"I'm betting there are willows along the banks, and if so, I'd like you to harvest some bark—from the younger trees if you can get it."

"Ya'll are going to make some poultices, I'm guessing. I seen the Comanches do that."

"And some tea if we can get her to drink. I learned about this from one of our Tonkawa scouts. At least I never saw it do any harm. It's supposed to help with pain and healing and fights off infection. I don't have anything better in my medicine bag."

He plucked his knife from his pocket and clutched the splintered arrow shaft that stuck out from just below her left breast, which fortunately was not large enough to interfere with the task. He cut and hacked his way through the shaft, quickly breaking off most of the broken arrow and leaving no more than a two-inch stub that he smoothed down before he tore away the remaining scraps of fabric that surrounded the arrow's entry wound. Then he took one of his kerchiefs, wet it in the hot water, and washed the swollen flesh surrounding the wood stub and finally rubbing the wet cloth over the stub itself.

"Now I want to clean around where the other arrow is lodged, and then I'll pull that out first and see how she reacts. I'll need to have you get down here and help steady her."

"She's sort of a scrawny gal. Shouldn't be that hard to hold her."

"If we're lucky, but folks in pain can call up a lot of strength when they're trying to escape it all."

When Ezra was on the ground, following Con's directions, he wrapped his arms around the young woman's waist, pressing against her with his hip.

"I just don't want her to turn onto her back till we've got the arrows out," Con said.

Con turned his attention first to the arrow driven between the shoulder blades, again clearing away any fabric and cleaning the area around the arrowhead. The shoulders of the flint head could be seen just below the opened flesh. He saw no reason to cut the opening further, so he clutched the shaft as near to the arrowhead as possible and yanked. It came free followed by a stream of blood which he quickly dammed with his gauze. The patient moaned and tried to roll free, but Ezra held her snuggly, and soon she calmed.

Con sighed. "Barring infection, that wound wouldn't be fatal, I'll need to do a few stitches, but we've got to move and get the arrow shaft out of her body while we've got her here. I just hope she doesn't suffer any more than she did with this one."

After cleaning around the projecting head, he took one of the kerchiefs, wrapped one end about the arrowhead to keep his fingers from slipping, pushed one knee against her back and locked the fingers of one hand about the arrowhead's shoulders and grasped the fingers of the other hand about the portion of the shaft that had emerged. "I've got to get this on the first try, Ezra, or God knows what more damage I'll do inside. So hold tight. Here goes."

He tugged gently at first, but the arrow's shaft did not budge, and the patient moaned and started stirring. No time to waste. This time, he put all the strength he could muster into the effort, and he could feel it moving free. But the woman started screaming, her cries echoing through the river valley. He leaned back and kept pulling till the shaft broke free from flesh, and he lost his balance, nearly tumbling over. He righted himself and started tending to the gaping, bleeding wound, while the young woman kept squirming and crying.

Then she yelled, "Get away from me, you bastard."

He took her speaking as a positive sign. "We're here to help you, ma'am. It's alright." He turned to Ezra. "You can let her go now, Ezra. Maybe you can see about the willow bark. Just get what you think might get us through till tomorrow. If she can drink soon, I might use a bit of your whiskey."

"She likely needs it more than me right now."

Chapter 5

AS DUSK APPROACHED, it was still impossible to carry on a conversation with the young woman, but she had drunk some whiskey and later a tea made of willow bark during brief moments when she was conscious, and Con thought she might be getting some relief from the concoction. Regardless, she was taking some liquids, which was important with the blood loss she had suffered.

While Con finished the stitching and dressing of the wounds, Ezra put the horses up in the lots where the loafing shed was located. There was enough grass there to satisfy the critters for the night, and they would seek out pasturage for staking them out tomorrow morning. They left the woman alone briefly while they moved the bodies to the cemetery location. Con tended to the grave digging and burials, and Ezra returned to be with their patient.

Con was pleasantly surprised to return and find that Ezra had taken the canvas covering from the pack animal loads and made a lean-to shelter from some of the low hanging cottonwood branches. He had stacked some of their supplies on the two sides to furnish a windbreak. It would be tight, but the three of them could sleep there, and they could not even consider putting the woman off by herself somewhere. He figured he and Ezra would be sleeping in shifts, not only to guard against the possible return of the attackers but to tend to the patient. Of course, if the Indians returned, they were as good as dead anyhow.

Ezra prepared biscuits, bacon, and beans again for supper, but since they had bypassed a noon meal, Con welcomed the food as a feast. They sat at the fire and ate, resting a bit for the first time since their arrival at the farmstead. Con said, "After supper, you can get some shuteye first if you want. I'll wake you up in a few hours."

"Won't argue that. Been many a moon since I worked this hard, and I'm feeling my years tonight. It's a nice night, and I don't fancy sleeping next to a woman that might be dead when I open my eyes. I'm going to take my bedroll away from the tree and lay it out under the stars. When you wake me up, I'll move in and sit beside her, and you can take my bedroll since she's using most of yours."

Con shrugged. "Whatever suits you." He got up and commenced cleanup chores. It was an unseasonably warm night, and at least there was no need to worry about keeping the lady warm.

After completing the cleanup task, he picked up his Winchester and stooped to step into the shelter. Almost twenty feet away, he could hear Ezra snoring. The old devil apparently never had trouble falling asleep, because the previous night Con's own sleep had been delayed and disrupted by the chorus of snorts and snoring interrupted only by a booming fart now and then. While they traveled together, he hoped to devise strategies for as much nighttime separation as possible.

He sat down next to the woman who was breathing steadily but quietly as she slept. It was a miracle she still lived. He did not hold out much hope for more than another day or two, but he admired her toughness, and she certainly would not die alone. Later, he found himself struggling to stay awake, and his chin started to drop to his chest just as a raspy, halting voice came from beside him. "Who the hell are you?"

He started and turned to the young woman who lay just a few feet away, her head propped up on his rolled-up deerskin jacket. He scrambled to his knees and looked down at her. Her eyes were wide open, boring in on him with near rage. He said, "My name is Con Callaway. What's yours?"

She closed her eyes as if struggling to recall her name. Finally, her voice still hesitant and raspy, she said, "I'm Virginia Harwood. Where are my sisters?"

"Let me get you something to drink." He reached for the canteen that contained the willow tea and shook it before he slipped an arm under her upper back, lifted her up, and pressed it to her lips. She drank greedily for several minutes before he took the canteen away. "Let this settle some, and then I'll give you more."

"Tastes like horse piss."

"You drink a lot of horse piss, do you?" He chided himself for his sarcasm, but Virginia Harwood, on the edge of death, seemed to be picking a fight.

"You didn't answer me. Where are my sisters?"

"Miss Harwood, I know nothing about your sisters."

"You are a lying bastard. The animals you ride with took them."

Now he understood. "Listen to me closely. I am not with the Comanche who attacked what I presume is your home. My partner and I found you here. We thought you were dead at first, but we have been trying to help you through this. You will have to decide whether you believe me or not before we can talk more about this."

She was silent, closed her eyes for a spell and seemed to drop off to sleep.

He moved away and settled in to keep watch again, realizing it was past time for Ezra to take a shift but knowing he would not sleep anyhow. If drowsiness struck him again, Con decided he would get up and wake his partner to take over.

"I've got to piss—bad." It was Miss Harwood's voice, and while it was no more than a loud whisper, there was desperation in the tone. This problem had not even occurred to him. He had figured he was just on deathwatch duty.

He shifted over by her side. "Do you think you can walk ten feet or so if I help?"

"I'll try."

With multiple wounds, especially internal ones, he hated for her to move, but he could not let her sleep in her own waste, and he had no notion how she might straddle one of the cooking pots here. He got up, pulled away the blankets, lifted her into his arms and carried her a dozen or so paces away from the shelter. "I can't carry you to the privy," Con said when he eased her feet on the ground.

"Got to get my britches down."

He knew nothing about the logistics of such things, but he unbuckled her belt and unbuttoned her denims and eased them and her underpants down to her ankles while she held onto his shoulder with her right hand. She almost pulled him down when she suddenly squatted, and continuing to hold onto him and balancing herself with her left hand pressed to the ground, she started to pee. He grabbed the tail of her shirt, which was previously his, and pulled it up so it would not get saturated in the process. He thought she would never stop the flow, but finally she did.

"Help me get to my feet," she said, her voice somewhat stronger now. "If you will help, I'll try to walk back."

"Are you sure, Miss Harwood?"

"I'd like to try. And you can call me, 'Ginny,' I guess, after that bit of intimacy."

She must have decided that he was not her captor, and she appeared not totally without a sense of humor. "And I go by 'Con.'"

They walked slowly, resting briefly between taking a few steps. When they reached the canvas shelter, Con saw that Ezra was standing off to one side watching, shaking his head from side to side. He felt Ginny stiffen when she saw the newcomer. Con said, "This is my friend Ezra. He has been helping care for you."

"Howdy, ma'am," Ezra said, doffing his hat.

She nodded, but her knees buckled, and she started to fall. Con caught her, lifted her into his arms and carried her to her blankets and gently eased her down onto the ground bed. She said, "I got dizzy."

"You've got to be in terrible pain."

"I hurt everyplace, but I don't know how I can even be alive. I remember now. One arrow went deep into my body. It can't still be there."

"You were hit by two arrows, and you had a gunshot wound in your shoulder, but the slug passed through." He decided to spare her further details for now. He noted, however, that her voice was stronger, and he was amazed that she was not suffering agonizing pain from the arrow that dug through her body. But he had no doubt that the worst of her pain was yet to come, along with the infection and symptoms from whatever internal damage had been done.

Ginny said, "I'm hungry."

Con looked up at Ezra who had moved in behind him.

"I got a few biscuits from supper yet. If she'll eat one and drink some willow tea, I'll share a few chocolate Necco Wafers I got stowed away."

"You never offered to share any with me."

"I save Necco Wafers for the ladies. Now, you let me sleep through my shift, why don't you grab a few hours of shuteye, and I'll look after this young lady for a spell."

Chapter 6

GINNY OPENED HER eyes as sunrise cast its glow over the prairielands. She could smell bacon frying in a skillet easily piercing the veil of campfire smoke, but she was not hungry now. Her overriding concern now was the pain, the unrelenting stabs in her abdomen were worsening by the minute. She could make out the form of the older man who had stayed with her during the night till she dropped off to sleep again.

The next time she woke, the younger man—Con—had been at her side staring off at the sky, obviously deep in thought. Comforted by his presence, she said nothing and closed her eyes again, snatching the sleep that helped fight off the pain that was increasing. She found it difficult to complain considering what had happened to the others in her family. It was different now, though, and she realized that death was lurking nearby, ready to bring her peace. But she had things to do first.

She heard a horse whinny off to the shelter's left side. It couldn't be. She thought Artemis was dead or taken by the raiders. Con appeared now, leading the blue roan mare, and Ginny began to cry. "My baby. You found my baby."

"I thought she was likely yours. She was standing next to you when we rode in. She took a bullet in her hip. Ezra got that out. He's got a special way with critters, and he said she didn't fight him much. She'll favor that side a few days, but she'll be fine. I'm going to stake her out where you can see her, and if you need to relieve yourself when you're stronger, maybe I can lift you into her saddle and take you over to the privy, upgrade your facilities some."

"Thank you. I'm so glad to see her and know she's alright. I raised her from a foal." A surge of pain in her gut made her grimace and take a deep breath.

"You're hurting. Let me stake your mare out and then I'll see what I can do."

Shortly, he knelt beside her and placed a hand on her forehead for a bit. He said nothing and removed it. "I'm going to redress your wounds and see how they're doing."

"Not just yet. We're going to have an understanding first."

"What do you mean?"

"I'm not a total idiot. I've got a fever, don't I?"

"It appears so."

"Then just tell me when you check these things. I want the truth, the hard truth when you're touching me and looking at my body. Don't sweeten it with sugar, just tell me straight what the hell you're seeing and thinking." Her eyes met his dark, brown eyes, and she hoped he saw her anger.

Con said, "You will know exactly what I'm seeing and thinking. Now, with your permission, I want to check those wounds."

"Go right ahead."

"We need to take the shirt off."

"Help yourself. I suppose you've already seen what little I've got to show when you were working on me before."

He unbuttoned her shirt, and she was able to raise herself on one elbow at a time while he slipped the garment over her shoulders. First, he lifted the gauze patch on the shoulder. "A little reddish around the wound, but nothing I'm worried about right now." Next, he checked the wound between the shoulder blades. "Looking good. That one didn't go very deep, and it doesn't appear there was any poison on the arrow tip as we sometimes find."

"You've seen lots of these?"

"Army for five years, chasing Comanche with General Mackenzie most of that time."

"Yeah, I suppose you have seen a few then."

"Now I'm going to take a look at the other two."

"Two? I thought I was hit three times."

"I guess I didn't explain. This arrow entered below your ribs, and the point pushed out your back."

"Oh, my God. I was skewered like a chunk of beef. It was that Comanche with the wolf pelt over his head and back. He was up close when I faced him. It had to tear up my insides. I'm as good as dead."

"You are still alive. Let me look at the wounds."

He pulled back the dressing below the ribs, and when he probed about the wound, she shrieked. His grim look answered her questions.

Con spoke softly. "Infection has set in. We'll use our poultices, but it will be mostly up to your body to whip it. I'm going to look at the exit wound now. I cut the arrow shaft to a stub on your front side and pulled it through from the back."

The mere thought of it made her weak and nauseous. "Go ahead and check the back wound." She could not see his face now, but his silence spoke. "Bad, isn't it?"

"Yes, but not as bad as the front."

She could not delay things that needed to be said. "Where did you bury my parents?"

"Your parents and a boy were buried near the graves of two others. We buried a dog there, too."

"The dog was Skipper. They shot him when he was trying to help my mother. He was my cattle dog. I'm glad you buried him there. Can you remember names?"

"I have a tablet and a pencil in my saddlebags just behind you. Just a minute." He retrieved the items. "Give me the names."

She hoped she died as soon as she said what she had to say. "The names of my brother and sister who died from diphtheria several years ago are carved on the crosses. The brother you buried is Richard—we called him Ricky. My father's name is Manfred, and my mother is Helen. Again, the dog is Skipper. I told you that I am Virginia, and I want to be buried next to Skipper."

"I hope that won't be necessary."

"What I have to say next is most important. The raiders took my sisters. Noreen is eleven and Krista is nine."

"I had no idea. I'm sorry."

"Sorry isn't enough. I know I'm a stranger to you, and I'm not the begging kind. But please, I'm begging you. Promise to try to get my sisters back. Contact the Army at least."

He did not answer immediately, but when he did, Con spoke very precisely, "I don't make promises lightly, Ginny." He paused, and she felt her heart skip a beat. "But when I do, I take them very seriously. I promise that I will try to find Noreen and Krista and get them back from the men who took them, and when I do, I will see that they are properly cared for."

"I can die with some peace then. Thank you, Con. You and Ezra are like angels sent by God to help."

Chapter 7

BY LATE AFTERNOON Ginny was burning with fever and delirious, incapable of carrying on a rational conversation, and her intermittent screaming said she was enduring horrifying pain. Sometimes, she went silent, and Con thought she had died, but each time he found she had simply found the blessed refuge of sleep. Meanwhile, he continually bathed her face and body with ice-cold water from the well.

Ezra repacked the wounds with the willow poultice, although Con was skeptical that it helped. He returned the mare called Artemis to the fenced grass with the other critters. She would not be used for trips to the privy since Ginny had evacuated both bowels and bladder on her blankets, sometimes a sign that death was imminent. Ezra had offered his own bedroll for replacement, and Con washed the soiled blankets at the pump. They were now hanging on a tree waiting for the sun and a nice breeze to dry.

Ezra came up behind Con as he bathed the sick young woman. "Want me to do that a spell, Con? You been at this a long while."

"No, I'm fine, but thanks." In truth, he did not want to leave for fear her last breath would be drawn during his absence. He could not explain why.

Ezra said, "Some of her innards must be working with the mess she made on the blankets."

"We just don't know. It's not possible that the arrow passed through without doing some damage. We can only hope it is the type of damage that can heal on its own. Of course, it doesn't matter if the infection wins out, and there's not much else we can do about that. I've never seen soldiers at this stage who lived."

"Nope. I seen a few folks get this way, but they never got up."

As dusk approached, dark clouds rolled in and covered what remained of the blue sky. Con forced himself to eat the chipped beef and beans Ezra prepared and willingly ate the brown betty he had concocted from dried apples and biscuit crumbs. He only wished that Ginny could eat a portion. He worried more, however, that they had been unable to get her to drink since early afternoon. Her life would burn out much sooner without water.

Con tended to the water pump that evening, attaching the cupped end of a pipe to the spout and pumping the handle to pull up the water that traveled via the pipe to a tank in the pen where the horses and mule had been lodged. Ezra was more than glad to pass on water pumping chores and stayed near Ginny while Con watered the critters.

Just as Con finished, thunder roared, and a bolt of lightning lit up the sky. He hurried and retrieved the drying blankets from the tree limb and dodged under the crude shelter.

"Looks like you'll be staying in tonight, Ezra. You can have these blankets. I'll just curl in between the two of you and take any leftovers." He knew Ezra would not argue, because for some reason the old timer was averse to waking up beside a dead person.

Suddenly, the rain began a soft patter against the canvas. A few minutes later, it began to hammer. Con had been in many worse winds, but this one was enough to shake the shelter. He was confident the refuge would hold, though. Ezra had fashioned and secured the structure. He might move at a slow and deliberate pace, but when he took on a task, he generally did it right. Any wind should be coming from the backside, so they would not likely take in too much water.

It was cooling some now, and he lay down beside Ginny, lying on part of the poncho he had spread out in the shelter under the bedding. Soon, Ezra lay down on the other side of him and shared half of his top blanket. Con finally gave in to exhaustion and dropped off asleep, blissfully unaware of the torrential rain and the crashing of the thunderstorm. This was far from the worst he had been through during his Army years.

He woke instantly at the sound of Ginny's mumbling next to him. He lifted himself on one elbow. "Ginny, I'm right here. What is it?"

"Thirsty."

He could barely make out her voice, but he reached for his own canteen, thinking she might drink more without the willow bark taste. He carefully placed his arm about her back and raised her up some and then with the other hand pressed the canteen to her lips, allowing just a few drops at first. Her right hand came up and clutched the canteen, Ginny took charge, drinking greedily before he pulled the canteen away.

"More," she said.

"In a few minutes. You will get sick if you drink too much too fast."

"Now."

"Just wait."

There was anger in that raspy voice, and he took that as a positive sign. He placed a hand lightly on her forehead. It was like a heat stove in the cool air, but he would swear it was not burning like earlier. "How's the pain?" he said.

"Just lovely."

He did not know whether she was spitting sarcasm or out of her head. He guessed it was sort of a stupid question when he thought about it. It occurred to him then that the storm had stopped, and stars were sparkling in the heavens. "Now, you can have another drink." He helped her, but she was very possessive of the canteen.

Finally, though, she surrendered it to him and allowed him to lower her back down to the ground bed. She's got a chance, Con thought. He knew that some in her condition had a final surge before death claimed them. Virginia Harwood was one dang tough young woman. For the first time, he held out hope for her. He had seen miracles on the battlefield, and maybe this would be one of them.

During the remainder of the night, Ginny drank several more times, and Con became convinced that her fever was, indeed, abating. By sunrise her voice was stronger, and he examined the wounds again for possible redressing. He decided not to tamper with dressings on the shoulder wound and the mid-back arrow puncture when he found that bleeding had been insignificant since his last look and swelling appeared to be reducing.

The wounds from the arrow that passed through her abdomen's left side were another matter. Where the arrowhead had broken through the backside was red and swollen, but not nearly so much as the entry wound where a discharge of dark blood intermingled with yellow pus oozed from the opening. Con pressed the edges of the fissure gently and a mass of the stinky stuff squeezed through the opening. This was why he had not fully closed the wound with stitches because he had expected drainage needs if Ginny lived long enough.

Still, he was baffled. He had no way of knowing what the extent of internal damage was, but Ginny's condition otherwise appeared to be improving by the hour. All they could do was wait. She was a tough varmint and was not giving up the fight.

He cleaned up the mess around the wound and saw that her eyes were fixed on him as he applied a new compress. He could feel the tension in her body and sensed she was in pain. "Am I hurting you?"

"That's alright. You're keeping me alive, I guess. Why?"

"Why not? A man does not come across a young woman in your condition and just say 'too bad' and ride on."

"Some would."

"Not most."

"How long before I can ride?"

"I have no idea. Whatever I would predict, I suspect you would cut in half anyhow."

"Each day that passes puts Noreen and Krista farther away. I am going to live, and I am going to find them and kill that damned wolf warrior who put the arrow in me. And since I'm going to make it, you are released from your promise to look for them."

"It won't do any good to leave if you're going to fall out of the saddle along the way, and you don't have any idea where you are headed."

"I'll find them."

"Not without help. Ezra and I have talked. We will go with you."

"Are you serious? You and Grandpa?"

"Ezra lived with the Comanche. I fought them. We might be able to help some."

"But I can't expect you to do this."

"We've got nothing better to do for now. Ezra's positive that the warrior with the wolfskin cape is a renegade known as Angry Wolf. He works with the Comancheros.

He raids and takes anything of value, especially horses—and sometimes children. The Comancheros see to the marketing of the merchandise."

"That would explain why the Negro and at least one white man, maybe two, were with them. What do they do with the children?"

She would not like his answer. "They take them to Mexico to sell to bordellos or raise them with the band to eventually give birth to children. The band's population is dwindling, and it hasn't been unusual over the years for the Comanche to take in children as slaves and then convert them to the tribe. Chief Quanah Parker's mother was such a child."

"If they went to a bordello, how would we ever find my sisters?"

"First we must locate Angry Wolf."

"I'm hungry."

Con called over his shoulder to Ezra who was stirring hot coals in the firepit. "Ezra, the lady says she's hungry."

Ezra limped over to the shelter. "The same young lady that called me Grandpa? My hearing ain't gone yet."

Ginny looked up at Ezra with sad puppy dog eyes. "I never knew my grandparents, and now my folks are gone. Won't you be my grandpa?"

Con could see that she had completely disarmed the ornery cuss.

"Well, young lady. I ain't got no grandkids of my own. I suppose I could do that. Come to think of it, 'Grandpa' don't sound so bad."

"Thank you, Grandpa. This means a lot to me."

Ezra said, "How about some hotcakes this morning, Ginny? I snuck in a jar of strawberry jam, and I still got bacon I can fry up. And I got coffee brewing. Maybe it's time to perk you up with a cup or two of coffee."

"Oh, Grandpa, that sounds wonderful."

Ezra beamed and went off to put breakfast together. This young woman was slick as a greased snake, Con thought. He made a mental note not to ever underestimate her. Still, in all fairness, she might be bestowing an honor of sorts upon Ezra. Time would tell.

When breakfast was ready, Con propped her mare's saddle behind Ginny's back and helped her sit. Ezra brought a tin plate of hotcakes and bacon with a mug of coffee and fork for her. "I went ahead and slathered jam on the hotcakes, Ginny. Hope its not too thick."

"Thanks, Grandpa. There's no such thing as jam too thick."

"Now, you and me's thinking the same, girl."

Con sat down beside her with his own breakfast, so he could assist her if necessary. He saw quickly that his help would not be needed. Her hands were steady and her appetite ravenous, and she cleaned her plate before he finished his own breakfast. She downed her coffee, and Ezra was immediately there with the pot for a refill. He did not offer to refill Con's, so he got up to pour his own.

As they both stood near the dying fire embers, capturing a bit of heat on this brisk morning, Ginny called. "This coffee's already working its way through. I can hold it for a spell, but you suppose I could get to the privy?"

Con walked over to the shelter. "You can't walk that far, and I can't carry you that far. Do you think you can stay on your mare if I lead her? I really don't like the idea of jarring that wound and maybe starting up the bleeding again."

"Would you rather clean piss and shit off the blankets again? You talked about putting me on the horse before. What's the difference now?"

"Truth?"

"Truth, always."

"I figured you were going to die anyhow."

"And you've changed your thinking?"

He hesitated. "Yeah, I have. I think you're going to survive this, but it is as near to a miracle as I've ever seen. I'll go fetch your mare and bring her over here to saddle up."

Chapter 8

GINNY SAT ASTRIDE Artemis on the north bank of the Canadian River, relaxing to the sound of water rushing over the rocks. It was high noon. Well over two weeks had passed since the Comanche raid, and she had been able to walk around the yard without fighting spells of dizziness for only several days. Regardless, she had been stepping into the stirrup and mounting Artemis on her own before the dizzy spells ceased.

She no longer required an escort to the privy, and she knew she was starting to be a little testy when Con moved to help her with anything. He meant well, but she had never been gracious about dependence on others for anything. She felt a twinge of guilt because she knew she owed her life to Con's efforts, but still she found herself almost resenting the fact.

She cringed at the thought that Con had seen virtually every inch of her naked body and cleaned up her messes like a baby. He had even bathed her several times from a water bucket, running the wet cloth over her entire body although, after she was able, allowing her to tend to her most private parts. She tried not to think of what he might have done during her delirium, especially after she soiled the blankets.

He still dressed the wounds, but at least he was not seeing so much of her when he did it now. He always behaved businesslike when he tended to the wounds and seemed sensitive to her modesty, which was not surprising since he had already filled his eyes many times. But earlier, she had thought of him as a doctor for whom a woman of necessity bared much of herself on occasion. That time had passed, and now she thought of him more as just a man, and a quite handsome one at that.

And she thought he had been looking at her the past few days as more woman than patient. She was uneasy now about the time they would be spending together during the coming days and weeks. She wanted no part of a romance with any man, and he had better not get the notion that she would spread her legs for him, or she would send him packing. They had work to do.

Of course, she might just be flattering herself. She was reed-thin right now, and her chest was almost flat as a board. With a little distance, she could pass for a boy easily enough, up close maybe a female scarecrow. She knew from several sorry experiences, though, that women in the west were scarce enough that a horny cowhand looking for a poke had a way of turning blind.

Her memory still refused to erase the day a week or two past her sixteenth birthday when she was riding in the pasture that a male rider appeared on the trail from the north. She should have reined her mount around and raced away, especially since Skipper had not yet entered her life as protector, but she had chosen to keep riding, figuring she would just nod a greeting and ride on. She had made a bad choice, because when she met the unshaven man, he had been ready for her, abruptly turning his big stallion into her gelding, jarring her loose from the saddle and toppling her off the horse.

He was on her like a cowhand on a roped calf and cracked her on the side of the head with his pistol butt. He dragged her off into a draw, and when she regained her senses, he had already stripped her of her britches and was having his way. She could still smell his rancid breath and see the rotten-toothed smile. He had held her for several hours that day and taken her three times before she slipped his six-gun from its holster and put a slug in his neck.

She suspected that the man had been coming from No Man's Land to the north where outlaws thrived. It did not matter where he was headed. His destination then was to a dinner for coyotes and buzzards and such. Anyway, she had found twenty-five gold double-eagles in his saddlebags, leaving her five hundred dollars richer, and made off with his weapons and big bay stallion and tack. She decided she had been the most expensive poke that no-good ever had.

The gold coins were still buried on the ranch, but, of course, her father had claimed what she told him was a riderless horse and the tack. She did not tell him about the loss of her virginity because he would have accused her of luring the man to his sick behavior. Manfred Harwood did not hold women in especially high esteem. Her father would have claimed the money, too, but she had not been fool enough to tell him about it.

She saw Con mounted on his buckskin riding her way from the east on the trail that edged the river. When he saw her, he waved and rode her way. She waved back and reined Artemis out to meet him. When they met, she said, "I wondered where you went. I haven't seen you all morning."

"Just scouting your land. I assume that huge limestone rock east along the river is where your south and east lines meet."

"You saw the letters 'CCC' carved in the rock?"

"Yeah, that's the one."

"That's where our lines intersect. Step across that east line, and you are in Indian Territory."

He nodded without comment.

Ginny said, "We've got about five hundred acres. There is a limestone rock at each corner, but this one's two or three times as big as the others. They've all got the same letters on them."

"How long has your family been on this place?"

"Ever since I turned ten. That would mean not quite ten years. I've spent nearly half my life here."

"You were out here during the Indian wars then."

"My father set up a trading post and general store here. He called it 'Harwood Place.' The big sign is ashes now, I guess. He bought buffalo hides from whites and Indians. The Comanche tolerated the business because Pa provided a market for extra robes and furs and could trade for goods they couldn't obtain otherwise. Pa brought in some men and built the trading post first and then attached the house to it. We were lucky if we saw a town once a year."

"You obviously went to school someplace."

"Fortunately, Ma was a former schoolteacher and strict taskmistress, and we had an unbelievable library acquired by trade and during rare trips to Santa Fe. That's one thing she stood her ground on with Pa. Her children were going to get an education so they wouldn't be forced to spend their lives here unless that was their choice. She would have pulled up stakes and left with the kids if he fought her on that score, and he knew it."

"Who did you buy this place from?"

"I can't imagine what difference that would make to you, but I have no idea. How many ten-year olds would know about that?"

"On another matter, you've been after me to get on the trail of your sisters. Do you think you'll be up to riding out in the morning? We'll go as slowly as we need to. I'm thinking we should head south to Fort Elliott. Even at a slow pace, we should make it in no more than three nights on the trail."

"Why Fort Elliott?"

"You need to be checked by Army surgeons, and there's a big general store and trading post just outside the fort proper where we can get resupplied. I can also talk to some of the soldiers I know that should still be stationed there. I'm not much more than a year out of the Army. I might be able to learn something about Angry Wolf."

"I'm tired of having my wounds messed with. I'm almost completely healed, and you don't need to be looking me over anymore, either. It appears you've taken care of things alright. I don't want a bunch of strangers checking me out."

"We can see how things are going after we get there. Do you think you can get your things together and be ready to ride out in the morning?"

"What things? I've got nothing. No extra clothes. No blankets. Nothing. I'd like to borrow the shovel when we get back to camp, though."

He looked at her quizzically but said nothing. She was glad he was not the prying sort. He never made her feel like she was being cross-examined by a lawyer like those she had read about in books. She said, "I'll bet Grandpa's got something ready to eat. We'd better hightail it back to camp, or he'll be scolding us."

After lunch, she rode her roan mare to the burial ground for the first time since the slaughter of her family members. She dismounted and was surprised to find crude wooden crosses with names of her parents, brother, and even Skipper carved in them. They were evidently hewn from scrub trees or branches harvested from near the river. This was why Grandpa Ezra had asked her to print out all the names. Tears rolled down her cheeks as the cold reality of her losses finally struck her. Somehow it had all seemed like a bad dream till this moment. She could not help them now, but if humanly possible she would recover her sisters or learn their fate if it took the remainder of her life.

"I will be back," she whispered. "I vow I will find Noreen and Krista and return here with them, God willing."

She mounted Artemis. First stop was behind a hillock that rose some fifty feet beyond the cemetery. When she reached the stone she was seeking, she dismounted slowly, grabbed the shovel she had tied behind the saddle and walked over to the stone and pried it away from the spot where she wished to dig. She spaded the soft dirt and sand away about a foot deep until she saw the top of the leather bag she stored there. She could not bend far enough to pluck it out, so she lifted the bag with the shovel, then hoisted it into her saddlebags. There would be $312 worth of gold and silver coins that she had secreted from her father in addition to the five hundred dollars she had taken from the dead rapist.

She then rode over to the burnt remains of the stable-barn. It occurred to her that Con and Grandpa could see her now from the campsite. And she was stumped. She should have realized that she would be unable to move the debris by herself. She planted her hands on her hips and pondered a solution. She hated like blazes to ask for help. She knew that her money was safe from these men, but she did not want to explain what this was all about. Then, out of the corner of her eye she saw Con walking her way. She sighed and waited.

When he approached, Con said, "If there is something in that mess you're looking for, I'd be glad to help."

"It's in the northeast corner, buried no more than a foot and up against the foundation. The spot is covered by a stack of small stones."

Con held out his hand for the shovel. "You just tell me what you want me to do." He waded into the rubble and made his way to the corner, pushing away stubs of charred timber as he went.

"Here?" Con said when he reached the corner.

"Yes. You will be looking for a metal box."

In less than a half hour he had the rocks cleared away and a rusty metal box in his hand. He returned to Ginny and placed the box in her hands. "Finished with the shovel?"

"Yes. And thank you for doing this."

"You could have done it yourself if you weren't stove up from the wounds. I didn't want you to tear my handiwork open." He turned away and walked back to the campsite.

Ginny poured the contents of the box into the empty side of the saddlebags. She did not know the amount of her father's personal stash but figured it would be substantial. She would tally the total amount when she could capture more privacy. She had seen him hiding the money three or four years earlier. She had not touched it but always planned to give it to her mother should she decide to leave a marriage where she was no more than a useful slave.

She was suddenly exhausted. She let Artemis carry her to the campsite, and she nearly fell asleep in the saddle. Con evidently recognized her situation and helped her dismount.

"I'll stake Artemis," he said. "You head for the bedroll."

She would not argue this time. She stumbled over to the shelter, collapsed on the blankets and fell instantly to sleep.

Chapter 9

"DID Y'ALL SEE that cornerstone?" Ezra asked, as he ambled over to Con who was packing the white mule, Chester.

Con tossed a look over his shoulder to confirm that Ginny was not nearby. "Yeah, I saw it yesterday when I was scouting around the area. Since we are camped along the Canadian, I figured my so-called land shouldn't be too far distant. I would have never guessed we were already on it."

"I seen them letters on the rock when I was hunting rabbits a few days back. I can't put together more than a few words, but I know the letters, and for sure a 'C' when I see it. I wanted you to know before we pulled out of here, and I hadn't had a chance to talk to you since you started looking after that purty filly. You going to boot her off the place?"

"Not likely, but the title needs to get straightened out if she comes back here someday. I suppose she'll need a law wrangler for that. Anyhow, I think she's got enough troubles without having to fight me over some grass I'm not even bonded with. I've been thinking about the cattle she's leaving behind. With water and grass, they'll survive over the summer and won't go too wild, but some will wander, and plenty could get rustled if the wrong folks come by and figure out nobody's watching over them."

"Yeah, she mentioned that but says nothing matters if she don't get her sisters back."

"I think that's why she lived. She's set on finding those girls and is just too dang stubborn to die."

Ezra said, "Here she comes now. I'm guessing she was making one last visit to her family in the cemetery."

"Yeah, she's carrying a lot of weight on her shoulders right now. I still worry about that arrow that went in through her belly and almost bored its way out through her back—-afraid there could be damage that hasn't made itself known yet. I'm hoping to get her to one of the surgeons at Fort Elliott, but I'm not sure she'll go."

"Maybe Grandpa can work on it after we get there."

"Now that she's perked up some, it seems like she's quit listening to me. It's almost like she doesn't like me much."

"I ain't never figured out female thinking, and I ain't even gonna try with Ginny."

"She's got you wrapped around her little finger. When she's around you're like a dang pup trying to please her."

Ezra spat a wad of tobacco into the dust at his feet. "Worse ways to spend my time."

"Let's saddle up and get away from this place."

At the beginning of their journey the riders tried to follow the route the raiders had taken. Even though the rains had washed away much of the evidence, remnants of piles of horse dung still marked the trail as well as occasional hoofprints from unshod horses.

When the trio reined in their mounts for watering at a stream, Ezra pointed at the evidence left by the renegades. "They ain't going to hide a trail of that many horses," Ezra remarked. "They got near a herd of the critters."

Ginny said, "They didn't take more than a half dozen from our place. We always had a few around that Pa took in trade and then sold or traded for something else. The last few years, he let me make most of the horse deals. I could do that at the stable and not get in his way."

"I gather you handled the cattle operation, too," Con said.

"Yeah, that's why Pa let me take over the cowherd, too. He was a merchant, not a rancher. He probably would have whipped me with a belt if he'd known I was taking a commission on the horses and sold a few of the calves on my own when I was dealing with buyers who came out from Fort Elliott or one of the big ranches."

"Seems only fair," Ezra said. Con wasn't sure it was quite honest.

Ginny said, "I couldn't drive cull cows and yearling steers and heifers to market on my own, but I always wanted to be part of a cattle drive. Running fifty or sixty cows, we would have needed a few extra hands to drive our own. That would have taken all the profit. Others checked with us every year to buy what we had for sale. The Army wasn't looking for a thousand head."

Virginia Harwood had a knack for looking out for herself, Con thought. She obviously had a contentious relationship with her father but had resisted any efforts to turn her into a frightened mouse. At some point in her life, she had apparently decided to take the man on as a challenge, and she probably occasionally drove him near crazy.

Midafternoon, Con could see that Ginny was pushing her limit. The glaring sun had turned the plains into a fireplace, more reminiscent of July than early June. He caught sight of a scalped bluff that rose from a wooded area to the west that he estimated would be no more than ten minutes' ride. Trees generally signaled water, and rocky bluffs tended to turn up shelter of one sort or another.

"Swing west," he hollered, pointing to the bluff.

Ezra nodded, and Ginny cast him a doubtful look but followed. When they rode up to the forested area, Con reined in Quanah and looked over the area.

"Nice spring feeding the stream from the rocks," Ezra said. "Fill the canteens and water the critters."

"I had in mind setting up camp and spending the night. Lush grass along the stream. No sign of rain, so we can sleep under the stars, maybe find a clearing in the trees to give us a little cover."

"You didn't ask me," Ginny said.

"No, I didn't."

"What if I want to ride longer?"

"I'm tired. You'll do it without me. Maybe I'll find you in the morning."

She glared at him and dismounted, leading her mare to the stream.

That night, Ginny tossed down the bedroll they had been sharing at the farmstead camp. "These are yours," she told Con.

He sighed. "And where are you going to sleep?"

"I want some distance between us now. I don't need any medical help during the night."

"It's warm out tonight. I don't need them, or I can take one of the blankets, and you can have the other two."

"I suppose you'll be ordering me what to do next."

"I'm just saying we can share the blankets, and you can put whatever distance between us you want."

Ezra intervened. "Folks, time to have us a talk, maybe one we should have had before we hit the trail. Now as I see it, we're gettin' into some dangerous business in the days ahead, and it ain't no good to be fussing with one another. And somebody's got to be in charge of this outfit."

Ginny said, "We're looking for my sisters. I should be in charge."

"Sweetheart, you don't know this country. You can run a ranch and all kinds of things and look after yourself just fine, but don't take no offense, you just ain't ready to take on responsibility for all of us when it comes to facing what's ahead."

"Then you be in charge."

"Nope. I do just fine most of the time in charge of my ownself, but I ain't no leader. I can give my opinion, just as you can, but somebody else has got to have final word."

Her eyes narrowed. "That leaves Mister Callaway."

Ezra said, "He was an Army sergeant, served five years in this godforsaken country. He should be the leader and last word. If we got to vote on this, I'll have to give him mine and risk making you disown me. And Sweetheart, you know you cannot do this alone."

Con said, "I've got a bad habit after all those Army years of just making decisions and giving orders. I'll try to do better about consulting with you two, and I apologize, Ginny, if I've been too bossy. I just want to see this mission be successful." He handed her the two blankets.

She accepted them and said, "I know you saved my life, and I need you both. I'll try to be more patient." But this night she laid her blankets down a good ten feet from Con.

Chapter 10

THE NEXT MORNING, after two hours in the saddle, the travelers came across the charred remains of another farmstead. Four fresh dirt mounds off to the side of the house signaled that the victims had already been discovered and buried. They dismounted and walked around the buildings, trying to piece together the story.

"A farm family," Con said. "They likely had a milk cow or two, but the nearest fields have been plowed, and it looks like corn is starting to come up. This isn't the best land for cultivation, but it looks like the farmer knew his trade. God knows why they chose this area to farm. No neighbors in sight, probably a good day away from Fort Elliott and supplies, and land more fit for grazing than farming. I guess he would have had a market for grain at the fort."

Ezra said, "I suppose he figured the Indian wars was done. Well, mostly, but they won't be all done for a spell yet. From shod tracks comin' in from the east, I'm guessing an Army patrol come by and did the burying."

"Yeah. We'll probably learn more about it when we get to Fort Elliott."

Ginny said, "I wonder if any more children were taken."

Con said, "These people likely were known around the fort. We'll find out when we get there. I doubt if the raiders got any prize mounts, probably nothing they couldn't have taken without killing and burning. These folks likely had a few draft horses, maybe one or two riding mounts but no more. Anyhow, there's nothing we can do here. We'd best be riding on." He looked at Ginny. "Do you need a rest, Ginny?"

"Of course not, and I wish you'd quit asking."

"Yes, ma'am." She seemed to be getting testier by the hour, but he supposed this scene had not inspired pleasant memories. She did not take kindly to his fussing over her, though. Time to quit. He would just keep an eye on her and call for a rest when he decided she needed it. He would find an excuse to stay over at Fort Elliott for a few days to give both riders and critters a rest. It would take time to elicit the information they would require to decide their destination after the fort stop, and, of course, resupplying would take some time.

They continued to follow the path of the Comanche for another hour until they came to a fork where the raiders had apparently split up. They reined in, and Con dismounted and walked down the southeast branch first. These horses appeared to be headed in the direction of the fort, but the horses cut a wide swath and were scattered about. The riders were not soldiers or they would have been in formation, likely single or double file for a patrol.

Ezra hollered at him, "All but one or two unshod heading southwest. That would be the Comanches."

He walked back and joined Ezra and Ginny. "I think the others are the Comancheros in the war party. They will sell the horses at the fort and likely rendezvous with their Comanche friends at some agreed upon place."

Ginny said, "But will the Army buy the horses from those men?"

"Not immediately. But there are generally several horse traders that have set up corrals and shelters within a few miles of military posts. They'll buy the horses for two thirds of what the Army will pay and then sell the animals to the Army a month or so later. A trader probably has connections with the quartermaster or whoever is acting as the horse buyer, and for a commission that person won't ask questions. Decent horses in this country always find their way to a market. We will want to take time, though, to see if any of the Comancheros are still around Fort Elliott. If they have some money most of that kind can't resist pissing it away at a tavern and bawdy house, maybe lose the rest on gambling. They would know where to find Angry Wolf."

Ginny said, "So you are saying we aren't going to follow the Comanche now? They would be the ones who have my sisters."

"It's been three weeks or so since your place was hit by the raiders. You tell me if I'm wrong, Ezra, but they probably hit this fork more than a week ago after raiding other settlers along the way. The Comanche have likely made it through Palo Duro Canyon and onto the Comanche War Trail by now. Even if we can follow their trail for a spell, they'll lose us in the canyon. It's over a hundred miles long and close to twenty miles wide in places. Without herding horses, they'll likely cover forty miles a day, and they know where they're headed. We don't."

"You make it sound impossible to catch up with them," Ginny said.

"We're not going to run them down if that's what you mean. I spent five years trying that. We've got to catch them in their lair, at their village."

"And how do we find that?"

"I'll ask around at the post. It's a good bet they will be crossing the Pecos River in southwest Texas. My main concern is whether they continued on and crossed the Rio Grande."

"You are thinking they could end up in Mexico?"

"There are mostly Apache hideaways in the Mexican mountains, but Comanche have been known to retreat there. That could be a bigger problem for us. The Army was not allowed to cross the Mexican border—not officially anyhow—and I don't know that country."

Ezra said, "I do. I lived in that country with the Comanche band I lived with for a spell. Of course, they was moving all the time—there's a name for that. Sometimes I remember."

"Nomads," Ginny said.

"Yep. Never stay one place too long. Anyhow, that's rough country down there. I doubt if we'd ever find them, and if we did, the three of us ain't got a chance of whipping them warriors. Likely them that hit Harwood Place was just a war party off a lot bigger bunch, and so far, they've escaped the whole dang U.S. Army."

"Grandpa, I won't quit ever. God saved me to rescue Noreen and Krista. I believe that. I'll find a way even if you two decide to ride away from this."

Ezra sighed. "I swear, girl, sometimes you're like a ornery bobcat looking for a fight. Me and Con ain't going nowhere, but sometimes you act like you're trying to chase us off. Just hear my whole story before you jump in and start yowling."

Con enjoyed letting Ezra fuss with her for once. Maybe he could settle Ginny down some.

"Now," Ezra said, "as I started to say, we don't got much chance taking on all them renegade Comanches. Our best chance is to ransom them girls for gold coin. I'm betting this Angry Wolf knows about money. I got a bit over thirty double eagles I'd give to a ransom."

Con said, "I can come up with nearly two thousand dollars. I think between us we've got more than enough for ransom."

Ginny's face flushed with embarrassment. "Thank you both, but I made off with some money I'd saved and a lot more that my pa had buried in the stable. I think I can pay a ransom. And I'll try hard not to question your loyalty to the mission again. Sometimes my mouth gets ahead of my brain as I know you've already figured out.

That likely won't change anytime soon. But how do we bargain with the Comanche without losing our scalps?"

"That's what I was coming to," Ezra said. "I know somebody who does that work. He's rescued or ransomed thirty or forty kids over the past ten years, mostly from Comanches. Last I knowed, he considered hisself retired from that work, and there ain't much need where Comanches is concerned. It's mostly Apaches yet these days. He gets paid for this work, of course."

She said, "How much?"

"Can't rightly say. Maybe a thousand dollars to get him back to work. He's married with a wife and passel of kids and teaches school. He also runs a ranch with his pa. He ain't likely looking for another job. But if he'd help us, I guarantee he'll find where them renegades is holed up and figure out a way to deal for ransom."

"I'm wanting to kill that bastard Angry Wolf, too, and a few others if I can find them."

"It could be you can't have everything you want if you expect to get them girls back."

Ginny said, "I know. I just need to have a talk with myself. Who is the mythical man who does this magic? You're asking a lot to swallow the notion that a schoolteacher can saddle up and do these miracles."

"Name's Grit. Grit McKay."

"Grit. Now that's quite a name."

Con joined the conversation. "I've heard of him. Grit McKay is a legend. I read a long newspaper story about him. His real name is Angus Duff McKay the third. He was a war hero for the Confederacy at Antietam and Missionary Ridge and Gettysburg. Collected a bucket-full of medals, they say. Some of his children were adopted after their parents were killed during Indian raids."

Ginny said, "His side lost."

"The war's over, Ginny."

"I lost my Grandfather Harwood fighting for the Union in that war. I never got to know him. I talked to folks who came by the trading post. Maybe we won't be shooting at each other, but that war won't be over in a hundred years. Anyway, where do we find this great man?"

Ezra said, "About a two days' ride east of San Angelo and Fort Concho. We'd be passing through that town to get where we're going anyhow. It's the only way to get there with supply stops and such on the way to the Pecos River."

"Well, I want to ponder this. Let's move on to Fort Elliott and get our business done there."

Con figured the decision had been made. Ginny just liked to let the others stew a bit. They would be riding on to Fort Concho, where he could learn more about Angry Wolf after a swing east to pay a visit to Grit McKay.

Chapter 11

SHORTLY BEFORE NOON a day later, the riders caught sight of Fort Elliott. The scene was not quite what Ginny expected: no palisades or other defense barrier, only buildings, many adobe, organized precisely along the sides of the parade ground. Surrounding the fort were scattered structures of every sort, including a good number of tents which she assumed were occupied by civilians.

As they neared the fort, Con said, "The barn-like building west of the fort is a trading post and general store. Next door is a tavern that's got meals if you're hungry enough and aren't too particular. This used to be a central buffalo hunters' camp. They call that conglomeration 'Mobeetie,' and it's supposed to be a town, but it's got a ways to go before its respectable. It's a rough place populated by outlaws of all sorts and the folks who serve them. It's not wise to venture there after dark."

"I never heard of the town."

"It used to be called 'Sweetwater,' since the area is near Sweetwater Creek, but I guess there's another town with that name, and the U.S. Post Office wouldn't accept it. I was told that Mobeetie means sweet water in one of the Indian tongues."

Ginny said, "I see what looks like a livery stable with corrals and such. Will we put up our critters there?"

"I hope to rent space in the Fort Elliot livery. Former Army can usually do that, and they should have space with troop reductions that have taken place since most of the Comanche and Kiowa went to the Fort Sill reservation. We might never see our mounts again if we leave them at the Mobeetie livery. I'm hoping we can buy some puptents from the post trader at the commissary and then set up camp as near the edge of the fort as they will allow. We'll need to venture out to the Mobeetie general store before we ride out again, but Ginny, please don't go there alone."

"Why not?"

"Like I said, this place is overrun with dangerous people."

"Who lives in all those tents?"

"Some of the business owners. There's a big turnover here. And there are some...uh...businesses carried on from the tents."

"Like whores, I suppose." Con flushed a bit. Lord, he should know by now that she had not lived a sheltered life.

"Yeah, and some special liquor sales and peyote sales."

"I've heard about peyote. I think it's a cactus, but it can do strange things to people. Indians use it in some of their religious ceremonies, I read."

"Yes, there's been some fussing about it on the reservations. You chew it or grind it up and make tea or just plain eat it. I guess it can be smoked, but I understand that slows down the effect. I've never tried the stuff but had a few soldiers end up in the guardhouse in worse shape than being booze-blind."

"I always chewed mine," Ezra said. "Just used that instead of tobacco sometimes. Don't want to do it when you need your brain working. Sends you off to dreamin', sometimes good ones, but then I had a few times that scared me and bedeviled me something awful, and I give up the stuff."

Ginny decided she could live just fine without peyote. She didn't need more nightmares than the ones she had lived night after night since the raid.

They approached the official entrance to the fort that was marked by rifle-bearing soldiers standing on each side of a wagon road that led to the interior of the fort proper. She noticed that Con reflexively saluted, and that a young fuzzy-cheeked guard with straw-colored hair looked at his companion, obviously looking for guidance on how to react.

Con rescued him by speaking. "Privates, we are seeking admission to the fort. We are hoping to rent space at the livery for our horses and mule for a few days. We also have a Comanche raid to report. I am a former sergeant with General Mackenzie's Fourth U.S. Cavalry regiment."

The blond private responded, "Well, sir, we got to get somebody's permission to let you through."

"Is Sergeant Jasper Michels still in charge of the livery here?"

"He is, sir."

"Why don't you tell him that Con Callaway is seeking entry and asking to see him."

"Well, I can do that. I will be back shortly."

The young soldier disappeared and returned within ten minutes with a short, stout sergeant with a brushy, graying mustache that did not hide the broad smile on his face. The sergeant hollered in a deep voice, "Con Callaway, what in God's name are you doing here? I figured you gone for good."

Con dismounted and stepped forward with his hand extended, but the sergeant ignored the hand and clutched him in a bear hug that about knocked him off his feet. Con said, "I just had to see Jasper Michels again."

"I ain't buying that by a longshot. When you come around, it's always to take advantage of this poor old Dutchman. What do you want now?"

"Well, we need to lodge four horses and a white mule after you meet my friends." He introduced Ginny and Ezra who remained saddled. "Later, I'll be pumping you for information."

"See, I said you always showed up to take advantage of me. I got to be darn careful when it comes to your smooth tongue. Yeah, I got plenty of room in the stable these days. Let's get them tired critters put up, and then we'll talk a spell."

Ginny and Ezra dismounted, and they followed, leading their horses as Sergeant Michels and Con, with Quanah and Chester in tow, stepped out ahead engaging in serious conversation in soft voices, obviously not wanting her to hear. She had no doubt, however, that the sergeant was getting the story of the attack at Harwood Place and their mission. The sergeant tossed a look over his shoulder from time to time, and his somber face told all.

At the stable the sergeant ordered two privates to tend to the mule and horses after the travelers unloaded the pack animals and put the gear and supplies in an empty storeroom assigned by the sergeant. "Put your valuables in there, too, if you want," Michels said. "I ain't got enough work to keep my men busy these days, and I'll keep a guard within sight of the storeroom."

Ginny was uneasy about leaving her gold coin-filled saddlebags behind, but she could not lug the gold around all afternoon. Besides, if they were going into the Mobeetie area, she worried that she would attract undue attention. Con showed no reservation about leaving his saddlebags, so she stuffed some coins in her pocket and abandoned what she considered her fortune.

When they finished at the livery, Sergeant Michels said, "Ida's at a church social, so we can't provide lunch today, but you're expected at our quarters for good German food for supper tonight. Con knows where to find us."

As they walked out of the stable, Ginny could see that Con was pondering something. "Spit it out," she said.

He looked at her with aggravation written on his face. "What makes you think I've got anything to say?"

"You've got to be careful. I can read you like a book."

"That doesn't give me comfort, that's for sure. But okay, I was going to suggest that you visit one of the post surgeons before we head to the commercial area outside the fort. You really need to have those wounds checked."

"Why? They're nearly healed, and I'm getting stronger by the day. The pain's going away. A dang sawbones will think of something to do, grab a chance to feel my little apples if nothing else. Forget about it. I'm not seeing a surgeon."

"They're professionals. They are trained to help folks with medical problems."

"Well, let them help those folks and leave their roaming fingers off me. No surgeon, and if you say any more about it, I'll think of a way to make you pay. And I'm hungry. It's past lunchtime, and I'm going to find a place to snag a sandwich or something. You two can do what you damn well please."

Ezra was chuckling. "I'd listen to her, boy, if I was you."

"I surrender. Let's go eat. The last time I was here, we could choose between Sweetwater Tavern and Sweetwater Tavern."

Chapter 12

GINNY HAD NEVER been in a tavern before, and she found nothing in the Sweetwater Tavern that would encourage additional visits. Immediately, upon stepping into the dark barroom where any sunlight was dimmed by dirt-caked windowpanes, she was struck by the rank odor of sweat intermingled with horseshit. She was accustomed to the smell of animal excrement and not ordinarily offended by it. She had cleaned the stalls daily at Harwood Place and didn't mind the smell, but this mix from men who likely bathed rarely was near nauseating. And the tavern was filled with men standing shoulder to shoulder at the bar.

Most of the tables were occupied, but a soldier stood up and waved them toward a vacant corner table next to one he shared with three comrades. They were playing poker and enjoying drinks it seemed, and she assumed they were not on duty. Out in the middle of nowhere, she guessed there was no other place to go outside the post for leave of any kind.

"Thank you," she told the soldier as she leaned her rifle against the wall, and they sat down and claimed the corner table. She saw that it was covered with crumbs, slivers of meat, and drippings from spilled beer. She supposed it would be wiped off when a waiter or waitress appeared. Alas, no one came to their table.

After a fifteen-minute wait, a woman Ginny guessed to be in her late twenties sauntered up to the table with her eyes fixed on Con. Her dress top was cut low to reveal generous cleavage. Her long, black hair might have been pretty, but it needed washing like everything else in the place, Ginny thought.

The woman, still looking at Con, asked, "Drinks?"

Con smiled. "Yes, but can we order something to eat?"

She spoke with a soft, seductive voice. "We got sandwiches, Honey. That's about it till suppertime. I'd recommend the ham. I wouldn't feed the beef to a dog. There was some rotten, moldy edges when it got cooked up a few days back."

Con looked at the others. "You're my guests. What will it be?"

Ezra said, "Ham sandwich and a beer."

Ginny said, "Same."

Con said, "The ham sandwich and coffee."

The waitress lifted her painted eyebrows. "A real drinking man, huh? That's refreshing, Honey." She turned and walked away, needlessly swinging her butt a bit much, Ginny thought. And both Con and Ezra were watching every swing of that butt. Men were disgusting creatures.

"What happens after we're done here?" Ginny asked.

"We'll stop at the post commissary and get what we can there and then whenever we ride out, we'll stop at the Mobeetie general store and try to fill any missing needs."

"I'd like to stop at the general store when we've eaten. I need some changes of clothes, and I'd like to buy some blankets, so I can put together my own bedroll."

"I guess we can do that. I figured we would stop there when we left the fort anyhow if the commissary doesn't have everything we need, but you wouldn't want to put your bedroll together on the run—or pick out clothes. We wouldn't get out till suppertime."

"Are we going to be able to get out of here tomorrow?"

"I don't know. Jasper said that Captain Leroy Richards is acting commandant at the fort. I rode with him when he was a first lieutenant. An excellent officer, and he will talk straight with me about what we're up against as far as the Army is concerned. I'll check at his office when we get back to the fort and find out when I might be able to talk with him."

Ginny said, "We've got to get moving. Time's wasting."

The waitress returned with the orders and set them on the table. The woman still pretended Ginny was invisible and did not acknowledge her presence beyond placing the mug of beer and sandwich plate in front of her. Ginny guessed that tables did not get cleaned in the tavern, but the little witch took a cloth and wiped the table area in front of Con before setting his plate down. "I'll be back in a minute with your coffee, Hon. There's a fresh pot brewing, and I thought you might like that."

"That's very kind of you, ma'am."

"My name's Lulu, Hon. Please just call me Lulu."

He smiled. "And my name's Con. Thank you for looking after me."

Ginny almost gagged at the interplay between the two. Then Lulu dug her fingers between her breasts and plucked out a small, folded piece of paper and handed it to Con before turning away and leaving to retrieve the coffee she was likely lying about. Con opened the folded paper, glanced at it, and tucked it in his shirt pocket. He obviously was not going to share the contents.

She took a sip of the beer and nearly spat it out. It was bitter as sour milk and so warm she wondered if it had been taken off the stove. She had never drunk much beer but occasionally stole a bottle from the stone springhouse where her father had stored bottles of beer for customers and himself in a trough of water that ran through their stone springhouse. She had come to enjoy a bottle of beer on a warm day, and Pa was not good with numbers so long as she did not overdo her pilferage. She would never join the temperance movement, but brew like this would have kept her out of the springhouse. On the other hand, Ezra seemed not to notice, and she slid hers to him. He looked at her and nodded his thanks.

When Lulu returned with Con's coffee, Ginny asked, "Do you suppose I could have a cup of coffee, too?"

Lulu looked at her with sad eyes, "Oh, I'm sorry dear, this was our last cup." Ginny stared at her in disbelief, as Lulu winked at Con and walked away wiggling that damned ass again.

Ginny looked at Con and said, "How can they be out of coffee when yours was made fresh?"

He shrugged. "You are welcome to mine if you want it."

"I don't want your damned fresh-made coffee. I'll get me a drink of fresh water from my canteen when we get back to the fort." She took a bite from her sandwich. The bread was a mite stale, but the ham was okay. Deciding it was edible, she downed it quickly.

"We'll eat well tonight, I promise. There is no better cook in the world than Ida Michels, and you will love her."

Ginny figured that any woman after Lulu the Bitch would be an improvement. She just wondered what was going on between Con and that woman.

Con got up to go to the bar and pay the bill, but before he left, she saw him drop a silver dollar on the table, which Ginny assumed was for Lulu. He was crazy. The meals with drinks wouldn't be more than two dollars. For the service she got, Ginny would not have left the woman a nickel.

While Con was settling the bill at the bar, Ginny looked up and froze when she saw two men step through the batwing doors like cocky roosters. A rangy man with raw scars peppering one cheek, not more than a kid, looked around the room, and his eyes set on her. He nudged the other big, bearish man with a black beard who turned his head and stared at her. She froze. He was the man she thought of as "Grizzly." At first, he appeared shocked, but his eyes and face quickly turned to rage. This was the man she had stabbed at Harwood Place, and he was already making his way toward her with his young companion following behind.

She turned toward Ezra. "These two were with the raiders. The scars on the young one's face came from Skipper."

She knew she did not have time to grab her Winchester before they reached the table, but Ezra's fingers were inching toward the six-gun holstered at his waist.

But Grizzly had already latched onto her arm and yanked her from the chair. "I thought you was dead, bitch. No way you could be alive. You come with me, and we're going to talk."

The young man already had his six-gun trained on Ezra. Grizzly started to drag her away when Con latched onto his shoulder with one hand and slipped the big man's pistol out of the holster with the other, dropping it on the floor. He pulled him around and drove a fist into the big man's nose. Ginny, released now, stumbled back and landed on the floor. She saw the younger Comanchero swing around to fire his weapon at Con, but Ezra sprang up with quickness that belied his age and drove the butt of his own pistol into the back of the younger man's skull, dropping him like a gunnysack full of corn.

Grizzly, blood running over his lips and into his beard, charged Con, striking him with a glancing blow just below the eye before Con feinted and rammed his fist into his opponent's gut and hammered another to his jaw.

Grizzly was swinging wildly now but landed a few more hits to Con's face before Con moved in close and began punching and jabbing, again and again. Then he dodged away while Grizzly kept swinging at the air before he attacked once more and with full force drove a sledgehammer-like fist between the eyes. Grizzly stumbled backward and tumbled to the floor, unconscious.

There was a dead silence in the large room, all eyes fixed on Con before he spoke. "These two men are Comancheros and were part of a Comanche war party that killed this lady's parents and brother and took her two little sisters with them. We are taking these men to the fort where they will be held until the law deals with them. Any man who tries to stop us will be taking on the United States Army."

Ginny climbed back to her feet, her head spinning over all that had transpired in several minutes' time. She saw that the soldiers at the adjoining table were all standing now.

The soldier who had waved them to the corner table said, "We'll walk back to the fort with you folks, sir, in case you need some help."

Con spun around. "Corporal, that would be much appreciated. Maybe you can help me drag the garbage outside, and we'll try to get them back on their feet."

With the two Comancheros sitting on the boardwalk and starting to regain consciousness, the corporal, a lanky, clean-shaven young man, came up to Con. "Sergeant, I'm Corporal Tom Best. You wouldn't remember me. I was in a different company and a private when I saw you win the championship at Fort Sill. You took on a bigger man that time, too. You could have been a professional boxer. I thought you looked familiar when you walked into the tavern, but I didn't realize who you were till I saw those fists swinging."

"Well, Corporal, at least I had some padded leather wrapped around my fist in my boxing days." He held up his hands and displayed the raw knuckles on his left hand.

The Corporal looked at the hand and said, "You ought to stop at the post surgeon's and get some salve for your knuckles and see if you should get some stitches on the side of your right eye. That handkerchief you're pressing to your eye is blood soaked."

"I might just do that once we get these no-goods locked up."

"I'll see they're locked up in the guardhouse. You will likely want to report this to Captain Richards himself in the morning. I know for a fact that this afternoon he's meeting with some Washington bigwigs that came in on the stage."

"I'll do just that."

Ginny was standing next to Con, and Ezra leaned against the tavern's front wall on the other side of the entryway. Con Callaway was the last man in the world she would have guessed to be a boxer. Somehow, he just seemed too refined for fisticuffs. Regardless, his face looked like a horse had stepped on it, but she was not going to accompany him to the surgeon, or she would end up stretched out on a surgery table herself before she escaped the hospital. What she really wanted to do was find a way to kill the two bastards sitting on the boardwalk before she left the fort.

She lifted her rifle and levered a cartridge into the chamber and stepped toward Grizzly when Con grabbed her arm and pulled her back.

"No," he said. "You will just make things worse."

Fuming now, she looked up and glared at him. "I'm not a child."

"Then act like it."

They stood there silently for several minutes before Ezra sidled up next to Con and said, "Young feller. About that paper you got in your shirt pocket."

"What paper?" Con's hand went to his shirt pocket. "Oh. What about it?"

"You ain't in any shape to be needing it."

Con chuckled. "I wasn't planning on using it anyway. Do you want it?"

"Yep. I'd take it kindly."

Con handed him the note. "Give Lulu my regards."

Ezra nodded and took the note, giving it a glance before stuffing it in his trouser pocket.

Ginny had forgotten about the paper Lulu gave Con. Now her curiosity was almost more than she could bear. What was going on?

Chapter 13

SERGEANT JASPER MICHELS greeted the three visitors at the door of the small residence located in the quarters set aside for married enlisted officers. "Come on in folks," Michels said, studying Con's face and grinning. "They tell me I ought to see the other guy. Sorry, they don't give no trophies and such here."

Con figured that word about his altercation had likely spread to the fort before they returned. "Those two animals were the only trophies we needed. I just want to be sure they never see the light of day again."

"You'll have to take that up with Captain Richards. You rode with him a time or two, didn't you?"

"Three missions. I'm glad he's here."

"He'll be in a bad mood. He was spending the afternoon with two stuffed shirts from the War Department. They're talking about closing down Fort Elliott. Don't make me no mind. At the government's speed, it will take at least five years, and I'll be on to someplace else or retired by then."

Before they could sit down in the parlor, a tall, buxom woman, attired in a colorful flowered dress, emerged from the kitchen. She saw Con, brushed a few errant hair strands from her face and rushed to him, almost knocking him off his feet when she fell into his arms and planted a kiss on his cheek. She was a sturdy woman but not fat, just big and several inches taller than her husband. She pulled back, and sparkling blue eyes studied his face. "Oh, Con, why did you have to get in a fight your first day back? Jasper told me, and you've even got stitches below your eye."

"Better than a lead slug, Ida. I'll be fine, just not as purty as usual."

She laughed, "And you always were such a handsome cuss, had all the single ladies drooling, and a few of the married ones, too."

Jasper said, "I hope that don't include my wife."

"You'll never know, you old scoundrel. Besides, I've caught you looking at some of the ladies now and then and read those thoughts you shouldn't be thinking in your head."

"I'll retreat from any war of words with you. I ain't won one yet. I just hope you got some supper for these folks soon. They got to be near starving."

Ida turned to Ginny and gave her a warm hug. "And you're Ginny. Jasper told me about your family. I'm so sorry. We'll talk later, if you like. You're going to stay in our spare room while you're here, and I'm betting you would enjoy a hot bath."

Ginny brightened. "You're sure it won't be too much trouble?"

"Lord, girl, you don't know how hungry I am for company. And you will all take your meals here. You've got a long trail ahead, and you don't need to start it with the slop the Army feeds—and Con will get into another fight if you go back into that so-called town to eat."

She left Ginny speechless and stepped over to Ezra and embraced him. "And I can't forget Ezra. Such a good man, helping Ginny the way you are. Welcome to our home. And everybody just call me 'Ida.'"

Con figured Ida had totally won over all the guests with her warm greetings. Wait till they ate.

Ida said, "Now you all take your places at the dining table. I've got five places set." She gestured to a table at the end of the parlor just off the kitchen entryway.

Ginny said, "May I help you serve, Ida?"

"If you like, dear."

The women disappeared in the kitchen and soon Ginny returned with a huge plate and set it on the table. "Ida says this is schnitzel, slices of breaded pork."

Ida followed with a huge bowl of potato salad with bacon pieces, and soon they had green beans and fresh-baked bread on the table. They sat down to eat and Ida offered a blessing, giving thanks for the food and asking for the safety of their guests in the days ahead.

Ida said, "The coffee's brewing, and I will have something to fill your cups shortly. And save room for Black Forest cake."

"I saw the cake," Ginny said, and for the first time Con saw a childlike smile that made her even more beguiling. "I had never seen one, chocolate layers with a sweet cream or pudding between and cherries poured over the top, even some between the layers."

Later Ginny volunteered to help Ida clean up, and Con could hear the ladies chattering in the kitchen. Ida was getting more congenial conversation out of Ginny than Con had during more than three weeks he had known her. Somehow, it seemed like he usually ended up in verbal combat with her.

Jasper and Con retreated to rockers on the front porch, and Ezra gave profound thanks to the hostess for a scrumptious meal. He told her he was tired out and was heading off to catch some sleep, accepting Jasper's offer of the cot in the stable office.

Con had already decided to claim a spot in one of the nearly vacant barracks, but Ezra wanted no part of that. Of course, Con knew the ornery cuss had another stop on the agenda before he headed for his cot.

He and Jasper sat down on the porch, watching Ezra hobble across the parade ground. "He's headed out the gate," Jasper said, handing Con a cigar. "If he's fixing to visit Mobeetie, dark ain't a good time to go."

"Full sun didn't work out all that well today," Con said, tracing his fingers gently over his tender face. "But Ezra won't likely be headed for the tavern. He's going to make a visit to Lulu."

"Lulu?"

"Yeah, a young lady that served our lunches today." He took a lucifer from the little tin he carried in his trouser pocket and lit the cigar, savoring that first puff. He had never cared much for cigarettes, but he rather enjoyed a cigar when he had the opportunity three or four times a year.

"One of the tent ladies?"

"Yep. I never figured the old guy would have that much fire in his drawers, but he was sure taken with Lulu. Good for him, I say."

"Gives me hope for the future," Jasper said, lighting up his own cigar. "Wish we could share a whiskey bottle, but Ida's taken up with the temperance folks. I got to take my spirits at the stable, and not just before I'm headed home. She's a wonderful woman, and I'm always surprised she keeps me around, but when she gets her mind set on something, it ain't worth a fight to take her on."

"Well, I gave up the drinking. I went on a few drunks that about got me booted from the Army, and I got demoted for brawling drunk one time. I was lucky I had a company commander who explained to me that I was like he was, one of those men who touches a drink, and he can't stop. He said if I wanted to fight somebody maybe I should take up boxing. I did, and I won the company a few championships."

"Hell, you was the best in the whole danged Army. I was surprised you didn't try to make a living at it."

"I figured out that I'd end up with my brains beat out sooner or later, and I'd sort of lost my taste for fighting."

"So what are you going to do to make your way from here?"

"I don't know. I've got to live through this chase I'm on first."

"Well, you got a darned pretty filly to chase with."

"She is that, and she's got no idea what she does to a man. But I don't want to spend a lifetime fussing with a female. I'll move on if I get through this mission with my scalp."

"Aw, fussing ain't so bad when you got other compensations."

"Like good German cooking?"

"Well, that, too."

"I need to change the subject. What do you know about Angry Wolf?"

"Nothing firsthand. I don't get in the field anymore. Has he got something to do with these raids? A patrol from here buried a family at a burned-out place a few days back."

"I told you about Ginny's family. The leader wore a wolfskin cape, and Ezra said that would be Angry Wolf."

"Yeah. That sounds like what I've heard about him. And he's got one of the few bands that ain't gone into the reservation. They say he's twice as fierce as Quanah ever was and one mean son of a bitch. Him and his people still think they can drive the white man out of this country."

"Are there any troops trying to track him down?"

"Nope, not from Elliott anyhow. We don't got men to spare these days. I think that's what Captain Richards will tell you."

"I know the Army doesn't know exactly where Angry Wolf's village is or they'd have a force after him—or I like to think so."

"I ain't heard anything about that. Maybe Captain Richards can help. Somewhere across the Pecos for sure."

"We're going to visit a man named Grit McKay about the possibility of helping find Ginny's sisters. Did you ever hear of him?"

"Yeah. Everybody's heard of old Grit. Recovered all them kids from the Comanches. Generally got a pretty good price. Sometimes he made a deal for ransom, and others he just went in and took them somehow. You couldn't go wrong to sign him on—if you can afford him."

"I guess we'll have to see what he's asking and what he thinks they might be asking for ransom."

"If they still got them girls. You said the Comanches was working with Comancheros."

"Yeah. We took two into the guardhouse today."

"Well, that's good. If they connected up with Angry Wolf, they'd be pushing to take the girls to Mexico. That don't mean Angry Wolf won't do it, but he might not be so quick to do it because he wouldn't know the contacts and likely not speak their language. Of course, if there were other Comancheros with the Injuns, they might go ahead on their own. Hell, who knows?"

Chapter 14

THE WATER WAS cooling in the wooden tub now, but Ginny savored her soaking in the water. Poor Jasper had hauled the tub's contents upstairs to provide her with this luxury, first carrying buckets of water from the outside pump, and then moving it again after Ida heated part of it in the big kettle to add to the cold water in the tub. Ida had supervised the task to be certain the water was just right.

Ida offered to scrub Ginny's back with lye soap and was horrified at the healing wounds on her young friend's body. "Praise the Lord, Ginny. It's just not possible for someone to survive what happened to you. It's truly nothing short of a miracle. God had work for you to do."

"He wants me to bring my sisters back, I guess."

"And Con Callaway was your doctor?"

"I suppose you could say so."

"It's amazing. Con and Ezra were like angels sent at just the right time to help you."

"I believe that, but a better time would have been a few hours earlier when the Comanche attacked Harwood Place. I told them they were like angels, although sometimes they don't seem so much that way. Con was more like the devil when I watched him pounding his fists on that ugly Comanchero this noon. And sometimes he gets so bossy, I'd like to punch him myself."

Ida laughed. "That comes from being an Army sergeant. I married one of those, and it took a spell for him to accept that I was his superior officer when it came to certain things. With patience and persistence, they can be trained."

Ginny could not keep from smiling. Ida Michels had a knack for coaxing smiles. Ida assisted her out of the tub, wrapping a big towel around her. "I have a flannel nightgown you can use during your stay," Ida said. "I love having you here, and I know Con has a lot to do tomorrow, so I'm certain we get to have you with us at least one more night."

"When we got here, I wanted to move on as soon as possible, but now I don't mind indulging myself another night. I need to find a way to purchase some riding clothes tomorrow and undergarments. I don't want Con looking over my shoulder when I'm looking at underpants. He's taken enough of my privacy. When I thought I was dying, he washed every inch of my body in cold water, and he's still changing the dressings on the wound below my breast. I'm not sure it even needs changing anymore. It bothers me sometimes that he's seen me naked so many times."

"I'm sure he didn't pay any attention, dear. He was just trying to help."

"Do you really believe that?"

"No. But I am sure he liked what he saw."

Ginny closed her eyes and grimaced. "That doesn't help a bit. And these wounds are going to leave such ugly scars that I'd be embarrassed for any man to ever see me naked again."

"They're healing nicely for how serious they were. I do think the one on your abdomen needs attention for a few more days, but not much longer. Con hasn't been doing it to invade your privacy. He's not that kind, I assure you. I can change the dressing tonight and tomorrow night, and we can find something for you to take with you so you can do that yourself from now on."

"That would be wonderful."

"And if you like, I will take you shopping tomorrow. I think we can find everything you need at the commissary tomorrow. They do have a room set aside for women's garments, although for riding britches, and an extra shirt or two, you might have to settle for men's things, but we'll get something that fits you better than what you've been wearing lately."

Ginny was buoyed by the thought of shopping with Ida and felt a bit guilty for the happiness she had enjoyed the past few hours. She knew this would end soon enough.

Chapter 15

CON FELT BETTER after a shave and cold shower at the water barrel that was hoisted on a small tower near the water pump. Canvas tarps anchored to poles allowed for a bit of modesty and furnished some buffer against the wind. He preferred the convenience of bathing in the nearest stream or creek, but a man never knew what had joined the water upstream, and a few times he had picked up a near herd of leeches.

He had left his filthy clothing with a woman at washer's row, and now he was on his way to visit the acting fort commandant Captain Leroy Richards. He entered the office and was greeted by a corporal at a desk. He said, "Good morning, Corporal. My name is Congrave Callaway, and I would like to speak with Captain Richards sometime today if possible."

The corporal got up from the desk. "If you will wait just a moment, sir, I'll check with the captain. I know he's expecting you." He disappeared through a doorway behind the reception desk.

He should have known that word of the new prisoners would have reached him as well as the story behind their incarceration. The corporal returned shortly, followed by a tall officer with thick, salt and pepper hair and mustache. The captain eased past the corporal and stepped out to greet Con with a welcoming smile and extended hand. The men exchanged firm grips, and Captain Richards said, "Sergeant, it's a joy to see you again. I hoped our paths might cross again one day. Come into my office, and you can bring me up to date."

"Thanks for seeing me on such short notice, Captain. I know you're a busy man, and I thought I might have trouble getting in to see you."

"For a soldier who saved my scalp at least twice? I think not, Sergeant." When they walked into the commandant's office, the captain gestured toward his desk and closed the office door behind them. Con took the chair in front of the desk, casting his eyes about a room devoid of any wall hangings, not even the captain's West Point diploma or certificates for the medals he had earned during Civil War service, where he had reached the rank of brevet colonel.

The captain sat down behind the scarred desk that was stacked with papers and said, "I don't really have all this work to do. I met with War Department bureaucrats yesterday, and they wanted to review all this old paperwork, which, of course, they wouldn't understand. I'm hoping I get sent to a battlefield command soon, maybe west to the Apache wars. I'm not cut out for a desk job."

"I've got to admit it seems strange not seeing you in the saddle, Captain."

"But you didn't visit to hear my bitching. I know you were at work with your fists again, and with your eye swollen nearly shut, it appears you took a few blows. I thought you were finished boxing when you left the Army."

"Me, too, but I was sort of forced into this match."

"Well, the surgeon reports your fists left a man with a broken jaw and a nose that's going to look like an African warthog's."

"I can't say I'm sorry. I wonder if the fella can talk?"

"I don't know. Except for some dizziness, the surgeon said his partner's okay. If you want to question them, you can visit them at the guardhouse. I'll sign an authorization for you to show the guard. But tell me what this is all about."

Con gave the captain a summary of the slaughter at Harwood Place and the abduction of Ginny's sisters. He also told him about the discovery of the other burnt-out farm a day north of the fort.

"I'm aware of the place north of here," Richards said. "We had a patrol come across that farmstead a day after it must have happened. Buried a young couple, an old man, and a little girl not more than three years old. They couldn't tell if there were other children that might have been taken captive or not. It had to be the same bunch that attacked Harwood Place. I'm sure those two you brought in came here with the stolen horses and sold them to one of the outfits near the fort, and they'll eventually make their way to our herds."

"You buy stolen horses?"

"These folks are clever, and I'm afraid we have a man or two among our troops working with them. Wranglers come here from Fort Union to the west and, of course, Fort Sill, to claim extra horses for the Army. Sometimes they even deal directly with the traders, and the mounts don't pass through our hands. The Army's always hungry for more horses."

"Do you have troops out tracking the war party?"

"No, I'm sorry to say. Not only are we short of men right now, but our orders are also 'non-pursuit.' Our mission is to protect farmers and ranchers in the Texas panhandle area and to discourage raids with regular patrols. I just don't have enough men to engage in a chase, and it would put me in the position of disregarding orders. Besides, do you really think that our forces, made up largely of men who have never fought Indians, would surprise somebody like Angry Wolf?"

"No. I'm joining the search for those girls with not a great deal of confidence."

"So you won't leave the young woman?"

"No. She is stubborn as a mule, and I really believe she'd go on alone if it came to that. Do you know anything at all about where Angry Wolf might be?"

"I really don't. You mentioned contacting Grit McKay. I've met the man, and I couldn't give you better advice than that. I'm betting he will either have a good idea or know someone who does. Of course, I understand he hasn't been doing this kind of work since most of the Comanche went to the reservation."

Suddenly, gunfire and yelling outside interrupted their conversation. Captain Richards sprang to his feet. "What in the hell is that commotion out there?" He charged around his desk and headed for the door, and

Con got up and followed. The gunfire was sporadic by the time they reached the door that opened next to the parade ground, and when he and the captain stepped outside, they saw that chaos reigned near the guardhouse at the opposite corner of the parade ground. Between smoke pouring out the barred windows and a dust cloud forming a near-black curtain, the structure was barely visible.

Several dead or wounded soldiers lay on the ground at the edge of the drifting, dark cover, and a surgeon and stretcher-bearing soldiers were rushing toward the unfortunates. A bucket brigade was forming near one of the water pumps. Con and Richards headed for the guardhouse, and Con caught sight of his new friend Corporal Tom Best breaking away from the melee and rushing their way.

When they met, the corporal stopped and saluted the captain, who returned the salute and said, "What happened, Corporal?"

"I'm picking it up in bits and pieces, Sir, but it appears eight to ten hooded riders swarmed into the guardhouse, shot the outside guard, and a couple went inside, took out the interior supervisor, got his keys, and released one prisoner. The two civilians we locked up yesterday were the only occupants. There were more shots inside, and two explosions that set the guardhouse on fire."

The captain said, "Nobody's been inside yet?"

"No, Sir. I don't know what we'll find in there, but I got a bucket brigade going, and with the stone walls and such, there ain't much to burn. The roof doesn't seem to be on fire, yet anyhow. Fifteen minutes, and we should be able to see the damage. I'm afraid for the inside guard. They killed Private Smith, the outside man, and you could see for yourself, Sir, that a couple of soldiers headed that way to help got taken down. Don't know their condition."

"Did one of the prisoners escape then?"

"Yessir. I was coming from the stable. It looked like they had just one spare horse, and I saw that big, bearded feller that the sergeant here whipped good yesterday staggering toward the horse with some help. They got him mounted, and then they rode out. I could see the dust trail. It looked like they were headed for Mobeetie, but they won't be there but a minute I'm guessing."

"Thank you for taking charge, Corporal. There will be a commendation entered in your records for a job well done."

"Thank you, Sir. Now, with your permission, I'll see to getting things cleared, so you can inspect it."

When Corporal Best left, Richards commented to Con, "That young man has a future in the Army if he doesn't bail out like some I know."

"He does, Captain. And he told me he's hoping for a career in the Army unlike the fella you're talking about."

They walked slowly now, giving the firefighters time to clear the air. The dust had settled, and the smoke was thinning, granting a view now of the building. Richards said, "Without a wall or parapet or even a fence, I've always worried about attacks like this. No barrier of any kind. Folks can just ride in and out as they please. It made this place vulnerable to Indian attacks when first built, but fortunately things were taming down some by then, and the fort was still protected by sheer numbers. I double the guard at night. I should have kept it doubled or even tripled the guard, I suppose. I frankly didn't see how these men could be that important to anybody."

"Don't second guess yourself, Captain. Nobody would have expected this, and that's why it worked for the attackers. I just don't understand how they got a force that size to help with an escape."

"The man must be more important than either of us thought, and Angry Wolf certainly appears to have more influence with the Comancheros than I would have guessed."

Con said, "But Ginny said she saw no more than four Comancheros among the raiders—the two we brought in and then a colored man and another who might have been Mexican. There could have been a few more that she didn't see, but those wouldn't have been enough to put together the large force that apparently hit the fort this morning. And I still wonder why they didn't strike at night even with the extra guards."

"Moving in the dark has its limits. Our guards tend to be more alert at night. The darkness spooks a lot of men on sentry duty, and the enemy can't see their targets as well. And the element of surprise. Who would have expected this attack at an Army post in the middle of the morning?"

"Yeah, that's true enough."

The smoke had cleared now, and the corporal waved them to the guardhouse. When the two men approached the door, Corporal Best said, "The clay floor is slippery from the water, Sir, so you might want to step carefully. Two dead men inside, one of the prisoners and Private Jacobs."

When they stepped inside, the private was stretched out in front of his charred desk, his rifle not far from an outstretched hand. Con thought the young man had tried to mount a defense, but everything had happened too fast. They walked back to the cell block. He noted that the fire had not damaged the structure significantly. The smoke had evidently come from mattresses and furnishings.

They found the prisoner on the floor near the half-open cell door. Con knelt beside him. A single bullet wound in his temple. The burns around the wound suggested the pistol barrel had been pressed against his flesh. Killed by his own comrades, if those types even think of each other that way. Anyhow, the man had been dispensable, possibly a nuisance during any escape, and he might have known a thing or two that the invaders had not wanted shared.

Con said, "Captain, were you able to obtain any names for the prisoners? Ginny always called the big man 'Grizzly.'"

"Oh, yes. My clerk will have the names. I don't remember the name of this young man, but it was no doubt made up. The man you refer to as Grizzly even printed his name out for us. The first two letters are initials. The name was 'U.R. Dead.'"

"A man with a sense of humor. Can you send some troops to try to find these men?"

"Of course, I'll do this now. They've killed soldiers. We've got to try to bring these men in. My guess is that some will head with Mister U.R. Dead to join Angry Wolf. Those that were just hired guns have already disappeared in Mobeetie, and our chances of nailing them are slim to none. There are three or four hundred no-goods in that town, most living in tents, and nobody's going to help us figure out the identity of those hooded men. Anyway, I've got to go issue some orders. How soon will you be moving on?"

"Likely tomorrow morning. Now I've got to go give Ginny Harwood the news about her friend Grizzly or U.R. Dead or whatever his name is."

Chapter 16

GINNY WAS TIRED and discouraged. The search for Noreen and Krista was going nowhere. It had been ten days since they departed Fort Elliott, and she missed Ida Michels terribly. They had become fast friends in a few days' time, and she found that she rather enjoyed her first experience of being spoiled. They shared tears at their parting, but Ginny had promised to visit upon return with her sisters. The brief rest had strengthened her, but the blistering sun and a hard ride was taking its toll after over ten days in the saddle.

She regretted now that she had snapped at Con when he informed her of the guardhouse escape, blaming him because he had stopped her from killing Grizzly. She realized she might be sitting in the guardhouse at Fort Elliott herself if she had shot the man. Her temper was hair-trigger these days, and that was not her nature. Unfortunately for Con, the man who saved her life was the nearest target.

They were resting and watering their critters at a stream in the midafternoon. She turned to Ezra. "Grandpa, you have been to this Diamond M Ranch before, right?"

"Once. But it's been maybe ten years. We're in the neighborhood, though. I'm sure of it. I suppose we shoulda swung by Fort Concho to check, but this saved us a couple days." She supposed that was true if Ezra and Con knew where they were going.

Con said, "Well, Jasper's sketch says we shouldn't be far. I've crossed the Concho River plenty of times, so I know that's what we've been following, and this stream has got to be Frog Creek. Jasper's map says a giant cottonwood would mark the stream that fed into the Concho and I've never seen one any bigger than the giant we saw this morning. If we follow the stream southeast for a half day it is supposed to pass within fifty yards of Diamond M headquarters."

Ezra said, "Yep, it's comin' right up."

Con said, "I'd like to ride another hour, and if we don't find it, set up camp and hope we reach the place early tomorrow."

Half an hour later, Frog Creek started flowing downslope and the riders looked out onto a vast prairie. On the horizon stood enough clustered buildings to make up a small town, Ginny thought.

"I'll be danged. That's the Diamond M, but the place has growed more than a little since I last seen it," Ezra said.

It took another fifteen minutes to reach the building site, and as they neared, Ginny saw an enormous two-story house that dominated the ranch headquarters site. Challenging the headquarters house for size, however, was a newer stone structure with a flagpole in front, flying the red, white, and blue flag with thirty-eight stars, whipping in a stiff wind. Although Ezra had informed her the man called Grit was a highly decorated Confederate veteran, the War of the Rebellion was apparently over for the folks who occupied this property.

Ginny assumed the stone building was a school. Near the structure, which she estimated was set about a hundred feet south of the house along a wagon road, was a building that looked like a small bunkhouse. Farther back were several stables with corrals, a big barn, two bunkhouses and assorted smaller buildings. All appeared to be simple, solid structures, designed not to impress but entirely with function in mind.

They rode up to hitching posts in front of the house and dismounted, and a black and white shepherd dog leaped off the veranda and raced toward them. He had apparently been trained not to bark at every visitor, so as not to scare the horses. The dog reminded her of Skipper, and for a moment the memory caused her to fight back tears. His tail wagged, and his eyes signaled he was glad for company. He came directly to Ginny, and she knelt to accept his kisses. "You sweet thing," she said. "You are just what I needed."

They hitched the horses and mule to the rails. A few ranch hands were hollering and breaking horses at the corrals, but it was quiet near the house and school which she supposed was not in session with summer settled in now. They started for the house and the door opened, and an older man with a full head of salt and pepper hair emerged from the house. He stepped out onto the veranda, offered an affable smile and said, "Howdy, folks. Come on in."

They stepped onto the wide porch, and he gave Ginny a slight bow, took her hand and kissed the top. "Welcome, young lady, to the Diamond M."

He was a strong six feet tall, lean and muscular with sun-bronzed skin and deep crow's feet extending from clear blue eyes. He was a handsome devil even at what she guessed to be a bit more than sixty years.

"Thank you, sir," she said.

"Oh, I'm not 'sir.' I'm Duff. Duff McKay."

"And I am Ginny. Ginny Harwood."

"Pleased to meet you, Ginny."

He extended his hand to Ezra and while they shook, his eyes focused on the old mountain man. "I know you. Give me a minute. Ezra Stumpf. It's been a long time, old friend."

"My Lord. It's been near ten years. How in blazes did you remember my name?"

McKay grinned. "Some folks are unforgettable."

"A man could take that several ways."

"Take it as a compliment."

Duff turned to Con, again offering his hand. The two exchanged firm grips, and Con said, "I'm Con Callaway, Duff."

"Well, let's get in the house and talk a bit. You'll be staying for supper, of course, and we'll find decent beds for the night. After we get acquainted some, I'll take you over to the stable, and we'll get those critters put up right. I've got a hand or two to help us out down there, so it won't take long." He looked down at the dog. "You can come in, too, if you want, Whizzer."

When they walked into the house, Ginny thought at first she was walking into a big banquet room. The doorway took them directly into a dining room with three rows of long tables that combined would sit over thirty-five people, she estimated.

Duff said, "The sitting room's off to the right. We'll head in there and get you seated. Would you drink some coffee, maybe try one or two of the cook's doughnuts?"

"Sounds darn good to me," Ezra said, and his companions nodded agreement.

The sitting room, or parlor, was a third the size of the dining room. With a stone fireplace, and stuffed leather chairs and couches sufficient to seat a dozen, it was a cozy room, and she suspected it had been carved down some at one point for an enlarged dining area. She claimed one of the stuffed chairs and noticed that an orange and white tabby cat had been disturbed from its nap and was looking at the intruders with annoyance but was not conceding space. Whizzer sat down on the rug at her feet, obviously waiting for ear scratches.

"That's Ranger on the chair next to you," Duff said. "He's friendly when he chooses, but nobody moves him from his spot. He and Whizzer play sometimes but when Ranger chooses."

Ezra and Con dropped onto a settee nearby.

Duff said, "I'll be back soon. The cooks should be in the kitchen working on supper, and my wife, Rosita, and daughter-in-law, Jess, will be in later. Those two and some of the kids look after the hogs. The cowhands are insulted to be asked to work with pigs, but they sure don't mind eating ham and bacon and pork chops. We're a long way from any town and feed a lot of folks, so besides our cattle and horse operation, we've got to make room for hogs and chickens, too."

When Duff left, Ginny looked around the room, which she immediately decided was arranged for comfort not pretentiousness. But more than one cook? Outside of wives and daughters, a hired cook was almost unheard of in the west she lived in.

"He didn't mention Grit," Con said. "I hope he's around."

"He's a schoolteacher," Ezra said. "Maybe he's over at the school. Last I knew, him and Duff run the ranch together, but Duff never was keen on the school business."

"With a school built just steps away, it looks like Grit won that fight."

Soon, a young Mexican woman entered the room with a tray that included a coffee pot and four mugs. Duff followed with a plate of doughnuts. "This is Camila Gonzales, Rosita's niece—mine, too, now," Duff said. "She will get you served and then leave the coffee pot and doughnut platter on the tea table in case you would enjoy more."

"Good afternoon," Camila said, displaying a perfect smile, and began filling the cups and passing the doughnut plate.

Ezra snatched two. "Ain't no sense in pretendin' I might not eat a second."

When Camila left, Duff said, "Camila and her friend Mary, along with supervision from my stepdaughter, Juanita Hamilton, handle cooking for the family, the ranch hands, and the entire school when it's in session. School finished for the summer a few weeks back. We had twenty students outside the ranch families this past year, a dozen of them boarders during the school week. You probably saw the lodge next to the school. It's partitioned into girls' and boys' sections with an adult supervisor in each. Over my complaints, Grit has turned the school into a major business—one that we barely break even on. Lord, he's hoping to add a high school soon and even talks about a college someday. There won't be room for cows on this place. It'll be filled with kids."

Ginny thought there was a fair amount of pride in Duff's words, notwithstanding his grumbling.

Duff said, "But I don't think you came to talk about school. What can I do for you folks?"

Con spoke. "We came to see if Grit might be able to help us recover two young girls that were taken by Comanche." Sparing details, he told the rancher about the killing of Ginny's parents and brother and capture of Noreen and Krista.

Ginny noticed that Duff McKay's eyes narrowed under a wrinkled brow, and his friendly smile turned into a frown. Duff said, "Grit's not in the child recovery business. Those days are past. He promised me and his wife, Jess, too, when we backed him on his school plans. Besides, he can't even sit a horse right now."

"I don't understand," Con said.

"Darn fool went and broke his leg trying to break a bronc the day after school was out. Took on a black stallion nobody else was able to handle. Well, it tossed him and then stomped him good. We were lucky that Jess is good at doctoring and that her twin sister, Jennie, was here at the time. Jennie was home from Texas Medical College in Galveston, where she'll finish up and become a full-fledged doctor in another year. She was known as 'Medicine Fox' when she lived with the Comanche. I suppose she'll be wanting to turn this place into a hospital next."

Ginny said, "She lived with the Comanche?"

"Yep, more than ten years. She was taken when she was ten. Married a Comanche warrior. You'll see her little girl tonight. Anyhow, they got Grit splinted up, and he's walking with some crutches, but he's a long way from riding a horse. Thank God, because he wouldn't let me get rid of the stallion. He's going to take on the devil before school starts up again, he says."

Ginny was disappointed and distraught. They had lost all this time, and Grit McKay was not going to be able to help them.

Con said, "Well maybe your son can offer us some advice and ideas as to how we should go about this."

"He'd be riding with you if he could no matter what anybody else said, but, yeah, I'm sure he'll help you out however he can. He'll be back to the house soon with supper coming up. Let's get your horses put up. We might even run into Grit down by the stable."

Chapter 17

THE TRAVELERS FINALLY met the legendary Grit McKay shortly before supper, when he made a less than graceful entry into the house supported by a pair of crutches and assisted by a sinewy young man with bronze skin and slightly aquiline features. Grit was a tall, trim man with coffee-colored eyes, lightly tanned skin and thick, dark hair endowed by his Spanish mother, according to his father, Duff, also known as Angus Duff McKay II, who explained it had been his intention to marry a Scottish woman before his first wife, the late Mariana Diaz, captured his heart and diluted the Scottish line when she gave birth to Angus Duff McKay III, nicknamed "Grit."

Con concluded instantly that the Indian assisting him must be Grit's and Jessie's adopted Kiowa son Rover, officially named Angus Duff McKay IV. The complicated family composition had been explained by Duff after the critters were put up for the night, but Con was still trying to sort everybody out.

Five cowhands were already eating and talking animatedly at the far end of the dining area. Since no students from the Liberty School were present, several tables were vacant, but ten or twelve places were set for family, including two with wooden boxes propped on chairs, presumably for Grit's and Jessie's three-year old twin daughters, Heather and Shiloh. Jessie and her mother-in-law, Rosita, had already been introduced and immediately claimed custody of Ginny and taken her upstairs with her saddlebags to show her the room where she would be sleeping. Con and Ezra had been assigned to the vacant school dormitory.

Duff introduced Grit and Rover to Ezra and Con, and they all exchanged handshakes. Con was surprised to find that Rover spoke perfect English after being with the family for three or four years, but he supposed that with the schoolhouse just next door and his father the head teacher, the eighteen-year-old had not been given much choice. There was obviously more story there that Con would like to hear but would be unlikely to have the opportunity to do so.

Duff sat at the head of the table with his wife, Rosita, as the family and guests ate. Con sat to Grit's left and Rover to his adopted father's right, across the table from Grit's wife, Jessie, who sat between the twin girls, with Ginny nearest the head of the table sitting next to one of the twins. Ezra had escaped to the cowhands' table and was already regaling the men with tall tales.

Farther down the table, Con figured out the identity of the other children, Tobe McKay, who looked to be about fifteen, and Franny McKay, perhaps ten years, siblings whose parents were killed by Comancheros, found and adopted by Grit and Jessie. Finally, the other girl, tanned-skinned and with her mother's red hair, had to be ten-year-old Rebecca, formerly known as "Red Bird," the daughter of Jennie, who was Jessie's identical twin. They made up a challenging family group, Con thought, but all appeared to be thriving.

Speaking softly, Grit questioned Con as they ate. The tone was friendly, but the man was clearly all business. He nodded toward Ginny who was engaged in an animated conversation with Jessie over the head of the twin who separated them. "Tell me your story. What brought you here? Dad told me a little bit, but I would like to know more."

Between bites of succulent roast beef, fried potatoes, and beans, Con gave Grit a summary of what he knew. "The raiders apparently were a mix of Comanche and Comancheros. The Comanche leader wore a wolfskin cape of some sort. He shot the arrow that passed through her body. I still can't believe she lived through it. The soldiers at Fort Elliot were convinced the warrior was known as Angry Wolf, and I had heard of him during my five years in the Army. Ginny can fill you in on the attack details after supper. As I told you, we had an encounter with several men at Fort Elliott, and she was certain that two of them had been with the raiders."

"Your attacker was no doubt Angry Wolf. Even during the Red River War years, he didn't run with the other bands. He carried on his separate wars in alliance with the Comancheros. I'm betting he has a fair amount of gold coins stashed someplace. He understands the white man's money and speaks fluent English. His father was a half-blood Comanche. Married a Comanche woman but took her with him to live among the whites where he felt more at home. He scouted for the Army, and they lived on Army posts, and Angry Wolf was schooled till he was close to ten. Then his father was killed when a soldier mistook him for an enemy warrior. His mother returned with him to her people. When he lived among the whites, he was known as John Wolf. I think his hate for the whites came from his father's unfortunate death."

Con said, "I had never heard about his background. This makes him even more formidable. How old do you think he might be?"

"Early thirties, I'd guess, but he has been a leader since he was a youngster. Some, like Quanah Parker, are just born to it, I think. This is a man you should never, never underestimate."

After apple pie dessert, they adjourned to the Diamond M library, a spacious room with every wall book-filled from floor to ceiling, broken only by a large fireplace in one wall. The room included two large desks, one of which was a rolltop, assorted tables, and stuffed chair seating for eight to ten people arranged to facilitate conversation. Ginny and Con shared a settee, and he was pleased that she chose to sit beside him, taking it for a sign that Ginny was declaring a truce in the war she seemed to be engaged in with him.

Ezra claimed his own chair, and the only others in the room were Grit, Jessie and Rover. Grit would not have needed his assistance to move around the house, and Con wondered about the young man's presence. He had not heard the Kiowa speak more than a few sentences, and he appeared to worship Grit and followed him like a puppy sometimes, but tonight Con sensed that his attendance signaled more.

Everyone waited for Grit to speak, and he did not keep them waiting long. “Folks, in speaking with Con tonight at supper, I think I have a fair understanding of your mission. Please feel free to break in with a question anytime or tell me if I have anything wrong. First, I must say that I find your search for the girls very compelling, and I am very interested in joining you on your journey.”

“Grit...” It was Jessie.

He continued, “But I’ve already got my orders from Jess here. I can’t go. And in my present condition, I would eventually be a burden that might interfere with your success. I would be in the saddle if I could, but I cannot.”

Ginny said, “But can you tell us anything that might help?”

“You have been told by others that the band you are seeking is led by a man named Angry Wolf. It is very likely that he has retreated by now to a place known by some as the ‘Wolf’s Mouth.’ I have seen this place when it was not occupied.”

“Where is it?” Con asked.

“In the Mexican state of Chihuahua, the Sierra Madre Mountain region in a place called Copper Canyon, which is in reality a half dozen or so connected, deep canyons, and there are countless sub-canyons that branch off those. It is in one of those sub-canyons that you are most likely to find Angry Wolf at Wolf's Mouth, named by the Comanche for the war chief whose followers occupy the place and for the difficult entrance making a person think of entering the mouth and throat of a beast. I will sketch a rough map before I go to bed and give it to you in the morning, but you likely won't need it."

"Why not?" Ginny asked.

"Someone who has entered the Wolf's Mouth has volunteered to ride with you. I am not happy about it, but he can be a stubborn sort."

Ginny said, "Who is this person?"

"He is in this room. My son, Rover."

Con turned his eyes to Angus Duff McKay IV. Rover's dark eyes met his gaze unflinchingly, but for the first time, Con saw traces of a smile on the young Kiowa's face.

"You know that country?"

"I know most of the Southwest, especially Texas and New Mexico, and I have crossed the Rio Grande to Mexico many times."

Grit said, "That's why he is called Rover. He was orphaned when he was ten or eleven years old and left his Kiowa band, traveling from band to band among the Kiowa and Comanche. He always entered the village bearing a recently killed deer or other game, so he was welcomed. Sometimes, he visited a few nights, others maybe several months, but he always moved on. He speaks Comanche and Kiowa, and, since refining his language skills at our school, fluent English and Spanish. Any of these could prove helpful during your journey, but, most of all, Rover knows the land."

Con asked Rover, "You will be welcome, of course, but why would you do this?"

"I love the Diamond M and my family and friends here, but I must move a spell. It has been too long in one place. If you had not come here, I planned to ride out soon to wherever the Great Spirit guided me. I suspect He sent you here so I could join your mission."

Grit said, "I'm hoping he will get the roaming out of his system and return here. He is eighteen now and has moved extremely fast in his formal schooling. I want to work with him another year so he can test into a college."

Rover rolled his eyes. "There is no better man than my father, but he has his dreams, and I have mine."

Jessie interceded. "These two are both a bit strong-willed, but Rover is free to do as he wishes, and we will never stand in his way."

Grit said, "He'd just run over me anyhow, but I can't help offering a little guidance. Anyway, the most assistance we can give you from the Diamond M is Rover, and it won't be long before you see why, I promise. He will take you to the Wolf's Mouth. I'm not sure what you do after you get there."

Con said, "What are the chances the Comanche still hold the two girls?"

"Hard to say. Many of the Indians who jumped the reservations still have visions of expanding their bands, increasing their numbers again. It is possible the girls are being held to become future wives and mothers. Sometimes they need slaves. Angry Wolf would probably be more inclined to keep them. The Comancheros would prefer to sell the girls either as slaves or to a bordello." He looked at Ginny. "I'm sorry. But those are the realities."

"But how do we find out?" Ginny asked.

"Somebody will have to go into the Wolf's Mouth and ask. If the girls are there, you would first try to negotiate a ransom price. The Comanche would likely be open to this. Do you have gold money?"

"Yes," Ginny said.

"They like to bargain. Offer only a bit of what you can pay first. But do not take the money with you into the canyon, or they may just decide to take it and keep the girls and remove your scalps while they are at it. You must establish a place for an exchange of money for the girls where you cannot be surrounded. That will be a challenge, but it can be done."

Ginny said, "How long will it take us to get to the Wolf's Mouth?"

"I'd guess anywhere from two to three weeks. You've got a long journey ahead. You will be able to move at a decent pace till you cross the Rio Grande and while riding over desert country, but when you near the foothills and mountains on the Mexican side, you will be going at a snail's pace. And keep in mind that Angry Wolf's warriors and Comancheros aren't your only danger. Apache hide out in that country, too, and the state of Chihuahua and its border towns are infested with bandidos of every sort. Soldiers patrolling that area aren't generally cordial to American visitors. Avoid them if you can. You will need to resupply down that way, but make your stops brief and keep an eye out for trouble."

Con figured that wouldn't be enough. One way or another, plenty of trouble was what they were facing.

Chapter 18

CON HAD HOPED for an earlier start, but their party rode away from the Diamond M before eight o'clock. They now had not only another rider but an extra pack animal, a zebra dun mare. Rover McKay, astride a big blue roan stallion, led the mare with the ease of a man born in the saddle. He appeared so relaxed, Con wondered if he might fall asleep. Even as an old cavalryman, he was certain he had never felt that much at ease on his mount.

Rover was a congenial sort, but he was not inclined to casual talk. Perhaps that would come later as he got better acquainted with his comrades. He was dressed like an ordinary cowhand with his hair trimmed shorter than most. It occurred to Con that if he had not been told of Rover's Kiowa ancestry, he would have guessed him to be Mexican. He had been told, however, that most Mexicans were mestizo, a mix of Spanish and Indian bloods. The bow and quiver of arrows hitched to Rover's mule, however, would eliminate the speculation of many.

Whatever his ancestry, Rover was a handsome young man, lean and sinewy, probably just short of six feet tall. It surprised him when he noticed Ginny studying the newcomer, and he was struck by a twinge of jealousy. Rover and Ginny were within a year or two of the same age, so he supposed it was not unnatural that she might be attracted to an eighteen-year-old male. He reminded himself that he had no claim on Ginny and no intention of pursuing her affections. He had simply taken pity on her and volunteered for this mission, and then he would be moving on.

He edged Quanah nearer to Rover and his stallion. "How long do you guess it will take us to get to San Angelo and Fort Concho, Rover?"

"By wagon, three days and three nights. We can cut a day and two nights off since we don't have a buckboard. I was going to talk to you about that. We'll hit the shortcut in about an hour. We will be forced to ride single file half the time, but there is good grass and water along the way."

"You just lead us, and we'll follow."

He nodded and nudged his stallion ahead.

That evening, after Ezra's favorite "three B" supper of bacon, beans and biscuits, the four sat at a campfire no more than twenty feet off the trail with the critters staked out within sight of the camp in patches of grass that edged the trail. They would lead the horses and mules to the nearby stream again in the morning to drink their fill before departure.

Ginny got up to head into a cluster of trees near the camp to tend to bedtime business when Rover said, "Wait, Ginny, let me circle the campsite before you go out there."

She looked at him quizzically. "I'll be fine. I won't be but a few minutes, and I don't need company for my business."

"Somebody could be following us. I won't be long."

She shrugged, "Go ahead if it suits you."

Rover returned shortly. "All clear."

Ginny said, "Now you've made me skittish."

"It may be nothing, but the birds, maybe a half mile behind us, were acting disturbed ever since we headed down this trail. They would settle down after our passing, and then something would excite them again and they would go flying into the sky. If it's a horse and rider or several, it doesn't mean they are trailing us. As you can see from horse dung on the trail, we're not the only ones who use the cutoff."

Con said, "Maybe we should take watch shifts tonight."

Ezra said, "Fine by me. I ain't hankering none for my throat cut or my head scalped tonight."

"A watch might be good," Rover said, "but if it is okay with you, Con, I'd like to go back on the trail aways and see for sure if anybody's behind us." He was already pulling off his boots and slipping into moccasins.

"Yeah, go ahead. Can't hurt."

Rover had disappeared by the time Ginny returned from her visit to the trees.

"What happened to Rover?" she asked.

Con said, "He's checking backtrail to see if we're being followed."

"Why would anyone follow us?"

"There could be a lot of reasons. Money. Eyes on a pretty lady. Men—and women—who take pleasure from hurting people. There are a lot of bad people in this world, always has been and always will be."

"If I'm the lady, I guess I thank you, but the way I'm dressed, I don't think anybody would guess it."

"Yeah, they would."

"Well, I guess we'll find out soon enough if anybody's out there. I want to know about tomorrow. I haven't heard Rover say. Does he still think we can make San Angelo by tomorrow night?"

"He hasn't said, but I think he would have told me if the goal was different than he originally thought. He seems to tense some when he's being pushed, so I just give him free rein."

"You never give me 'free rein,' as you call it."

"You're more like a wild horse that's never known what reins are."

"What do you mean?"

He just shrugged. He was not up to an argument with Ginny. At some point, no answer seemed to work better than a response when she was looking to pick a fight. "I think we should plan to find us a boarding house or hotel rooms in San Angelo. Because of its nearness to Fort Concho, they tend to have lots of visitors there, and that makes for some decent lodging. We can give Ezra a break from cooking and grab a few softer sleeps before we head out. We may not have another chance for some weeks."

Ezra said, "Ain't lookin' for no bed. Them things kill my back. I'll rent me a straw or hay pile in the stable, but I'd likely look for grub at some eating place."

Ginny said, "You sound like you're thinking we might stay more than one night."

"We'll arrive too late tomorrow for me to talk to anybody at Fort Concho. I'm hoping to find somebody still there that I know and see if I can find out more about Angry Wolf's bunch that might be helpful. And I've got other business to tend to."

"We can't be wasting time. This isn't a business trip."

"The time at the fort could be important. We're up against some tough odds, and we need to know as much as we can about Angry Wolf and see if there is any chance of Army help."

"The Army won't cross the Rio Grande."

"No, but if we're in Mexico and on the run from a war party, it might be nice to have an Army patrol waiting for us on the north side of the Rio Grande."

That seemed to give her pause. To nail down his argument for delay, he said, "We also need to resupply at San Angelo, and it won't hurt the critters to get some rest and a little pampering at the stable."

It was nearly an hour before Rover returned to the campsite. He appeared without a sound like a ghost from the darkness and squatted beside the dying embers of the fire. He spoke softly. "Only one man. I would guess him to be half-breed Comanche and white, thirty-five to forty years old. I will know him if I see him again because he wears a patch over one eye. I saw no reason to confront him because he would lie anyway if he planned to do us harm."

Con said, "We'd better keep watch in shifts tonight just to play safe."

Rover said, "I agree, but I doubt if the one man will make a move. It is more likely he is following us to determine where we are going."

"But who would care?" Ginny said.

Con said, "I can't imagine, unless it's your old friend Grizzly. If that's the case, this fella has been following us since Fort Elliott."

"But why? It doesn't make any sense."

"Revenge, maybe. Or he suspects where we are headed and wants to warn Angry Wolf. He was probably committed to take Angry Wolf his share of the horse money anyhow. If this man is following us after we leave San Angelo, we'd better have a talk with him."

Chapter 19

FORT CONCHO SEEMED a rather sleepy place in comparison to Con's prior visits when the Comanche wars were raging. It appeared from the number of colored Buffalo Soldiers they were encountering as he and Rover strolled along the edge of the parade ground that at least part of the Ninth Cavalry Regiment was still assigned to the fort. At Fort Elliott, he had been informed that Ninth and Tenth Buffalo Soldiers were being shifted west to the still ongoing Apache conflicts.

Con had asked a young soldier at the fort entrance if Sergeant Major Milton Greene was still stationed at the fort and had been pleased to find that his old friend was still on duty and occupied his office in the headquarters building adjacent to that of the post commandant. As the highest-ranking non-commissioned officer in a regiment, the sergeant major generally ran the day-to-day operations of the troops and often garnered more useful information than the commanding officer. In any case, that had been Con's experience with Miltie Greene.

When they entered the sergeant major's office, Con was surprised to find the sergeant major standing by a clerk's desk evidently issuing instructions of some sort. Greene was a giant of a man, tall with enormous shoulders and thick-chested but flat-bellied. The ebony skin of his clean-shaven face looked like it might have been polished. He did not look up till he had rattled off his orders to the young corporal who was obviously struggling to write his notes and keep up with the sergeant major's pace.

Finally, the sergeant major looked up and saw the visitors. He cocked his head to one side and studied Con for a few moments. "I'll be danged. I know you. Sergeant Con Callaway." He smiled broadly and stepped forward to grasp Con's hand and pump it with a force that left his fingers and arm numb.

"Yes, I'm no longer a sergeant, but I'd like to talk to you a bit if you can make time someplace. Oh, and this is Rover McKay. Maybe you've run across his pa sometime. Grit McKay."

"Pleased to meet you, sir," Rover said, seeming to take the handshake with ease. Con wondered if Miltie was sparing the young man.

"I've never met Grit McKay, but I've certainly heard of his exploits. Why don't you both come into my office, and we'll see if I can be of service."

They sat down at a desk in a spartanly furnished office devoid of wall hangings. Sergeant Major Milton Greene was slightly over forty years of age, but born in the north, had never known slavery and was a graduate of Lincoln University, formerly known as Ashmun Institute in Pennsylvania. Con figured that Greene would have been a colonel by now if not for the rule that prohibited Negroes from serving as commissioned officers, the sole exception being Second Lieutenant Henry Flipper, the recent first colored graduate of West Point.

Greene, looking across his desk at his two visitors, said, "Well, Con, how about telling me what you're up to."

"I'm looking for any information or suggestions that might be helpful." Knowing that Greene was generally impatient about wasted words, Con gave a very abbreviated version of the mission, noting that the sergeant major was listening intently, furrowing his brow and biting his lower lip when he was told about the slaughter at

Harwood Place. "We hope to find the two girls and bring them back," Con said.

"Damn, Con, I don't see how I can help you much. I know Angry Wolf by reputation, and I can tell you that you are up against an extraordinary man. During his early years, he was raised among the whites out here. He has a better sense of his enemy's thinking than most. But he's meaner and more conniving than any full blood Comanche ever was. I've heard of Wolf's Mouth in Copper Canyon. They say Copper is much bigger than the Grand Canyon in Arizona Territory, maybe three or four times as large. I don't know how you find Wolf's Mouth in the dang place."

Rover spoke. "I've been there, sir."

The sergeant major squinted one eye and looked at Rover. "Couldn't have been long ago. You aren't that old."

"Something over five years ago. I was thirteen then."

"Your parents were there?"

"No, sir. I was curious about that place. I was thirteen and an orphan then, and I rode down to Mexico on my own. That was before Grit and Jessie McKay adopted me."

"I see."

Greene still looked dubious but shrugged and continued. "Well, maybe you can find Wolf's Mouth then, but that's not enough to get those girls back. I'd say you've got no better than a fifty-fifty chance they're with the band. If they weren't killed, there's a fair chance they've been sold by now. They could be anyplace in Mexico or even El Paso or some other border town. And if they are with Angry Wolf, how do you even negotiate a ransom? I'm worried for you, my friends."

"I'm still thinking on that."

"As a former soldier, you know that you need more than the four of you to accomplish this mission considering you won't be dealing with somebody that has been inclined to talk in the past."

"The Army won't send troops across the Rio Grande."

"No, but there is nothing that says they couldn't have soldiers waiting for you, maybe a patrol of eight or a dozen men out scouting or training. You will be crossing the Pecos River at Castle Gap. It wouldn't be more than a few hours out of your way to swing by Fort Davis. I'll write a letter to Sergeant Washington there if you want to pick it up later this afternoon for delivery to the sergeant. Davis isn't far from the border. I'm thinking he could have some soldiers bivouacked on the Rio Grande about the time you would be expected to return."

"I'll take you up on that."

"One more thing. If you could pay decent wages, you can likely hire a few more men—ex-Buffalo Soldiers—to ride along if you see Tige Marshall at Lucky Five Freight. He manages the company along with his wife, Juana. They own a chunk of it now, I think. He's a former sergeant with the Tenth but would have mustered out before your time. Tige and the Lucky Five Ranch hire a good number of soldiers, and I'll bet he'd arrange leave for a few volunteers if you'd make up their wages."

"We wouldn't want so many as to attract undue attention, but what you say makes sense. I'll see if I can at least chat with Tige Marshall. I don't know how fast he could find a few men. Miss Virginia Harwood is getting quite impatient to get moving."

"If Tige is in, he will take care of it fast. I guarantee it, but dance carefully around his wife, Juana. If I know Tige, he will want to go himself, and she won't take to the notion. Juana is a wonderful lady, but she can be a firecracker if she's not getting her way. It won't help that she's with child again."

"One more thing. I would like to see a lawyer before I leave town. Is there someone you can recommend?"

"Frank Bell Russo. He's the best. Of course, he's also the only lawyer in town right now. Law wranglers tend not to stay too long in this part of Texas. Frank prefers paperwork, but he will go to court if pressed. The sheriff dispenses most of the justice outside of court since we haven't had a criminal prosecutor for a spell either. But I won't talk about that. The Russo office is located at the north end of Main Street. Frank will likely see you without an appointment if he's not tied up with somebody else."

After their meeting with Sergeant Major Greene, Con and Rover strolled away from the fort grounds which bordered the town limits. As they approached the town's main street and commercial center, Rover said, "Keep walking but look over at the man standing next to the stable door. That's the fella who was following us back on the trail."

Con glanced furtively to his left, and saw a figure leaning against the stable wall, a sombrero pulled low on his forehead, nearly hiding most of his face except for the whiskery, black stubble covering his cheeks and chin. The man's lips held a smoking dangling cigarette from one side of his mouth. He would not question Rover's identification of their follower, but Con did not see much that would separate him from a dozen other men in San Angelo. That changed when he raised his head to take a puff on the cigarette, and the eye patch was revealed.

Con said, "Why don't we separate at Main Street? I'll head north to the lawyer's office, and you can see if you can pick that feller up and keep track of him for a spell. I told Ginny we would meet her and Ezra at Pablo's Mexican Café at twelve-thirty. That gives us almost two hours. Try to be there with any report."

"If I am not there, do not worry. I will find you."

Chapter 20

FRANK BELL RUSSO, with neatly combed, thick black hair, a handlebar mustache, and wearing a blue, vested business suit, looked every bit like the image most folks would have of a legal counselor. He was on the short side but appeared trim and fit, unlike the few other lawyers Con had encountered. Con guessed the man to be in his early forties, and the lawyer's kindly sea-blue eyes and welcoming smile put Con immediately at ease.

Con sat in a comfortable leather-padded chair across the big oak desk from the lawyer. "How may I be of assistance, Mister Callaway?" Russo asked.

Con said, "Two matters. First, I was told that I have inherited a tract of land along the Canadian River in the panhandle. I have no proof of any kind to verify ownership. When I went to look at this property, I found that it was occupied by someone else." He briefly explained his uneasy relationship with a brother he barely knew and the ghastly scene he had come upon when he arrived at his so-called property.

Russo said, "What you describe is terrible. Those poor folks. If I understand you correctly, this young lady you are assisting and her sisters, if they are found, would be the only heirs to whatever interest the parents held in the land. This could present an uncomfortable situation for you, especially if her family resided on and claimed the property for more than ten years. A law called 'adverse possession' might allow her to make an ownership claim through the courts."

"That would not happen. I would never force her off the land if it turns out I have a legal claim. I would just deed it to her and her sisters. As near as I know there is no designated county seat with public records in the county where this tract is located. How do we find out who owns the property?" He pulled a folded sheet of paper from his vest pocket and pushed it across the desk to Russo. "This sketch my brother gave me shows the boundaries of the property. He didn't give me any other paperwork. Stones with the letters 'CCC' mark the corners."

Russo studied the sheet. "The description wasn't established by legal survey, but that's not unusual. You would likely want a survey completed before making a serious investment in the land, but first you must determine who has title to it. I have a colleague in Austin who can complete a title search there or find out where the land records are located. Since we don't have a rail connection here, it will take several weeks to obtain the results."

"That's no problem. It will be three or four weeks before I will be back this way." If ever, he thought. "Now, I have another matter."

"Yes."

"I would like to make a will, and I am departing San Angelo in the morning. A very simple will."

"I should be able to have something later this afternoon. Tell me what you have in mind."

"If I die, I want to leave all my property, including any interest I have in the Canadian River land, to Virginia Harwood. If she does not survive me by a month, I want everything to go to my aunt, Katherine Moore of Dodge City, Kansas."

"That is simple enough. You must name an executor or, in the case of a woman, she is called executrix. This is the person responsible, with the assistance of a lawyer, for carrying out the terms of the will."

"Since a lawyer will be needed anyhow, could you be executor, too?"

"If that is your wish."

"It is. And I want to pay you today for the work you will be doing."

"You may settle with my clerk out front. Five dollars for the will. I would ask for a twenty-dollar retainer for the title matter with the understanding that costs could be twice that depending upon what the Austin lawyer encounters and charges."

"That's fine."

"Now, there are some other details we should discuss about the will, and I should write down your proper legal name."

A half hour later, Con walked out of the lawyer's office and headed for Pablo's Mexican Café.

Chapter 21

CON WAS NOT concerned that Rover had not shown up for lunch. He was learning quickly that the young Kiowa had uncommonly good sense for an eighteen-year-old, wise beyond his years. His absence likely meant that he decided he should continue following his quarry, who evidently had abandoned his own spying for the moment.

Con and Ginny, who had insisted upon joining him, entered the stone building bearing a sign in orange, bold letters identified it as "Lucky Five Freight."

They were greeted by an obviously pregnant woman of Mexican ancestry whose beauty was not diminished by her condition. She smiled. "Good afternoon. I am Juana Marshall. May I help you?"

Con said, "Hello, ma'am. I am Con Callaway, and this is my friend, Ginny Harwood. We were referred here by

Sergeant Major Milton Greene. He thought Tige Marshall might be able to help us with a problem. I assume he is your husband."

Her brow furrowed, and the friendly face turned less friendly. She sighed. "Pardon me if the mention of Sergeant Major Greene's name does not excite me. He has a tendency to send my husband some nasty problems." She tossed a glance at the front window and grimaced. "But never mind, Tige is on his way here. He has been at our stables across the street seeing to some shipping business."

The front door opened, and a tall, muscular man wearing a rancher's Stetson strolled in. He nodded and offered a friendly smile. Apparently mulatto, his skin was only a shade darker than his wife's. He would be in his early thirties at most, Con estimated. He paused and looked at his wife.

Juana said, "Tige, this is Con Callaway and Ginny Harwood. Folks, this is my husband, Tige Marshall, who claims to be president of Lucky Five Freight."

Tige stepped over, doffed his hat to Ginny, and shook the visitors' hands. "Howdy. Juana says 'claims.' I'm the president on paper, but she runs this circus, and everybody around here knows it."

Juana said, "Mister Callaway says that Sergeant Major Greene sent them here to talk to you."

Tige Marshall's eyes brightened, and his smile grew. "Now this has got to be interesting. Why don't you folks step into my office and tell me what this is all about. I ain't talked to old Miltie in months. How's he doing these days?"

"Same old Miltie. All business. I knew him when I was riding with Mackenzie."

"You rode with Mackenzie, too? When was that?"

"I was discharged a bit over a year ago. I served five years, finished as a sergeant."

Tige led them into his office, gesturing for them to take chairs. Con noticed that Juana had followed and sat down in a chair nearest her husband off to the side of the desk. "I served five years, the last few with Mackenzie. I mustered out at Fort Stockton southwest of here. I did the last few years as a sergeant, too. I met Juana when I was here at Concho for a spell, and danged if she didn't hook me, so I headed this way fast before some other fell-er took the bait. Anyhow, you didn't come here for my life story. Tell me why old Miltie sent you."

Con said, "We're on a mission to recover Ginny's sis-ters from a Comanche band that's aligned itself with Comancheros. The leader is a war chief named Angry Wolf. Ginny can give you more details."

Ginny said, "My sisters are eleven and nine years old and were taken by these men. My parents and younger brother were killed during the raid at our trading post and small ranch north by the Canadian River. I was wounded badly and would have died if Con and his friend Ezra hadn't come along."

Tige said, "I've heard of Angry Wolf. Him and his bunch could show up anyplace. They seem to keep some distance from Concho and the other forts, but anything beyond a day out is fair game. So where do you expect to find the girls?"

Con said, "Our first stop is a place called the Wolf's Mouth in Copper Canyon. We must cross the Mexican border."

"Yeah, it's in the state of Chihuahua. Been there once to the rim of this Copper Canyon. Wasn't officially supposed to be there. Always wanted to see more of it."

"Tige..."

It was Juana, giving her husband a warning look. Con moved directly to his visit's purpose. "We visited Grit McKay, hoping he might join us, but he recently broke his leg. His son volunteered to come with us and will be very helpful, I think."

"You must be talking about Rover. I know him. You couldn't do better."

"Miltie suggested that we had little chance of recovering the girls with just four of us. He said you might be able to find three or four former Buffalo Soldiers to help. We will double whatever wages they're presently drawing and pay in gold coin."

"I know men who would be here in a minute with that carrot. Of course, the fellas I'm thinking of would likely do it free for the adventure. Some of us just got to mount up for the excitement once in a while."

Juana said, "Don't include yourself, Tige. We've got a baby coming in two months' time, and you've two other children to think about."

Tige asked, "When do you want to ride out?"

"Tomorrow morning. Sunrise if possible. We'll have the food supplies. They just need to bring their own personals, especially their weapons."

"I guess you can't waste time with those little gals held by them varmints. Meet here at our stable in the morning. I'll loan you a few good backup mounts and an extra pack mule in the morning. If you lose a horse out in Chihuahuan desert country, you got trouble."

"That's mighty kind of you, Tige."

"I want to help somehow."

Juana said, "I know what you're up to, Tige. I swear I do."

"Sweetheart, you know I wouldn't go if you didn't approve. But think about those little girls a bit, and then we'll talk after these folks are gone."

Juana just rolled her eyes.

Chapter 22

LATE AFTERNOON, GINNY and Ezra sat on a bench in front of the "Rio Concho Boarding House" where the proprietress, Thelma Rakestraw, would commence serving supper in an hour's time. Although Ezra slept at the stable, he had bargained to take meals here with the others of their party. The two-story, limestone house was perched on a hillock several blocks off main street and offered a view of the town and fort to the east against a panorama of rolling prairie and the fork where the North, Middle and South Concho Rivers meet to become the Concho River.

"Do you have any idea where Con took off to?" Ginny said.

"Nope."

"Sometimes that man gets so damned secretive, it's downright unsettling."

"Don't matter none to me. Maybe he's got a lady friend from his old days here."

For some reason, that thought enraged her. "He'd dang well better not be wasting our time on some trollop."

"Don't know 'trollop.'"

"Loose woman. Maybe a prostitute. One who sells her favors."

"Oh, I've heard of such."

"Yeah, I'll just bet you have."

They sat there silently for a spell, Ginny soaking in the warmth of a fading sun. She had never cared for cold weather much and had decided long ago that she would never sink roots north of Texas. If she moved on, it would be farther south. If she got through this journey, however, she was determined to return to Harwood Place with her sisters and rebuild and live on the land near where their deceased family members were buried.

"Con's walking up the slope toward us," Ezra said. "Don't look to be in a hurry."

"He's never in a hurry. Just moseys along like he's looking at roadside flowers."

"He's just thinkin' about things."

"Grandpa, you're always making excuses for him."

"Ain't making excuses. Just telling you how he is. And let me tell you, over the years I learnt I'd rather be following a feller like that than one who don't look before he steps in a pile of fresh horse apples."

When Con approached the bench, he gave a quick wave. "You two are going to wear your rumps sore sitting there. It's a perfect day for a walk."

Ezra said, "Ain't never perfect for a walk when your dang bones get as old and stiff as mine. You'll see someday, and it'll come faster than you think."

Ginny said, "It's sitting in the saddle ten hours a day that's making me sore."

"You ought to be calloused by now. Anyhow, you're just getting started on saddle time. Have you heard anything from Rover?" Con said.

"Ain't seen hide nor hair of him," Ezra said. "I hoped you might have met up someplace."

"I'm starting to worry about him," Ginny said.

Con said, "I won't worry unless he doesn't show up in the morning. That young man knows how to look after himself." He handed her a card, and she frowned as she read it.

"This is a lawyer's card. Frank Bell Russo, it says."

"Put this where you can find it if need be. If I don't make it back, you go to this man and tell him who you are. He can help you with things."

"What things? My pa had no use for law wranglers. He said they were all crooks and shysters."

"From what you've told me before, you didn't consider your father the last word on everything."

"Well, no."

"Keep the card. I'm hoping you don't need it."

She shrugged and put the card in her shirt pocket, perturbed by Con's constant cloak of mystery over his thoughts and actions. She was tired of never knowing what was going on in his head. She decided to tell him how she felt. "I'm not a child, and my sisters are why we're here this evening. I think I'm entitled to know what is going on. You hold everything so damn close that it's really starting to grate on me."

Con gave her a surprised look. "I'm not sure what you're talking about. I tell you everything about what we're doing."

"But I'd like to know why sometimes and what you're thinking before you tell us how it's going to be. I accept that you're the boss of our little outfit—for now anyhow—but I don't like not having some idea of the reasons we're doing something. I feel like the rest of us are soldiers in an army."

Con was silent for several minutes, and she feared he might react with rage and walk away. She did not want that. She knew that they could not do this without Con.

Finally, he spoke softly and calmly. "I guess I can understand how you feel, Ginny, but I think I explained this before. One more time. I was in the Army for five years. I took orders I did not question, and as a sergeant I gave orders that were not questioned by the troops. That's the way the Army works, but we're not in the Army here. Somebody must make final decisions, but there is nothing wrong with asking why or wanting to know what I'm thinking. I'm a quiet man by nature and not given to sharing much anyhow, but I promise not to be upset if you ask now and then. I doubt if I'll change much, but I won't take offense if you push for a reason."

Now she felt foolish. She wished he wasn't such a gentleman sometimes. When she challenged him, she always ended up feeling she lost after she won. "As you've no doubt figured out by now, I've got a temper, and I'm short on patience. Pa told me once I was always looking for a fight. I'll try to calm down a little. Maybe we can eventually meet halfway."

Con returned a sheepish grin. "It's worth a try."

Ezra chuckled. "You two make quite a pair, I tell you, but I wasn't doubting you'd start making peace sooner or later. Considering where we're headed, I'm glad it's sooner."

They were at the supper table when Rover came in and nodded, picking up an empty plate and going to the serving counter that separated the kitchen from the dining area and filling the plate with roasted beef, fried potatoes, and assorted vegetables.

There were only three other guests at the dining table besides his friends, and he claimed an empty chair beside Ginny, who filled his coffee mug from a pot sitting on the table. "Thank you, ma'am," he said.

She knew she could not discuss his mission in the presence of the other guests but felt they should talk about something. "Did you have a busy afternoon?"

"Yes, quite busy. I took an interesting walk in the countryside that took me to the river. There were five men camped there who appeared to be celebrating something."

"Oh, were you invited to the party?"

"No. I'm quite certain strangers would not have been welcome."

"You must tell us more about your walk later."

The meal dragged on for her, and when she saw that Rover was about finished, she retrieved a slice of peach pie for him from the counter. The other guests finally disappeared shortly before Rover downed the pie, and Mrs. Rakestraw was busy in the kitchen.

"Well," Con said, "what happened, Rover?"

"I followed our friend around town, waited across the street from two taverns while he passed his time there. Finally, mid-afternoon, he came out of the saloon with two others, and they started walking toward the Concho fork where they met up with two more men. They were so drunk I think I could have walked with them, and they wouldn't have noticed. It didn't take skill to follow these men and not be seen."

"That makes five men then. Could you hear any conversations?"

"No, but I slipped into some trees and got a decent look at them. They were a tough-looking bunch, but I guess that doesn't mean much. We won't look too respectable when we come back from the Wolf's Mouth. There were some things about these men that could be more than coincidence, though, from what I picked up in your talking at the Diamond M and on the way here."

"Well, don't keep us in suspense."

"There was a big man at the camp. It had been a while, but somebody had hammered the hell out of his face. I couldn't make it out really well from where I was, but his nose looked like a squash from mom's and grandma's garden, and his jaw and neck were wrapped."

"Grizzly. He's got to be Grizzly," Ginny said. Her heart raced, and her hand trembled so much she lowered her coffee cup to the table.

"There was a colored man there. I'd guess one was Mexican. The colored man stayed in the camp with the man you're calling Grizzly. A shorter, heavier white man came with the others from the tavern."

Con said, "This is strange. They picked up our trail someplace and followed us here."

Ezra said, "Likely just the one feller trailed us. When he saw the direction we was headed, he told his friends to meet him in San Angelo. We'd of caught on to the whole bunch trailing us 'less we was all deafer than a stack of posts. They got in mind killing us before we walk into that Wolf's Mouth, I'm guessing."

Con said, "They might change that notion when they see we've got some extra men."

"Yep, I suppose that's true enough. Then they'll head right for old Angry Wolf to let him know we're coming.

It's for sure they'll know when they see us heading south to the Pecos River crossing."

"Unless anybody has a better idea," Con said, "we'll be crossing at Castle Gap. I'd like to ride south to Fort Stockton, then west from there to Fort Davis."

Rover said, "Since we don't have wagons, there are other crossings, but Castle Gap is easiest, especially with pack animals, and once across you have a direct route to Fort Stockton. There have been a lot of ambushes at Castle Gap over the years. The Comanche War Trail feeds in from the north. The scattered bones of horses and even human remains that have washed up show it was a busy place at different times."

Con said, "Do you think you could follow those men camped at the fork until you know where they're headed? We really need to keep track of that bunch. If it appears they're setting up an ambush someplace, you could swing back and warn us. If you decide their destination is the same as ours, we need to know that, too."

"I could do that. Dad gave me his spyglass before we left the Diamond M. I'd left it in my saddlebags, so I didn't have it when I was afoot this afternoon. Anyhow, with the spyglass I can keep a good distance from those no-goods and still tell what they are up to."

Ginny said, "What if they are headed directly to the Wolf's Mouth? They would warn Angry Wolf that we are coming. Not only would that give him time to prepare for us. It could jeopardize the lives of Noreen and Krista."

"You are right, of course. It would be better if we could head them off some way and capture them. Your old friend Grizzly is an escapee from a military guardhouse, and I'm sure they would hold any others temporarily if we delivered our prisoners to Fort Stockton."

"I know I can identify any who participated in the raid on Harwood Place. I don't know how this gets sorted out legally, but I assume either military or civilian authorities will see that these men are tried and don't live to kill again." And she would do everything possible to prevent the nuisance of a trial, Ginny vowed.

Con said, "We should sleep on this. We had better grab all the shuteye we can tonight. We won't be getting much rest for a long spell."

Finally, they were going to start the quest to recover her sisters. Her patience was nearly exhausted. She felt she had endured one delay after another. It was time to head to the Wolf's Mouth.

Chapter 23

TIGE MARSHALL WAS at the Lucky Five stables to greet Con and Ginny the next morning. "Good morning, folks," he said. "I'll be riding with y'all. I've got three good men you'll meet in a few minutes."

The two dismounted, and Ginny said, "You mean Juana gave her approval?" she paused. "I'm teasing."

"Oh, sure. That wasn't ever in doubt. I just had to sweet talk her a mite."

Con glanced across the street where Juana stood in front of the office door, watching with arms folded across her chest resting on her pregnant belly. She did not look all that happy about Tige's forthcoming adventure.

Rover rode up with Ezra, each leading their pack animals. Con introduced the newcomers to Tige. Con looked up at Rover. "You'll be leaving soon, I assume."

"Just as soon as I find somebody to lead Pretty Girl. I can't be handling a pack horse while I'm trying to trail those fellers." Pretty Girl was his zebra dun mare that could also double as a backup riding horse if needed.

Ginny said, "I'll lead Pretty Girl. We've taken a liking to each other anyhow." She stepped over and took the lead rope from Rover. The Kiowa reined his blue roan stallion around and soon disappeared.

Con cast his eyes about the huge stable that had more stalls and alleyways than he could count. It appeared one side of the structure housed mules, and draft horses and riding mounts occupied the remainder. This was a big outfit, he thought, and it took a lot of men to keep it going. Tige and Juana Marshall had big-time responsibilities to keep this place running. Besides family concerns, he could see that Tige's absence dropped a big load on Juana. Impulsively, he walked across the street to thank the woman.

As he approached Juana, the scowl on her face dissipated, and a smile replaced it. She said, "Good morning, Con. I'll be praying for all of you till you all return. I'll stop by St. John's every morning. Of course, I do anyway since that scamp of a husband avoids church like the plague. At least our children get baptized and raised in the church."

"I'll be pleased to have your prayers, ma'am. I just wanted to tell you how grateful I am that you allowed Tige to join us."

"Oh, I couldn't say 'no.' We don't really do that with each other anyhow. He needs to go on this mission, and I couldn't tell him not to help those poor little girls. In case the baby comes, my parents and sister live here, so I'm not being left alone. Tige is more nuisance than anything during birthing. I'm not mad at him. I'm just making him carry a little guilt in the saddle with him this morning."

"Juana, I hope I find a good woman like you someday."

"Sometimes, men don't see what's right under their noses."

He wasn't sure what she meant but said, "I'll just have to keep my eyes open then. Anyway, thanks again, and we'll plan on seeing you soon. Anything you want me to tell Tige?"

"It's not necessary. He'll be over to kiss me goodbye before you ride out. May God be with you."

It must be something to have a woman like Juana going through life at your side, Con thought. She and Tige were different, cast in separate molds, but he sensed a connection that most would envy but rarely discover. When he reached the stable, three more colored men had emerged from the stable alleyway with two spare horses and a packed, dark brown mule with strange greenish eyes that did not appear all that friendly.

Ezra and Ginny had already met the newcomers, and when Con walked up in front of the entryway where they were standing, Tige introduced the men. "This here's Irish O'Toole," he said, nodding toward a mahogany-skinned, wiry man of average height. "Irish is foreman out at the Lucky Five Ranch, but I got him cut loose for a spell. Irish knows horses like the back of his hand, handy with vet work, and dang good with a rifle."

Con stepped forward and shared a firm grip with the man he guessed to be on the short side of thirty-five. "Pleased to meet you, Irish. Looking forward to getting to know you better."

"That goes two ways, Con. I can't wait to start. I promised Ginny we would find those girls and bring them back." Con noticed instantly that Irish spoke like a man of some education.

Tige said, "Then I've got Beanpole Hawley. We served with the Buffalo Soldiers together. He works with us in the freighting business—supervises the stable operation. A good man to have in a fight."

Con shook hands with a wiry man who stood at least six and a half feet tall and whose African blood obviously had not been diluted significantly. "And thanks to you, too, Beanpole."

Thankfully, when they shook hands, the tall man spared Con's, evidently aware of his obvious strength. Beanpole said, "Glad to get out someplace different. Ain't left this dang stable for a year it seems."

Tige said, "Don't believe everything Beanpole tells you. He rides shotgun on the two stages we run when we're shorthanded. He was gone ten days to Austin and back within the past month."

And finally, Tige said, "Meet Casper Woodson. He goes by 'Woody.' He rode with me in the Tenth, too. Used him lots as a sniper. Don't talk much, so he ain't bad to have around. He tends to the mules here, and he'll do most of the handling of Nipper on this trip—that's the ornery cuss on the end of the lead rope. If you ain't figured it out from the name, Nipper likes to bite, especially white folks." Tige grinned, and Woody, a short, stocky man in his early forties, offered a closed-mouth smile and nodded his head in agreement.

After shaking Woody's hand and thanking him, Con said, "It's time for us to be riding." He mounted his buckskin Quanah and reined the gelding south, leading his white mule Chester packed mostly with food supplies. Tige led a saddled dapple-gray gelding across the dusty street to where Juana stood. She wrapped her arms around him and accepted his lingering kiss with enthusiasm. Con smiled as he looked back. Juana and the man she loved would be just fine.

Chapter 24

ROVER ARRIVED AT a bluff overlooking the Concho River fork well before the Comancheros broke camp. He staked his stallion downslope and crawled higher on the bluff with his telescope. He was no more than forty feet above the river but three times that from the cottonwood cluster where the men had pitched several puptents, evidently to store supplies. Bedrolls were spread out on the ground nearby.

They appeared to have finished breakfast and were beginning to pack gear and take down the tents. Rover, stretched out on the ground, focused his telescope on the man he assumed was Ginny's "Grizzly."A hulking man, he lumbered about the campsite reminding Rover of a crippled version of the man's namesake. His mouth below a large, twisted nose appeared frozen in a scowl. He seemed to carry some authority, because he was obviously barking orders to the others, pointing animatedly at tasks that needed attention.

Soon, the eye-patched mixed blood who had followed them from the Diamond M mounted and rode away, following the river branch that fed into the Concho from the south. He was doubtless confirming the destination of Rover's comrades. He saw no point in following the rider. One man alone was unlikely to launch an attack. He would join the others later with a report. That was when a decision important to the searchers would be made. The Comancheros would most likely either move on to Angry Wolf's village in Mexico's Copper Canyon or attempt to set up an ambush of the searchers. He questioned whether they would be foolish enough to attempt an ambush once they learned of the reinforcement by the former Buffalo Soldiers. Still, this Grizzly seemed to be blinded by a lust for revenge.

When the others saddled up and left the camp with two pack horses, they headed in the same direction the mixed blood had taken. He figured they had established another route to Castle Gap, the likely Pecos crossing, but nothing would be faster than the well-used trail on the two or three-day ride Con Callaway and the others were taking. The Comancheros would be forced to push their horses hard to get out ahead of the search party before the Pecos. Since they would be aware of the fastest route to Wolf's Mouth, however, they could easily make up for lost time after they crossed the Pecos. He determined he would follow the Comancheros for a day and then report to Con.

The sun was blistering by midafternoon, and water was scarce. Fortunately, those he followed had obviously traveled the path before and had knowledge of the water holes. Rover always stopped to rest and water his mount a half hour after they did, trying to maintain about that much time between them. Their pace was slower than he had anticipated, winding between hills and passing through narrow canyons. He was surprised the mixed blood had not joined the others yet. The distance for him to locate the search party would have been negligible. Something was not right.

It was time to wait a spell. When they came to a small pass-through canyon, he dismounted, "Blue," he said in a near whisper. "I see lush grass along the canyon wall. It is time for a good horse's snack."

He led the blue roan stallion some fifty feet off the trail and staked him in the grass. He unhitched his bow and quiver of arrows from the saddle and climbed some twenty-five feet into the rocks that lined the wall, not far from the shallow canyon's rim. He pressed back into a crevice, nocked an arrow in the bowstring and waited. He knew that it was not all that likely he was being followed. Still, instinctively he saw that possibility.

After nearly a half hour's wait, he heard a horse whinny at the canyon entrance, likely sensing the nearness of his own mount. A riderless sorrel gelding entered the canyon, shortly followed by the mixed blood searching the canyon walls with his rifle held chest high, preparing to sight it with his lonely eye. He spotted Rover and raised the rifle to fire just as the arrow drove into his throat; the rifle clattered against the rocky canyon floor, and Rover's second arrow burrowed into the man's chest before he crumpled to the ground.

Rover climbed down from the rocks, half sliding over some shale. He checked the mixed-blood, having not the slightest doubt he was dead. He pulled out the arrows, ripping through the flesh. He scavenged the man's pockets, found a penknife and two ten-dollar gold pieces to drop in the deceased's saddlebags. He looked around for the sorrel horse and saw that the gelding was next to his own sharing grass. Using a lead rope stuffed in the half-blood's saddlebags, he anchored it to the horse, mounted his own and retraced his entry into the canyon. At first opportunity, he reined his mount onto a winding trail easterly in the direction of his companions.

Chapter 25

CON SLOWED HIS mount when he saw a figure on the wide trail ahead. Tige, riding next to him, said, "You see somebody, too."

"Yep. I think it's Rover from the blue roan he's riding, but he's got an extra horse."

Shortly, they met up with Rover. Con nodded toward the saddled horse. "That saddled sorrel is missing its rider."

"The rider doesn't have use for this fine gelding anymore, and I figured the least I could do was provide the orphan a home."

Con concluded that the young Kiowa had come out on top of an altercation with an enemy and would decide when or whether to tell the story. "I gather you've got some information for us."

"Yes, sir, I do. There are now four Comancheros in the bunch I was following. The one-eyed man who was scouting for them won't be reporting back. I suppose they might still try to set up an ambush, but the best spot would be Castle Gap where we cross the Pecos, and with the route they must take through the hills, I don't think they can beat us there. They will need to cut to our wagon trail soon if they want to hit us before, and there's just not a place where they could surprise us much. They'd high-tail it anyway when they saw our numbers."

Con said, "Any chance they'll just turn back?"

"Not likely. Ambush was just a possibility. And now with their scout disappearing, I don't see much chance they'll be looking to attack. They were always headed for the Wolf's Mouth. They'll warn Angry Wolf that we're coming. Knowing the country the way they probably do, they shouldn't have any trouble beating us to the Comanche stronghold."

"We should try to stop them before they cross the Pecos, then."

"Yes."

"And it appears Castle Gap is the place to do it. We need to get a greeting party down there, and the pack animals are slowing us. Rover, I'd like you to pick up the trail on the Comancheros again and hightail it back if they change course. Otherwise, stay with them all the way to the Pecos."

"I can do that. I'll grab some hardtack and jerky from your mule's load and then I'll be on my way."

Tige said, "Con, you send me and Beanpole on ahead, and we'll see them no-goods don't cross the Pecos. You'll have Irish and Woody here to help with the extra critters, and I guarantee you won't be short of guns if a surprise comes your way."

"Just the two of you?"

"Three."

Con twisted in his saddle and looked at Ginny who was astride her mare, Artemis. Her hat was pulled low on her forehead, but their eyes met, and he saw the determination that told him any argument would be futile. He turned back to Tige who was obviously suppressing a grin, evidently enjoying Con's discomfiture. "Another gun wouldn't hurt none," Tige said.

Thanks a lot, Con thought. "Well, collect what you need to eat in a cold camp," Con said. "We'll likely be nearly a day behind."

He dismounted and walked over to Ginny while she was stuffing her saddlebags with necessaries. "You know I don't like this idea of your going along with Tige and Beanpole."

"I'd have never guessed," she said sarcastically. "If you haven't noticed, I'm a full-grown woman, and I'm entitled to make my own decisions once in a while. I've been an obedient soldier for a good spell now. Today, I'm going on leave to tend to family business."

Con sighed, nodded a few times, wheeled and mounted Quanah with his white mule's lead rope clutched in his hand. He looked at Ginny again and found she was looking up at him. "Be careful, Ginny."

She quickly turned her head away and went back to filling the saddlebags.

Had he noticed that she was a full-grown woman? Damn right he had. He had seen darn near every inch of her naked body. He wasn't blind. At the time it had meant nothing. But lately, he had been undressing her in his head, and the memories of those nights when he had not expected her to live were starting to haunt him. And to make things worse, this woman and her ways were starting to grow on him. Feisty as she was, he liked her.

Chapter 26

GINNY RODE BESIDE Tige as they raced their mounts just off the wagon trail to avoid the ruts that formed traps for horses' hooves. She loved the speed and the wind whipping about her face trying to tear her hat away from the rawhide strip that anchored it beneath her chin. Artemis shared her enthusiasm for a good run. They would both tire later, but Tige seemed always aware of the horses' condition and the need for rest stops and water.

Beanpole trailed behind some, keeping his eye out for the ever-possible surprise. Both men exuded competence, and she understood Tige's lack of concern about numbers for their task. They did not need her to accomplish their mission, but she felt compelled to be a part of taking down those men who had been a part of slaughtering her family and abducting her sisters. In particular, she was obsessed with seeing Grizzly dead. She hoped that his demise might bring her a measure of peace. It had not been enough to watch Con hammer him to a pulp, although she cherished that memory.

That night they camped along a stream that Tige told her ended its journey at the Pecos River which he estimated was no more than ten miles distant. Unfortunately, it was nearly impossible to cross at this juncture because of high banks and a narrow channel that increased its depth to treacherous levels. The stream was lined with sumac shrubs, willow trees and cottonwood saplings that surrounded several giant oaks and a few ancient cottonwoods that towered over the stream. Beanpole had found a wide strip of lush grass along the edge of the trees, and that, along with fresh water nearby, determined their so-called campsite where there would be no tents or fire. Without comment, he spread his bedroll out near the grazing horses.

Beanpole seemed like a gentle giant who spoke only when asked a question or had significant information to impart. He had a sense of humor, though, laughing a lot and consistently displaying an easy smile on his face.

Tige and Ginny dropped their bedrolls in a clearing in the trees not more than thirty feet from Beanpole. She noticed that when she put her blankets on one side of the clearing, Tige waited till she had picked her spot before he chose the opposite side of the clearing. Still, no more than a dozen feet separated them. Her bedroll laid out, she picked up her saddlebags and stepped over to one of the big oak trees nearer to Tige, where she sat down, resting her back against it as she fished out tonight's jerky and hardtack. Tige turned toward her, sitting with legs crossed Indian style as he dug out his own meager supper.

Ginny said, "Will we be posting watch tonight? I want to take my shift."

"No. That's why Beanpole stays near the horses. They'll nicker or get nervous if anything or anybody comes anywhere near. Even without the horses, he's like a danged old dog, he'd sense it and have his gun ready to fire within a second or two. When I was on Army duty, I posted guards, but a sleeping Beanpole would beat them to the ready."

"Does he have a wife and family?"

"Nope, but he could if he wanted. Ladies love Beanpole no matter their color. Somehow, they want to spoil and mother the rascal, swarm to him like bees to new flowers. Let's just say Beanpole never wants for female company."

"I know Woody's a bachelor and keeps to himself pretty much, but Irish mentioned his wife."

"Yeah, now Irish is a different sort. Real name's Patrick. Guess that's Irish, but it's easy to see he ain't no Irishman. His father or grandfather must have been owned by an Irishman. Lots of slaves took their owner's last name. Just like me. I was born a slave and took my owner's name—Marshall. Irish's family was owned by an O'Toole way back. He says his grandpa bought his own freedom somehow, and like some other colored folks, he became a slave owner. His father had one of the biggest plantations in Texas before the war came. Irish got a good education at home by—I don't know what you call them."

"Tutor? A private tutor?"

"Yeah, that sounds right. Anyhow he can read and write and do numbers near perfect. Rose was born on the O'Toole plantation and got an education in her early years. They schooled the slave kids, but it was against the law. She's five or so years younger than Irish, but he had his eye on her for a long time. They got three boys now. One's just a little tyke. Lucky Five Ranch has treated him good. I think you know he's foreman there. Runs some of his own horses on the place, and him and Rose handle the animal doctoring. His family lost the plantation after the war, but he's smart as a fox, and could run his own ranch. I don't think the Lucky Five folks will let him get away, though. They'll treat him right like they have me and Juana."

"You should be proud with what you've done with your life after the war."

"I don't know, but I've sure been lucky."

"My father said that most successful folks make their own luck."

"It helps a man to have a wife like Juana. Smart as a whip, more patient than you'd guess and always got my backside covered. She's my best friend in the world. Talk about luck. I didn't make that luck. I just stumbled on to it."

"Maybe she got lucky, too. I hope I can know that someday."

"I got a hunch you will."

Ginny said, "What happens tomorrow?"

"We should make Castle Gap by early afternoon, and then we figure out how to set a trap for them varmints we're looking for. I got some hope your friend Rover will show up and give us some notice, but we ain't going to count on it."

She decided to tell him why she came along. "There's a man I'd like first chance to take down."

"Let me guess. That big Grizzly feller."

"How did you know?"

"In case you ain't noticed, old Ezra is inclined to storytelling. He told us how you knifed that feller when he tried to take you at Harwood Place. To hear him tell it, you cut that man up in small pieces. I don't see how he got put back together. Then you faced down old Angry Wolf, and he shot an arrow clear through you, and you hardly noticed. He thinks you're some kind of goddess or somethin'."

"Ezra exaggerated more than a little, I fear."

Tige chuckled. "I won't tell you what old Con did to Grizzly with his fists."

"I was there. He wouldn't need to exaggerate there."

"Well, it's clear that you was mighty blessed that Con and Ezra come along when they did. Good men, both of them. Old Ezra would die for you in a minute, and Con would, too. I guess they've proved that by hanging with you."

"I guess they have at that. And I owe you and your men, too."

"Ah, we just come along for some excitement."

For the first time, she almost burst into tears. She had been so selfishly focused on her plight and that of her sisters, that she hadn't given that much thought to the men who had stepped in to save her life and those who had signed on to her mission. She had almost been taking them for granted, especially Con. She hated owing anybody, and she owed him the biggest debt of all for not giving up on her when her death was nearly certain. She had kept an emotional distance between them too long, sometimes treating him like the enemy. She could and would do better. But first, she needed to tend to Grizzly.

Chapter 27

GINNY HAD NEVER seen anything quite like Castle Gap. She, Tige, and Beanpole had reined in their mounts at the east end of a vast mesa that would have blocked the trail were it not for a deep cut that split the Castle Mountains and allowed travelers to pass. "It's near a mile long and it barely lets a wagon through some places but would allow three or four times that many lined up side by side at others," Tige said. "The cut's over four hundred feet deep at its highest."

"The trail is worn to the rock," Ginny said. "It looks like it's seen a lot of use."

"Oh yeah. They say people been using it since them giant elephants was out this way. I ain't so sure about that, but the Injuns and them old Spaniards made good use of it. They still dig up some of that rusty Spanish armor in the rocks where Comanches or some such got the best of them. Buzzards, coyotes, and the like have done a lot of feasting in the gap. What they call fossils—just a bunch of old animal bones—are all over where rocks have caved away from the wall. At the river's end, we'll come to what's left of an old stage relay station. The crossing is called Horsehead Crossing 'cause of all the horse bones. Lots of fights and killing there, they say."

"And this is where Comanches traveled to cross the Pecos River?"

"Yeah. The renegades still do, and so do Apaches sometimes. Got to keep our eyes open for them devils, too. Like I said back a ways, the Comanche War Trail and lots of smaller trails feed into this one to let Injuns and others pass through the mesa. Walls are mighty steep some places, sloping at others and not so high, especially when we get near the south end when the gap widens and opens onto the land that slopes gentle-like to the river. Comanches mostly crossed here and went on to the Rio Grande and went into Mexico for raids, stole horses, kids sometimes, and senoritas for wives."

"Sarge, rider off to your right. Movin' at a slow trot." It was Beanpole's deep voice.

Ginny said, "It's Rover. I'd recognize that zebra dun mare anyplace, and he sits his saddle like he's part of the horse."

They watched as Rover moved toward them reining the mount in to a cautious walk down a steep winding trail that weaved through the rocks, disappearing occasionally behind a rocky mound shrouded by yucca and creosote bushes. Finally, the treacherous footing forced him to dismount and lead the mare until he reached the waiting riders.

"Good morning, Rover," Ginny said. "We've had our eyes open for you, wondering if you might pay a visit."

"Yes, ma'am. I figured I'd better get my fanny over here and let you know what's going on. Our friends are moving faster than I guessed they would. They obviously know this country, or at least one of them does. They're not more than three hours behind you. You need to get through the gap and set up for whatever you're going to do. I can go with you if you like."

Tige said, "I'm guessing they've connected with the Comanche War Trail by now."

"Yeah. That's helping them move faster than they were."

"I'd like you to head back some distance on the wagon trail so you're behind where the Comancheros will join up with it from the war trail. Then you just follow them through the gap and be ready to move in if you're needed, maybe find a shooting nest someplace so we got them no-goods boxed in."

"I can do that." Rover reined his mount around and headed back up the trail.

"We'll head into the Castle Gap," Tige said. "We want some space between us just in case somebody we ain't expecting is waitin' along the slopes. It takes better shooting to hit one than to fire at a bunch."

"Who are you thinking could be there?" Ginny asked.

"Most likely nobody, but there's other outlaws in these parts, and Apaches still raid up this far now and then. Just don't want to take chances. You follow me a good twenty feet back, and Beanpole will be tailing you about the same." He nudged his dapple-gray gelding toward the opening in the gap.

Ginny was in awe as they rode through the gap. The northern slope was covered with enormous boulders that would squash men like ants if they took a notion to break loose and topple to the floor of the gap. The south wall was steeper and higher, thick with cedars below the rimrock. As the gap narrowed, she saw small caves and stone overhangs, especially in the south part of the mesa that rose more steeply and higher in several tiers.

Tige signaled a halt when they neared the end of the gap, where the heights of the walls lowered substantially and became more sloping. Beanpole and Ginny rode up beside him. "This is where we set up," Tige said. "There's plenty of rock cover here. I want one of you on each side of the gap. Get high enough you'll be looking down on the Comanchero scum. See those two boulders in the middle of the gap? I'll take those, and when those men get close enough, I'll step out and give them a chance to surrender. If they decide to start shooting, I'll dive in behind the rocks, and you start shooting."

Beanpole objected. "Sarge, you do the slope. Let me face 'em head-on. It's more fun, and we can't risk losing you."

"We ain't losing anybody."

Ginny could not resist speaking her piece. "Why take prisoners? Ambush them and take them down. These bastards didn't give my family any chance. And prisoners would slow us down. We don't have time."

Tige said, "This ain't war. I just ain't one to shoot a man down without giving him a chance to surrender. If we take prisoners, we can drop them off at Fort Stockton. We was stopping there anyhow."

"And that Grizzly scum will escape again," Ginny said.

"If he ends up there, they'll hold him this time. Besides, he won't have friends around to break him out."

She prayed the Comancheros did not surrender. It was not her place to argue with this man who had volunteered men and himself to help recover her sisters. She looked around and spotted a stone outcropping on the southeasterly slope about twenty feet above the gap trail. She pointed. "How about I take that?"

"Good choice. Beanpole, you set up on the north, but first we've got to get our horses out of sight. We're only twenty-five yards or so from the end of the gap, and we can stake the critters off to the side someplace."

"You're the boss, Sarge."

She could see that Beanpole was a bit miffed that he could not claim the "head-on" spot. She was becoming fond of this gentle giant and realized how fortunate she was to ride with all the men who had joined her on this mission. She was starting to feel a special bond with all of them. It was like she was finding a new family, and she was caring for living people besides Noreen and Krista again. But she still wanted to see Grizzly dead before this day was out.

After they led the horses from the gap's southwest entrance and staked them in a smattering of grass that crept up through the near-stone surface, they took up their positions and began the wait. Her companions seemed at ease with the waiting, but Ginny found herself edgy and anxious. Time crawled at a snail's pace, and it seemed that too soon her bladder began to protest. She finally pulled her old pocket watch from her britches' pocket and saw that over two hours had passed. She needed to stay at her post.

Not a half hour later, she heard voices echoing from the east end of the gap. In another fifteen minutes, she saw her nemesis Grizzly trailing the three other men, leaning forward in his saddle as if in misery. It surprised her that he had not fully recovered from Con's beating. Good. Her empathy was frozen like ice when it came to that man. As they approached, she wondered why Tige had not stepped out. The Comancheros were within easy firing range.

Her question was answered when she tossed a glance from her perch and saw him rise from behind the cover offered by his boulders. "Dismount and throw down your guns," Tige hollered. "You're surrounded. We'll hold our fire if you surrender. Now."

The Mexican leading the group drew his pistol. "Go to hell," he said as he got off a shot that would have hit Tige in the chest had he not dropped behind the rocks. A rifle shot cracked from Beanpole's side of the gap, and the Mexican dropped from his saddle. The other Comancheros were shooting wildly now, trying to locate invisible targets.

Ginny raised herself to her knees, peering just over her stone fortress and lifting her Winchester to her shoulder blind to anyone but Grizzly. There was not more than forty feet separating them, and she was glad he saw her now and pointed his six-gun in her direction. She had already levered a cartridge into the chamber and aimed and squeezed the trigger, driving a slug into his beefy shoulder. His horse reared, evidently panicked by the close-range gunfire, and Grizzly slid off its back and landed face-up on the ground.

Ginny had already leaped over the rock barrier and was sliding down the shale slope on her buttocks, clutching her rifle in one hand. When she hit the ground, she headed for Grizzly who was struggling like a turtle on its back trying to right himself and get to his pistol which had fallen out of his reach.

"Stop," Ginny yelled, unaware that the guns around her had gone silent.

"I surrender, bitch," Grizzly said. "Look, my shoulder. I'm bleeding like a stuck hog. You got to help me."

She levered another cartridge, raised her rifle and aimed. "Like you helped my parents and brother and little sisters."

"I ain't armed no more. You can't kill me."

"Wanna bet?" She squeezed the trigger, the echoing explosion somehow more deafening amidst the silence. This time, the slug drilled a hole in the center of Grizzly's forehead. She stood there for several minutes staring at the lifeless form. She had killed a defenseless man, one she had hated above all creatures on this earth. It seemed that somehow Grizzly, who bore no more blame than any of the others, had been a symbol of the nightmare that had occurred the day of the attack. She should feel relief, even joy, but she did not. She felt like she could vomit, and seconds later, she did.

When she collected her composure and finally took in the scene around her she saw the blood-soaked bodies strewn on the trail, she noticed that Rover had arrived and dismounted nearby and was just staring at her. Farther away, Tige and Beanpole also stared.

"Aren't there things we need to be doing?" Ginny said.

"Yeah, you're right, ma'am," Tige said. "Beanpole, do you want to collect the new horses for the remuda and get them staked out with the others? I'll check the bodies and get the gun belts and weapons and anything else worth saving. Then we'll figure out if these gents is buzzard food or if we want to bury them someplace."

"Sure, Sarge, I'll see to the critters."

"Rover, we'll take care of this business. Do you want to head back to the others and let them know that the Comanchero bunch ain't a problem no more? We'll set up camp a ways beyond the south entrance of the gap and wait. We'll get together later tonight or in the morning depending on how far along the trail they are."

"I'll do that." Rover turned to Ginny. "Miss Ginny, do you want to go back with me or have you had enough riding for the day?"

"Thanks for the invite, Rover, but I'll stay. Maybe Tige can find something useful for me to do." And she did not want to talk to anybody else until she straightened a few things out in her head.

Chapter 28

DURING HIS ARMY years, Con had crossed the Pecos River at Horsehead Crossing a dozen times, he figured. The Pecos twisted like a giant snake from the Sangre de Cristo mountains of north-central New Mexico Territory through the southeastern part of that territory before entering Texas. The river passed through the Chihuahuan Desert country, which the searchers had just entered, and eventually emptied farther southeast into the Rio Grande River.

The frequent and sudden bends in the river's course sometimes confused travelers as to which side of the channel they were on. But the most serious challenges presented by the fast-flowing water were the steep and high riverbanks that made passage by horse, and certainly by wagon, nearly impossible at most places within fifty or more miles in each direction from Horsehead

Crossing. Here was a gate to the opposite side where the river widened and the banks tapered down gradually to the water's edge. Nature had done its part here, and migrants had done the rest over hundreds of years.

The crossing had acquired its name from horses' skulls that were scattered over the landscape on both sides of the river that had triggered endless speculation. Some thought they were remnants of a great battle. Others suggested that riders crossing the near waterless arid lands to the south had released mounts that overindulged, foundered and died there. Human graves, crude wooden crosses, no longer upright and most not readable, were intermingled among the skulls and added to the stories. Whatever the source of the deaths there, Con had always found Horsehead Crossing, located not more than a dozen miles southwest of the Castle Gap southerly entrance, an eerie place and was always glad to make the crossing and move on.

He held back while the others crossed the river, shallow and nearly a hundred feet wide where steep banks failed to contain it. For some strange reason, Ginny, astride Artemis, remained with him. Ever since they met up again not far from the south Castle Gap entrance last night, she had not been so standoffish. In fact, she had been hanging close and laid out her bedroll only a few feet from his. He liked her non-hostile presence and welcomed her nearness but knew it was best to say nothing.

They watched as Tige entered the water leading his packed mule. Ginny said, "Tige was sure fretting about that load on his mule, worried about getting it wet."

Con said, "I had never asked him, but I helped Irish unpack the critter the night we were separated. It's a heavy load, but that's a big old mule, and it doesn't seem to mind. Tige has a Gatling gun in there. Bought it from the Army when they were getting rid of surplus. Irish wasn't sure it was supposed to get into civilian hands, but he said Tige had lots of Army friends, both white and colored."

"A Gatling gun. I've read about them. They shoot fast and for long stretches. Right?"

"Right. This is one of the first box models, Irish said, but its outdated now. The first ones had to be handfed, but this one is fired by attaching cartridge boxes with about fifty cartridges. Use those up, and you attach another box. We never had one with our cavalry units during the Red River War. They were generally kept at the forts for defense. I guess Tige and Woody were something of a team with the gun in their company, and somehow their company commander wangled one to take in the field."

"I hope we don't need it."

"Me, too. And it does take some time to set up. I'll leave that to Tige. He seems to know what he's doing."

"After yesterday, I will vouch for that."

"You're different since yesterday."

"I suppose I am."

"I can listen if you ever want to talk about it."

"Maybe sometime. You helped bury those men, didn't you?"

"Yeah. We found a gully and rolled some stones over them. Ezra and Irish helped me. I think several wanted to leave the bodies for the scavengers. I was never good with that unless we were on the run. It bothered me. I can't explain why."

"You saw Grizzly then?"

"Yeah." That was all he was going to say about it. "Time for us to cross. A few are on the other bank, and everybody else is at least midstream. Ladies first, I'll be leading Chester and his load directly behind you."

All had removed their boots, and Ginny had attached hers to her saddlebags. He guessed that the water midstream would be no more than four or five feet high. He doubted she weighed many pounds over a hundred, so she and the blue roan mare would almost float. She would be fine. She rode as if born in the saddle.

That evening, they were well into the Chihuahuan Desert when they set up camp. Con decided they struck gold when Rover volunteered to join them. He roamed constantly along the fringes of the party, disappearing occasionally and then returning to report when he found a water hole or anything else that might be of interest to the others. Tonight they were camped in a small dead-end canyon with sandstone walls that had a spring erupting from one wall that offered a stream that ran along the base before disappearing. That it was a popular location was evidenced by a near carpet of dung left by deer, coyotes, and other wild species.

Ezra had harvested selected dung to supplement the meager wood supply he gathered along the way for cooking a simple supper of venison, biscuits and beans. The other men had handled cleanup, and the normally grumpy Ezra smiled approvingly.

Con stepped over to Ezra and said, "We should be at Fort Stockton the day after tomorrow. I'd like to get there by noon if we can. We'll stay overnight there and get an early start the next morning. Let me know if we need supplies, and I'll see what I can do about purchasing them."

"You're going to run yourself out of money unless you got a hell of a lot more than I think."

"I'm okay for now."

"You know, I got a hunch that little filly's carrying enough in them saddlebags to feed an army. You ought to have a talk with her."

"I'm not real comfortable talking about money."

"Them's her sisters we're supposed to be doing this for." Then he nodded to someone behind Con. "Speak of the devil. She's headed over here now."

Ginny came up to the men and gave Ezra a peck on his forehead. "Grandpa, I was just thinking about supplies at Fort Stockton. We've been loading up on food and such, but I haven't forked over a nickel except for a few things at Fort Elliott. Everybody's helping on this mission for me, and I haven't taken care of the funding. How have you been paying for these things? And I know we promised to pay the Buffalo Soldiers. That's my responsibility."

"Well, sweetheart, maybe you and Mister Callaway need to have a talk about these matters. He's been taking care of the money so far." Ezra made a strategic retreat claiming he had chores to tend to.

She looked at Con. "Why haven't you said something?"

"Well, Ginny, you've had to deal with a lot these past weeks. This isn't about money. I still have funds, and Tige said that the money for his crew can wait till we're back in San Angelo. I might have trouble covering that."

"I've got plenty for taking care of supply needs and hopefully to pay the Buffalo Soldiers, but I don't know what ransom we might be forced to pay Angry Wolf. Of course, that assumes he will even return my sisters for ransom money."

"If he will, we can pool what we've got. I'm hoping we can sell the extra horses and tack at Fort Stockton. We've all agreed that the money goes to you. Tige talked to his men and came to me and said they all agreed that the money goes to you to help those girls however you see fit."

"I...I don't know what to say. I started off hating the world, but I've had all this kindness come my way."

"There are a lot of good people in this world, Ginny. The bad ones just stir up more than their share of the misery, so it seems there are more of them sometimes."

"I don't know what I am. I murdered a man yesterday. In cold blood."

He reached out and took her hand. She did not resist as he feared she might. Aunt Kate had told him many times that sometimes folks just needed a gentle, human touch. "Walk with me," he said.

The sun had dropped behind canyon walls, and it was not so burning hot now. A soft breeze caressed their faces, and the only sounds were the soothing coos of desert doves nesting in the crevices that lined the canyon walls and the occasional nickering of the horses. They strolled leisurely along the canyon's perimeter. "It's so peaceful here," Ginny said. "I like the quiet with background music of the birds and horses."

"You do love your horses, don't you?"

She surrendered a quick smile and looked up at him. "I do. Pa set me on the back of a horse before I could walk, and he got me riding on my own before I was five. Mom was terrified and not happy about it. Pa and I were closer in those early years, but when I got to be twelve, we were fussing and fighting all the time. He changed, but I suppose I changed, too. Maybe that's what he didn't like—my changing. I wasn't his little girl anymore."

"I hardly knew my father. My mother died when I was born, and her sister, my Aunt Kate Moore took me and raised me, mostly in Dodge City, Kansas. As I've mentioned I have an older brother, Clifford Caesar Callaway the third, but we don't get along well. I stayed with him on the Triple C Ranch for a year after I left the Army. I liked the ranch work well enough, but Cliff was boss since he inherited the ranch from my father, and we butted heads all the time. The ranch is a good distance north of Harwood Place in the northeast corner of the Texas panhandle. Ezra worked there, too, for a short spell, and we both rode out the same day, going no place in particular when we saw the smoke at Harwood, and that's what led us to you."

"If God didn't send you, Lady Luck sure did."

"You're troubled about yesterday."

"Yes, I am. You know, you've heard me talking for days about how I wanted to kill Grizzly."

"Yeah, it does seem like you've mentioned that a time or two."

"Well, when we ambushed those no-goods yesterday, I took him down with a shoulder wound, but it wouldn't have killed him. We could have patched him up and taken him with us to Fort Stockton, but I walked over and with him staring up at me placed a slug right in the middle of his forehead. I put him down just like a suffering, dying horse, except he wasn't dying."

"And now it's troubling you."

"I hate what I was at that moment. And Tige and Beanpole were both just staring at me when I turned around. They saw the awful thing I did."

"I doubt if they were shocked by it. They haven't said a word to me. If there was any surprise, it was because you are a woman. Like it or not, men tend to have different expectations of women. They've probably done the same thing."

"You're not serious?"

"When you are at war, it's not unusual to receive 'take no prisoners' orders. In those instances, the soldier either leaves the wounded enemy to die or kills him. The expectation is that you will feed the wounded man another slug. Some officers will insist. It's nasty business, but I did it a few times to wounded warriors. I stopped short of killing women and children, but others didn't."

"Children? That would be a horrible thing to witness, let alone do."

"Those are the nightmares I carry with me. You are at war, Ginny. You saw what your enemy did to your home and family. No person who has experienced or seen these atrocities is going to judge you. Tige and Beanpole do not, and I certainly do not. Maybe it's not a bad thing that we remember these occasions, but we've got to somehow shake them off and move on. Your focus must be on saving the lives of your sisters. We can ease those nightmares by doing good when we can."

"Is that why you came with me? Easing your own nightmares?"

"Part of it maybe. I don't fully understand it. But Ezra and I do care. We didn't even talk about it. We just knew we had to do this for ourselves and a special young woman and her sisters."

He turned to Ginny when he heard her sobbing. He reached out to her with his arms open and she fell into them, soaking his shirt with tears till she was all cried out.

Chapter 29

GINNY FINALLY FELT she and her companions were making progress after they crossed the Rio Grande midmorning and entered Mexico's state of Chihuahua, a vast area made up largely of an extension of the Chihuahuan Desert. Still, their journey to Copper Canyon would take anywhere from another eight to ten days according to Rover, depending upon how critters and riders withstood the heat. Con and Tige had agreed that they would seek a camping place early afternoon.

Their visits to both Fort Stockton and Fort Davis were brief but provided opportunities to restock supplies for a long journey that would offer few, if any, trading post visits. Con had expressed concern about supply replenishment, but Rover was confident there would be sufficient hunting opportunities.

As to the horses and mules, Con had told her that this portion of the Chihuahuan, like that in Texas, was not pure sand but rather a mix of rock, dirt, gravel, and sometimes clay. The grass was lush only near limited water sources, but there were intermittent grasslands with a variety of grama grasses for adequate grazing from time to time. Tige said there were stories that grass was belly-high to a horse in places, although he doubted the truth to such tales. Regardless, the animals would not starve. This was a relief because she cringed at the thought of Artemis suffering from hunger. She would rather do without herself.

She rode beside Con today, as she had been doing increasingly since the night he held her during her rare crying outburst. They had not spoken of it again, but it seemed to her that night had torn down an invisible barrier between them, and they were more at ease and relaxed in their conversations now. And they each seemed more comfortable with silence between them. She liked that he was a man who did not need to chatter nonsense all the time. It was like they had suddenly become friends and were no longer strangers.

There was no trail over the vast land that lay ahead, and the riders moved more in a cluster than a column with Rover and Beanpole ranging ahead, fanning out to search for potential water sources and to keep an eye out for danger. When they slowed the gait of their mounts to give some respite to the critters, Ginny reined her mare nearer to Con. "Rover and Beanpole are looking for something besides water. Rover seemed mighty confident about finding water, so I'm curious about what they think they might find."

"Mexican bandidos, renegade Comanche, Apache, government federales, to name a few. Our horses and mules, not to mention saddles and tack, would bring big money here. There are gangs that roam this country, raiding ranches, stagecoaches, and travelers passing through. They're quick to squeeze the trigger when it comes to somebody getting in their way. They won't be sneaking in at night to whisp your critters away without you knowing it. They'd rather kill you while you are sleeping and then make off with everything you've got."

"I thought the Indians mostly hide out in mountain country—like where we're headed."

"That's true enough. The Mexican soldiers pretty much leave them alone if they're not attacking ranches and villages, but sometimes they can't resist. But they're out there looking for opportunities that might not attract the government's attention so much. Killing trespassers in Mexico likely wouldn't worry the federales any. In fact, there are some who would consider foreigners fair game. We sure can't count on their help if we run into trouble."

"What happens if we meet up with federales?"

"Well, they might escort us back to the border or toss us into a Mexican jail, which by reputation is worse than being dumped into a pit of rattlesnakes. Or they might decide to kill us on the spot. More likely, though, we could negotiate a bribe with their leader."

Ginny said, "And I thought we didn't have any worries till we reached the Sierra Madres and the Copper Canyon."

"Chances are we won't run into any trouble along the way, but in the Chihuahuan Desert country it's best not to take anything for granted, and we aren't. We're riding with good men who have been under fire countless times and know what they're doing. An ambush would be extremely difficult for an enemy to accomplish here in this wide-open land, so a surprise attack is unlikely. We wouldn't be facing a hundred men, so we just need a little notice to allow us to prepare."

"That's reassuring, I guess."

Con pointed to the southeast. "Rover is riding this way. Must have some news."

"Good news, I hope."

"He doesn't seem to be riding at a frantic pace."

"Rover never appears frantic about anything."

"That's true enough. Especially for a kid."

"A kid? I'll be twenty in September. He couldn't be more than a year or two younger than I am. Do you think of me as a kid?"

Con did not answer immediately. "No, Ginny, I sure as blazes don't think of you as a kid. I just turned twenty-four. Do you think of me as an old man?"

She laughed, "I don't know. You're getting up in years, that's for sure."

He looked over at her, cocked his head and squinted one eye. "I've never heard you laugh before. That's like music to my ears, and it becomes you."

She had to admit it felt good, but sobering thoughts quickly overtook her. "I haven't had much to laugh about for a spell."

"No, I guess you haven't."

When Rover reined his mare in front of them, she could not read anything on his stoic face. He spoke to Con, now accepted by all, including her, as the unofficial commander of the party.

"I thought you should know, Con. Somebody's keeping an eye on us. He's been following us for a good hour now. One man wearing a sombrero and riding a dang fine-looking black horse. He keeps his distance, but there's too much open country out here for him to be moving behind ridges and hills. I got a fix on him with my spyglass. He's got a cartridge belt tossed over his shoulder. I'm not sure if he even cares if we see him. Maybe you've already spotted him."

"Nope. I guess I've been sort of lazy, leaving that to you and Beanpole. Any notion who it might be? Federales scout? Bandit?"

"No uniform, so I doubt if he is with the army. He could be scouting for bandidos, or he might just be a vaquero from one of the ranches out here making sure we don't intend to make any trouble for them. The ranchers do have men posted here and there to keep an eye out for horse or cattle rustlers. To the north of us, there are big haciendas with almost a village of folks nearby providing workers and services. They're maybe ten miles apart, but they tail off and disappear the closer we get to the mountains. Apache and other Indians tend to discourage neighbors."

Con said, "For now, just continue to keep an eye on him. Check with Beanpole and tell him. I'd like to find a place to camp by midafternoon, hopefully something with water nearby and that we can fortify at least some to ward off any attack by unfriendly sorts. We'll try to catch at least several hours of shuteye and head out again after dark."

"I'll do that. The water is going to start being the tough part."

Rover wheeled his mount around and headed back in the direction of Beanpole who appeared tiny as an ant on the horizon. Ginny stared after him as he rode as if he were a part of the horse. "I love that stallion," she said, "so sleek and perfectly muscled."

Con said, "You are talking about the horse?"

"Well, him, too. I talked to Rover about mating that blue roan stallion to Artemis. Two blue roans ought to give me a fair chance at a blue roan foal."

Con was looking at her now, and she could see he was a bit miffed. He said, "You called Rover a stallion."

She shrugged. She loved teasing him, pleased that Con was revealing a trace of jealousy. She was not about to tell him she was starting to see Congrave Clinton Callaway as her stallion, not that Rover was not a handsome specimen, but she knew that his roving days were far from over. He was mature in many ways, but he was still an adventurous boy at his core.

"We'd better ride," Con said. "We don't want your stallion to get away from us."

Chapter 30

CON CAUGHT SIGHT of two riders off to his left, no more than drifting dust clouds, but he had seen such movements in his Red River War days, and they were usually the scouting fringes of a good-sized war party. He didn't like the looks of this. He sensed a gathering storm.

"What are you looking at?" Ginny hollered from five or so paces off to his right.

He pointed in the direction of the moving images. "Appears we've got more company," he yelled back.

"I don't see anything."

Ezra, astride his black and white spotted gelding and leading his sorrel pack horse, reined up beside him. "You already seen them, I'd guess."

"Yep, what do you think?"

"I'm guessing we got trouble coming our way. But what kind? Hell, it could be anybody."

"Why don't you ride up here with Ginny a spell? I'll go pass the word to the others. I'd like to see what Tige thinks. Just holler if you see something I should know about."

"That I can do good. I done a lot of hollering in my day."

When Con reined in beside Tige, he asked him if he had seen the riders, and the former Buffalo Soldier sergeant advised that he had not. "Well, I just wanted to alert you. I'm hoping we can get settled in someplace before we have visitors—if we have any."

"I'll pass the word on to Irish and Woody. I'm thinking we have bandidos scouting us out. Soldiers ain't likely to worry about scouting. They'd be more direct-like and just ride on in and state their business. And none of us, except Rover maybe, would catch sight of one till they was about on us. Bandidos would take their time, match our numbers to theirs, pick the most likely time and spot. They might decide we ain't worth the risk."

"What you say makes sense. Rover saw one man earlier, but he couldn't say for sure that the fella wasn't a lone traveler. When two more show up, that possibility doesn't seem likely."

"Nope. Let's just hope three men is all there is. If it turns out that way, they ain't going to bother us none."

"Do you really think that's going to happen?"

"Nope."

An hour later, they were galloping their mounts easterly at a steady pace when a massive dust cloud appeared on the southern horizon. The instant Con saw the dust, he recognized the source. Horses, and a good number of them, too. He judged them to be half a mile distant, but they would close the gap soon enough in the likely event they were not slowed by pack animals, and after a long day in the scorching sun they dared not push their own critters any harder. They desperately needed to fort up someplace.

Rover and Beanpole must have read his mind because, converging from different directions, the two joined up not more than a hundred yards distant and were waving them on. As they neared, Rover pointed northward and rode off in that direction while Beanpole headed to the back of the outfit to provide cover. As they followed Rover, Con tossed a look over his shoulder and saw that the pursuers had closed nearly half the distance, and he could make out riders now—a lot of them.

Ginny, astride Artemis, hollered at him from the right where she was easily maintaining his buckskin's pace. "Rover's headed for that butte."

Con nodded agreement. A ridged butte emerged from the flatlands like a giant molar. As they approached, he caught a glimpse of scrub cottonwood and willows at the butte's base and patches of green here and there. That signaled water. A scattering of rocks, having apparently caved off the limestone walls over the years, promised valuable cover. As their party members arrived, Con heard gunfire behind him and saw that Beanpole and Irish had reined in, turned toward the pursuers, and started unleashing gunfire on them.

Rover had already started pushing and stacking the ragged limestone chunks. Con yelled, "Stake your mounts and the packhorses off to the side away from where we're going to build our barriers. We want to keep them out of the line of fire, and they won't want to hurt the critters. That's a big part of what they're after. Make cover nests for one or two. There aren't enough stones or enough time to make a wall."

The gunfire ceased, and Con turned and saw Beanpole and Irish leading their horses toward the butte. The attackers, obviously bandidos of some sort, had swung back, reined in out of rifle range and were apparently discussing strategy. He retrieved his spyglass from the saddlebags before leading Quanah and Chester away from their piecemeal fortifications and staking them. He saw that Ginny had already staked Artemis and was helping Ezra with a stone barrier. She was lifting rocks that he thought would be beyond her strength. "I'll help you in a minute," he said as he passed her. "I need to talk to Beanpole or Irish."

"We're making this big enough for you, too. Just tend to your business."

He walked up to Beanpole, who was leading his horse to the others for staking. "Thanks for covering us, Beanpole. You bought us time to get organized. Any idea how many we're up against?"

"No time to get a count, but they got one less than they started with. I'm guessing that's what got them to think things over a spell."

"Well, why don't you get over there and put some cover together like the others are doing, and maybe you can take a few more down. I'm going to study the outfit with my spyglass a few minutes."

Beanpole said, "They got to do a heap of thinking. They's after our critters and tack and whatever dollars they can pick up—won't get a nickel from me. Of course, the guns would bring a fair price. But they about got to come for us afoot, or they risk losing their own critters. Ain't going to make no money that way."

"You're right about that."

As Beanpole walked away, Winchester in hand, Con lifted the spyglass and focused it on the bandidos. With the milling around of the men and horses, it was difficult to obtain a precise count, but he estimated there were ten to twelve men, mostly Mexican but perhaps three Anglo. They were a rugged-looking bunch, some with sombreros, others with an assortment of hats, unshaven, a few full beards and a lot of brushy mustaches. They were well-armed, some with cartridge belts slung across their chests.

Searching along the ground, he saw the bloody body of a man Irish or Beanpole had put away. He suspected there would be a fuss over who got the man's horse and tack as well as other belongings. He had encountered such men during his Army years, and it was a good bet one or two men would die over that quarrel. The one thing they had in common was that they preyed on the weak, often peasant farmers or small ranchers, maybe a stagecoach or wagon-borne family now and then. They would not fight to the death to take down the search party for the Harwood girls.

When he finished his survey with the spyglass, Con returned to the others, feeling a bit guilty that he had not done much of the manual work to fortify the place. They had five battle stations forming an arc with the butte wall at their back. "This is ours," Ginny said, waving him to the three-foot high stone stack where she was standing. "Ezra said he and Rover would pair up."

Con knelt on one knee beside Ginny who was feeding cartridges into her Winchester's magazine. "You're going to be prepared it seems."

"I already checked yours. You weren't. You are now. You were six cartridges short."

"Thanks. I'm bad about that."

"One could be the difference between living and dying."

"You didn't happen to do Army time did you?"

"Nope, but I would like to have been an officer maybe, so I could boss others around."

He did not want to pursue that topic and was glad when Tige stepped over. "They ain't sure what they want to do," Tige said. "I'm thinking they might make one run at us to see how much firepower we got. Then if they pay too high a price, they'll likely move on for better prospects. I could get 'Old Babe' out, but it would take a half hour, maybe more to get her ready to fire."

"I take it 'Old Babe' is your Gatling gun?"

"Yep, she'll work when it suits her, but she's been around a spell and needs some snuggles and coaxing before she's ready to get down to business. They tell me some old women is like that."

"Young ones, too."

"I heard that," Ginny said. "Both of you, please spare me your wisdom about women. I don't imagine either of you know much anyhow."

Tige said, "Well, me and Juana have been married a good spell, but I sure as heck don't got her figured out yet, so I guess I'll just keep my mouth shut tight."

Con said, "Too late. Our friends are starting to move this way. I don't think we'll need Old Babe anyhow." He hesitated a moment, noticing the bandidos were spreading out. "Ezra, let's try your old Sharps first. I'm betting you could hit one of the bandidos from here."

"Dang right, if I could see that far. They need to separate and move this way a mite, and then I can start taking them down like sittin' turkeys."

"Shoot when you're ready, Ezra. Everybody wait for Ezra to fire. I'd like Ezra and Rover to work their ways in from our left and Beanpole and Irish, since you're positioned to the right, you start from that side, and the rest of us will take the middle."

They all waited for the attack behind their stone fortresses. The bandidos did not force them to wait long. They fanned out and charged, most firing pistols because of the need to secure their horses' reins. Between range and inaccuracy astride a moving horse, they represented little threat to the defenders. Ezra's Sharps rifle roared, and the furthest left rider flew off his horse. Suddenly, gunfire nearly shook the desert floor. Con got off a few shots with his Winchester but could not say whether his rifle or someone else's had delivered the slugs that dropped two men.

He credited Ginny with one of those. She was shooting with intensity and care, exhibiting a soldier's discipline. She was not like any woman he had ever encountered, and he had known some smart, tough ones, including his Aunt Kate. Ginny, however, was still an enigma to him. About the time he thought he had her figured out, she displayed another side, and, of course, he could not come near to guessing how he stood in her eyes. Damn, he could almost forget the gunfire and just grab her and pull her over and plant a warm, lingering kiss on those tight lips.

It suddenly occurred to him that silence consumed the vast desert land now. While he had disappeared in dreamland for just a few moments—a soldier's invitation to death—the fighting had halted. The bodies of a half dozen men and one horse, lay on the desert in front of them. The others were snatching up the vacated horses and heading back south. It was over.

Beanpole and Irish headed out to check on the downed men. Ginny leaped up to join them, but Con clutched her arm and held her fast. "Stay here," he said. "Please. Go see how Ezra's doing."

"Grandpa's fine. He's standing up." A gunshot cracked, and she turned to the battlefield. Then another and another. Finally, one more. "Oh, my God. They're killing those men."

"I didn't want you to be a part of it. They put the horse out of its misery, likely the men, too. We couldn't take them with us. We can't lose the time to nurse them. We just walk away, and it's a question of whether the sunrays or the scavengers take them first. Now you know that others have faced the decision you made back at Castle Gap."

"But it was different. I killed out of rage."

Con shrugged. "Dead is dead when the other guy asked for killing."

Rover approached Con and Ginny. "Con, there's something you should know."

"What's that?"

He nodded toward the west, where the sun's glare was almost blinding now. "See that knoll down the trail we've been taking?"

"Yeah."

Rover said, "There were a couple of men watching our little fracas here. They disappeared as soon as things were settled. I caught them out of the corner of my eye when the shooting was going on, so I didn't get a good look. After she's watered, I'd like to take my zebra dun—she hasn't had a rider for several days—and see if I can figure out who they were."

"You need some rest."

"I'll have my bedroll and grab some shuteye when I can. We have a few hours of daylight left. I'd like to see what I can find while it's still light. I'll catch you up the trail someplace."

"We need you, Rover. Don't get yourself killed."

"It'd take more than two to kill me. I'm just uneasy about those men."

"Alright, see if Ezra's got some jerky and leftover biscuits to take with you. We'll meet up later."

Rover nodded and walked away to saddle the mare.

Ginny said, "Rover was worth the detour to Grit McKay's ranch, wasn't he?"

"Yeah. But we've got a passel of good folks riding with us, Ginny. We just might get this job done."

"You've had doubts?"

He did not reply.

Chapter 31

THEY DID NOT see Rover again for three days. The night travel made Ginny uneasy. She did not like being unable to see a significant distance into the landscape that surrounded them, but she conceded that it agreed with the horses and mules. Their breathing was less labored, and the critters were not so frantic to drink their fill when they came to the rare stream and occasional spring that bubbled up from beneath the sandy soil. The riders were not so sapped of their strength either.

It was nearly an hour before sunrise, and Beanpole had ridden ahead in search of a resting place that they could claim by midmorning. He was a competent scout, but none could compare to Rover in locating water sources. Somehow, she felt safer when Rover was with them.

As usual, she was riding near Con at the front of the riders and pack animals, but she started when a figure emerged from the darkness off to her right. She could not whisper because there was more than ten feet between her and Con, but she had to warn him. "Con, someone's coming off to my right. Beanpole should be well ahead of us."

"Coming in," the spooky figure hollered. "It's me... Rover."

She breathed a sigh of relief. "Rover, you scared the shit out of me."

"Well, I hope not for real. I thought you'd be glad to see me, that we'd have a party or something."

By this time, she had reined in Artemis, and the searchers had come to a halt. "We are glad to have you back. We were worried about you. At least I was."

"Don't know why. I knew where I was at."

Con said, "Then maybe you'll share that information with the rest of us."

"I'm not bringing good news. Those two men I spotted were Comanche warriors. I followed them as far as it made sense. I wanted to make sure they were headed where I suspected."

"And where was that?"

"It was clear they were headed to the Sierra Madres."

"You think they were with Angry Wolf?"

"You'll find Apache bands scattered about up there, but most of the Comanche are on reservations except for Angry Wolf. It's a good bet they were headed for Wolf's Mouth Canyon."

"Do you think they've been watching us long?" Con asked.

"I doubt it. I would have known. I think they saw the bandidos heading our way, and that whetted their curiosity. Comanche often have what we might call outriders that range away from the village, sort of half-guards and half-scouts. They'll ride out a long way looking for good hunting ground or horses that a band of warriors from the village might steal."

"But they wouldn't know why we're out here," Con said.

"The direction we're going could stir up some suspicions, I'm guessing. It's hard to say how well they could see us. But if they did, four coloreds, an Injun like me, and then a woman and a couple of white fellas would sure as blazes attract their attention."

"But a group our size shouldn't be seen as much of a threat," Ginny said.

"I don't know. I still don't like it that Angry Wolf is likely going to know we're out here."

Ginny said, "I never figured we were just going to ride into the village and introduce ourselves. It's hard to imagine they wouldn't know we were on our way well before we showed up anyhow."

Con said, "You're right about that. I guess this alerts us that it won't be long before we've got scouts keeping an eye on us as we move toward the mountains." He turned to Rover. "We'll count on you and Beanpole to keep an eye out. Between here and the base of the mountains, are there many good spots for an ambush? I don't worry about that so much out here in the flatlands."

Rover said, "There are such places, but I can lead you around them. I'm guessing they'll be watching us but won't be looking to attack us before we get to the mountains. They got a hundred ways to set traps for us there."

Tige stepped forward. "Con, I take it you never been this far into Mexico. Me and Beanpole took a patrol into the mountains following Apaches—what you might call an unofficial visit to see where the devils went. Well, we never found them but saw a part of the dang Copper Canyon from the rim. They say there's six canyons there that make up what they call Copper Canyon. Six different rivers run down the canyons and join up with the Rio Fuerte that takes the water on west and dumps it in the ocean."

"Did you enter the canyon?"

"Nope. We got the hell out. Wasn't a place I wanted to fight no Injuns, and Army brass wouldn't have liked it if they found out our captain had sent us there. He just wanted us to find the route where they might come back across the Rio Grande. Ain't no such thing. Probably don't cross the same place twice anyhow."

"The canyon's as big as the stories about it then?"

"Bigger. Con, that canyon's more than a mile deep in places, and the trails that will take you to the bottom are narrow and single file in places. I ain't got a notion how we find this Angry Wolf or get to him and his village."

Rover said, "I ran into Beanpole about an hour up the trail. He's found a good water hole amongst some rocks. No trees, and the grass is sparse, but it'll do for a day's rest. We'll find more grass and shade as we move west toward the mountains. You might want to stretch out a few of your canvas ponchos on stakes for shade if you don't want to burn up in the sun."

Con said, "Let's head for the water hole, and after we get settled in and have some breakfast, I want some more education about this place we're going. I think we'd better start figuring out how we're going to play the few cards we've got."

Beanpole was waiting to lead them no more than a half mile off the trail to a dilapidated, obviously abandoned, cabin that leaned to one side like it might tip over at any moment. The frame structure sat less than ten feet from a cluster of stones that were surrounded by a moat-like stream of water that seemed to go nowhere.

Rover said, "Dad told me that places like this are called artesian wells. Water underneath the ground is collected and saved in an aquifer, a big pool, and there's pressure in the aquifer that pushes the water through the surface. This is likely a small one, and the water that's not claimed doesn't go far before it's soaked back into the clay and sandy soil here. Other places, it sometimes pushes out enough water to form a stream."

Ezra, dismounted now, said, "Boy, I never heard an Injun talk like you. Them words you're usin' are danged highfalutin for the likes of me. I seen places like this now and then. Always just said there was an underground water well with its own pump."

Ginny said, "That partially explains the cabin here. It makes sense that a person would build near a water source. Still, why would you do this out in the middle of nowhere?"

"Some of us like nowhere," Ezra said. "This place was put up some years back. Good spot for a trading post. Maybe some feller traded goods with Injuns and other folks. A man's got something for trade, most ain't going to do no harm to you."

Con said, "Well, let's see what we can do about breakfast. Everybody get unpacked and water your critters and stake them out. Ezra, I'll help with your horses. Do we have something fit to eat yet?"

"Got the last of the bacon, and I can do biscuits if we can have a fire."

"Might as well. Anybody watching is going to see us, fire or not. I think others have kept the trees cleared off, but there are plenty of loose boards on the shack. I'll harvest some of that for firewood. It looks like I won't be the first."

Later, everyone kept a good distance from the dying fire embers as the group gathered to talk. Con spoke first. "It's time we started setting up some kind of strategy for the days ahead. I'm guilty of not having thought enough about this, and I think first we need to understand just how difficult this is going to be. Rover is the only one who has been into what's called the Wolf's Mouth, and Tige has been as far as Copper Canyon's rim, but I'm only beginning to understand that you just see a fragment of the canyon from a given place on the rim. Maybe Tige would like to elaborate on that."

Tige stood. "Y'all need to know that this ain't some canyon that you go to, and you view the whole thing from the rim. It's more like Palo Duro up in the panhandle country. It stretches out for miles and miles. I was told it's a couple hundred miles north and south anyhow and maybe half that east and west. Like some have been told, it's really made of six canyons along six different rivers. There's even a few towns in the canyon. One is called Batopilas in a canyon with that name, a good-sized silver mining town, but we won't be passing close to it. You got to understand that in that place ten miles is like fifty when it comes to getting from one place to another. I ain't got no idea how we get to this Wolf's Mouth from the rim. I'll leave that to Rover to figure out."

Ginny's confidence was shaken by Tige's words. She had never pondered logistics. She had always just thought about riding up to the village, demanding the girls, paying a ransom and riding away. Deep down, she knew it would not be that easy, but it had been easier than facing reality. Now reality was becoming worse than she ever could have imagined.

Con said, "Rover, how many days do we have in front of us?"

"Only two to the base of the Sierra Madre Mountain range. We will move at a slow pace there, partly out of caution, but the ground is rocky and we will start a gradual climb there. We must take care for the horses' sake. After two days, we begin our steep ascent into the mountains. Some of this will be very rugged, some not so bad. It will take a long day to reach the rim of the canyon where the Wolf's Mouth is located."

"Can we see the Wolf's Mouth from the rim?"

"Probably, with your spyglass, but you won't be able to make out the people or lodges if you were hoping to see the girls. Then some will descend into the canyon and spend a day getting to the Wolf's Mouth which is across a river and set in a branch canyon higher up again on a plateau. Copper Canyon includes countless sub or branch canyons, all much smaller than the six main canyons. The entry wall of the Wolf's Mouth has a jagged opening that is less than ten feet wide." He shrugged. "The jaws or mouth of the wolf."

Con said, "There is no way, I take it, that we can enter the Wolf's Mouth with rifle cover."

"No. And just inside the entrance, canyon walls include ledges fifteen to twenty feet above the floor, almost like the parapet of a fort that would allow warriors to shoot down at invading enemies. No army could surprise them there and likely would not take on the task anyhow."

"But we could set up cover outside the Wolf's Mouth?"

"Yes, I suppose. The question is where do you go once you get out?"

"I'll have to see what it looks like. Rather than go back up this trail where we enter the canyon, how long could we move north on the canyon floor? Is there an easier escape farther up the canyon?"

"I haven't been far that direction. I don't know. I'm sure there are many exits. I just don't know how difficult that would be."

Con turned to Tige. "Any thoughts, Tige?"

"I got to think on this a spell. We can talk more when we ride tonight."

Con said, "Can I assume it will cool off at the mountains' base?"

Tige said, "Yeah. At least we're going to start seeing more trees as we go along. We'll have shade and more water. Am I right, Rover?"

"Yes, and you won't need to be riding in the dark and won't want to on those trails."

Con said, "Starting tomorrow, we'll ease into getting our days and nights straightened out again. Anyway, we've got a few things to think about. Let's grab some rest and a little shuteye if we can."

Ginny stayed close to Con as he chatted with Tige and Irish for a spell after the others departed to improvise shade and layout their bedrolls. Tige said, "We got my Gatling. Don't forget that. Old Babe would sure as hell cover an escape once we got the gals out of the Wolf's Mouth."

"But what about those manning the gun? Eventually you'd run out of ammunition and be swarmed."

Irish said, "Not if we left the gun behind. The Comanche wouldn't know how to operate the thing, and we'd take a few small necessary parts and remaining ammunition."

Con said, "I had a notion you loved that old gun, Tige."

"I do, sure enough, but not enough to die for it."

"Well, we've got to get a better look at this place, and then we'll decide who's doing what."

When Ginny and Con turned away, she saw Ezra was already snoring just inside the open doorway of the shack. He had snatched the ready-made shade. "I laid out our bedrolls behind the shack. The back of the shack is to the northwest, and there is still nice shade there. Should last beyond noon anyhow."

She had laid their bedrolls out side by side, and she noticed he was looking at her with puzzlement. "I know," she said, "I usually keep a proper distance between us, but this is getting silly. Sometimes I want to talk, and I'd rather whisper than wake the whole camp." She did not add that she just wanted to be nearer to him for reasons she did not fully understand.

"You're more than welcome, and we're certainly well chaperoned."

"I even hauled our saddles over to rest our heads on."

"When did you do all this work?"

"It wasn't much work. I did it when you were helping with the fire and the horses. Being a female has certain advantages. The menfolk are always insisting on doing your chores. I'm not above taking advantage of such foolishness. I brought my poncho over here and spread it under the bedrolls. Yours is hanging on that old rusty nail. I thought if we need it later, we could figure out a way to use it for shade. Right now, I'm about to fall asleep standing up."

"Then maybe we should try to sleep lying down."

Fifteen minutes later they were both asleep on top of their bedrolls. Several hours later, Ginny awakened to find herself snuggling up against Con, her head resting on his shoulder and an arm slung across his chest. He lay on his back, his head tilted toward hers. Not as much as a foot separated their lips. What would happen if she planted a soft kiss on his lips? She was seriously tempted but was certain she would embarrass herself. Still, she did not disengage but instead closed her eyes and allowed a contented sleep to claim her for another hour.

Chapter 32

IT WAS LATE afternoon, and Angry Wolf sat in his tipi with one of his subchiefs, the village shaman, and the two scouts who had returned to the village with news that might or might not be important. Angry Wolf savored being the first chief to whom scouts brought their messages. The band included others of equal rank, and a chief's hold on power did not rest upon election but simply upon how many chose to follow him. For the present, his authority was unchallenged, but he was constantly aware that his position was tenuous. Of course, any who represented a threat tended to mysteriously die or disappear.

Angry Wolf's mother was full-blood Comanche and had married a half-blood who scouted for the Army. They had lived his first ten years on Army posts or in lodges nearby, where he learned to hate the white eyes and the

Anglo blood he wished he could drain from his body. He would never forget the isolation and breed taunts that had been imposed upon him by the other boys at fort schools and even by some adults.

The Comanche had welcomed him after the whites murdered his father and they returned to his mother's Comanche band, and he had found many mixed bloods among his true People. Even the great war chief Quanah was the son of a white mother.

The shaman, Moon Watcher, and subchief Coyote Foot, were only a few winters younger than his own thirty. None in his band had seen more than thirty-five winters. The old men had surrendered to the white man's bribes and rarely left the invisible boundary of the reservation, and even Quanah, younger than himself, had led the respected Kwahadi band to that prison. Neither Hawk nor Runs Fast, the scouts and former Kwahadis, were yet twenty, but he saw them as promising young warriors and sires of the growing band he was building—which he would soon announce was to be known as the Wolf band.

Although he retained the rudiments of English he had spoken as a boy, among the People he spoke only Comanche and used the other disgusting language sparingly when necessity was pressed upon him. Here he could speak the beautiful language of the People. "Tell us now,

Hawk and Runs Fast, of these men you saw that gave you such concern."

Hawk, the more talkative and instinctive leader of the two, said, "There was one white woman. I sneaked near their camp one morning to be certain. Slender like a prairie weed and brown-red hair that did not reach her shoulders. She wore a man's hat and clothing, even those clumsy, noisy boots the whites wear. From a distance she would pass as a boy or young man. Still, I would bed her willingly if I could."

"You would mount an ugly old woman if she would have you. Be patient. You will have a wife soon for that purpose. You may choose first from those we recently brought back from the reservation." He was quiet for a moment. The warrior woman he had killed would fit Hawk's description, but it could not be. She was dead.

The warrior woman haunted him, though. The mere thought of her raw beauty and fearlessness incited hunger in his crotch. He sometimes wished he had taken her for a wife and thought of babies he might sire with such a woman. Some warriors were already whispering of his greed at claiming three wives, however, when many had none. Perhaps it was best. If he had ever closed his eyes and fallen asleep after coupling, she likely would have killed him.

"Tell me about the others in the party," Angry Wolf said.

Hawk said, "There were two whites, one an old man and the other young with military bearing. The other four were Buffalo Soldiers. They were not in uniform, but there is no doubt of that."

"There were no others then?"

"One. He was dressed like the others, but he is one of the People, if not from one of our Comanche bands, Kiowa I would guess. He was their scout, and I fear he may have seen us. We took great care, and he did not follow us far, but I worry that he might know the location of our village."

"A strange group."

Coyote Foot, one of the few bare-chested men in camp and bearing the foot of his namesake on a strip of rawhide about his neck, said, "Why should we care about these people? We are nearly a hundred warriors strong, and we are within the safety of the Wolf's Mouth. They cannot come near without being seen, and with our numbers we will squash them like tiny ants."

Moon Watcher was less certain. A squat, chunky young man who had been a spiritual leader's apprentice before abandoning the reservation, was becoming a respected shaman among the band, and Angry Wolf had only recently begun to pay attention to his words. His visions were increasingly accurate after one sorted out the meaning.

The young shaman said, "I am uneasy about these people. They do not sound like miners, and the Mexican town of Batopilas is far from the course they appear to be taking. I have seen visions of travelers coming here, and there was a woman among them with a warrior's courage."

A shiver raced down Angry Wolf's spine. It would be impossible unless she herself was a spirit. "Hawk and Runs Fast, you must eat and rest and then return to find these people. Watch them and report back to me when you determine where they appear to be going. We must learn if our village is their destination. Moon Watcher, you will watch your moon tonight. Tomorrow morning, we meet again to find out if a vision came to you."

After the others departed, Angry Wolf stepped from the tipi and cast his eyes about their canyon hideaway. It was but a dot on a white man's map when weighed against the immensity of Copper Canyon, but in fact it was a sprawling place extending several miles in each direction on a large plateau-shelf above the main canyon floor. Locating it would be nearly impossible for a stranger and only slightly less challenging for those relying on directions from others—unless someone who had previously visited was among the party. The Indian could have visited the Wolf's Mouth, he supposed. Many came here summers before the death marches to the reservations.

Tipis and lodges were spread throughout Wolf's Mouth Canyon, but the only entrance or exit was through the wolf's jaws, making the sanctuary easy to defend. The People could be assembled quickly if attack was imminent, and sentries were always perched on the rocks above the opening.

The horse herds grazed where grass was lush along the river in the Copper Canyon floor below the plateau, although favored horses were sprinkled among the tipis and stick-mud lodges within the Wolf's Mouth, so they would be available immediately if warriors were called to battle or were preparing for a hunting party. Riders came and went constantly on one mission or another.

His tipi was one of four in a cluster near the center of the sprawling village, one each occupied by his wives and their respective children. Well, two tipis included children, three by his first wife and two by his second. The third wife was a Tejano captive who was called "Hissing Cat" for her feisty temperament. She had been with him for over a white man's year and was now sixteen winters old by her account. He had not yet been able to plant a seed in her baby garden but not for lack of trying. His other wives had not been summoned to his tipi so often since Hissing Cat's arrival and were jealous of her claims upon his attentions. Maybe a child would help bond her to the People and tame her spirit.

Now, since his return from the Texas raids, Hissing Cat, who insisted her name was and would remain "Ana Vasquez," shared her tipi with the two captive white girls, "Magpie" and "Dove". Magpie, the older of the two, was so named because of her constant chatter and obviously high intelligence in contrast to her younger sister who tended to be quiet and secretive. In some respects, Dove had to be watched more closely because she disclosed so little of herself, and he suspected this one of being a schemer, hiding a sharp mind that might even exceed that of Magpie. He should have sold them, but he had been enamored with the notion that they shared Warrior Woman's blood and would make fine breeding stock for young warriors in the years ahead.

Angry Wolf noticed that his wives, Swallow and Quail Whistler were busying themselves with preparing supper, apparently planning to roast some of the venison strips hanging from a nearby rack they had fashioned. The Dutch oven was next to the fire, so when flames disappeared into hot coals, they would be baking something.

It no longer bothered him that the oven was a white man's invention. After all, it was war bounty, having been taken from a farmer's cabin they had burned out. The dead occupants would have no more use for it. Many such items made journeys to village tipis.

Swallow and Quail Whistler brought peace to Angry Wolf's life. They never quarreled or struggled over petty jealousies and were attentive to all tasks expected of a woman. He supposed it helped that they were sisters, Swallow, his first wife, age twenty-seven now and her sister four winters younger. Swallow, pretty but on the plump side, was happy and enthusiastic when sharing his blankets, and willowy Quail Whistler was less aggressive and quieter but responsive, nonetheless. He chose them for coupling to suit his mood, and occasionally he invited them both to join him in his tipi blankets.

Hissing Cat was another matter. He was forced to beat her often to gain compliance. Sometimes he tired of punishing her and turned her over to the other wives for her beatings, and they willingly took on the task. At least he no longer had to force himself upon her when they mated, but despite her beauty and supple body, she was like coupling with a dead woman. He knew she did this to taunt him, and he was starting to hate her for it. Their times together were always brief, because like Warrior Woman would have been, he dared not fall asleep with her in his blankets when his knives or war axes were within the tipi.

He decided at that moment he would allow three moons for his seed to take root in Hissing Cat. If it did not, he would arrange with Comancheros to sell her to a bordello. He would not have her in the village. She had made no effort to learn the Comanche tongue and spoke to him and the other wives only in English. He, of course, understood her words, but other than the new girls, there were no English speakers occupying the village. Hissing Cat seemed determined not to become a part of the People.

Even now, she was not helping the other wives prepare the meal. She was somewhere with the white girls and Swallow's eight- and nine-year-old boys. All the children loved her, and she seemed to care for them all. He worried, though, that she would poison their minds somehow, cause them to question the ways of the People as they grew older. Hissing Cat did relieve the mothers of some burden, and she performed other chores when threatened with a thrashing, but she appeared determined to make his life miserable at every opportunity.

And now there were strangers riding their way. There could be many reasons for their presence nearby, but

Angry Wolf could not shake the sense of foreboding that they were bearers of trouble. If they came too near the Wolf's Mouth, they would meet death.

Chapter 33

ANA VASQUEZ WALKED with Noreen and Krista Harwood, studying the easterly walls of Wolf's Mouth Canyon, which was essentially a canyon within a canyon, she thought. Swallow's boys, Antelope and Mouse, had become bored with their adventure and dropped off to play with other boys. They would make their way back to Angry Wolf's tipi cluster soon enough to escape their mother's wrath.

She enjoyed the Comanche children and learning more of their language than Angry Wolf and the other wives suspected. Her father, who had known many Indians over the years, had taught her most of the universal sign language used by the plains tribes, and she taught the most common signs to all the children, helping them to communicate with each other. The Harwood girls were picking up Comanche words and phrases quickly, and unbeknownst to the parents, the Comanche children were adding many English words to their vocabularies.

They played many secret word games that would not have been approved by the parents, but at the risk of severe beatings, she was trying to help all the children prepare for whatever life threw at them in the years ahead. The girls' future was hazy right now, but the Comanche children would face reservation life much sooner than their parents believed. On the one hand, she sympathized with the Indians' plight and dilemma. On the other, she would never excuse the butchery that had been committed on her family and countless others, including the parents and siblings of Noreen and Krista.

She shared a survivor's bond with those girls and would never willingly abandon them, but they had complicated her escape plans. She could not leave without Noreen and Krista, but she would escape this hell. She just prayed that it was without a child in her womb. Even more reason she could not wait much longer.

She studied the jagged walls that extended above the plateau floor. Some places, the wall was as high as fifty feet, but at other spots, it dropped as low as twenty, and she was confident she could scale it easily enough. But with the girls? And then, what was at the top? The canyon did not have a conventional rim. She assumed that on the other side there was a near-sheer drop to the floor of Copper Canyon, the mother of all the canyons in this strange place. From her first and only sight of this place from the canyon below, she guessed that any wall to descend could be not less than a hundred feet. Of course, the western wall that consisted of a mountain backdrop was endless from where she stood and was not an option.

"Are you thinking about climbing out of here?"

Ana rested her hand on the flaxen-haired Noreen's shoulder. "No, not seriously anyway."

Noreen said, "We can do it. I know we can."

Krista, who was some ten paces away doing her own study, said, "And how would you get down? Ana might find a way, but we could not go with her."

Ana said, "I promised I would not try to escape without you. I keep my promises. Now we had better get back to our tipi or someone will come looking for us. Swallow and Quail Whistler will already be angry because I am not helping with supper."

"Will they beat you?" Noreen asked.

Ana shrugged. "Maybe. It doesn't hurt so much."

"You have welts on you sometimes from the sticks, but it is worse when Angry Wolf strikes you."

She said nothing, not wishing to worry the girls. She changed the subject. "Are you learning more Comanche words from the other children like I told you to do?"

Noreen said, "A few, but we don't talk that much, and the others outside Antelope and Mouse don't know sign language, and I don't think they like us. The girls are worst, and all they want to do is touch my hair."

Ana smiled. "They don't often see blonde hair like yours, maybe never. Now, my black hair is more like theirs, and Krista's would be different yet."

"The girls are afraid of Krista's. They think they might get burnt. We're both kind of freaks to them."

Ana, with the girls' help, collected an armload of firewood on their walk back to the camp, and although it yielded nothing but dirty looks from Swallow and Quail Whistler, she thought it likely spared her a lashing.

That night, she was relieved not to be summoned to Angry Wolf's tipi. After the girls were asleep, she grabbed a blanket and crept out of the tipi. Outside, she clutched the blanket about her and stealthily made her way toward the dung field where the woman went to relieve bowels and bladders. She hated the stench of the place and its communal character, especially mornings when many women might be sharing the open space.

Several times weekly, she was among the few assigned to scrape the solid waste into piles at the edge of the field, where it would be left in the sun to dry and eventually break down and disappear into the dirt. There were three or four such places for each sex at the village fringes. She took this route tonight, because she was not likely to encounter any warriors here, and women would give no thought to her presence. Wearing moccasins and a nearly worn-out doeskin dress that had been passed on to her by Quail Whistler, many would not recognize her even in the light offered by a full moon.

Stealthily, she moved past the dung field and toward the east canyon wall which she followed southerly to the low stretch of the canyon wall she had noted when she was with the girls late afternoon. She looked around, saw no sign of life, dropped the blanket and began to scale the jagged stone wall which she calculated was about twenty-five feet high at this spot. She stepped from cleft or jutting stone easily and gracefully like the cat for which she was named and quickly reached the top. She looked at the outside wall, spotted a narrow ledge not more than four feet beneath her and dropped down, her balance and sure-footedness sparing her from a fifty or sixty-foot fall to the floor of Copper Canyon.

Studying the wall illuminated by the moonlight, she was confident now that she could descend to the floor here. She had been a climber since she learned to walk, living in hill country with a family that earned a living raising a large herd of Angora goats that generated healthy profits because of mohair demand for fabric, especially in the East. The twice annual shearing was always a time of celebration for her grandparents, parents and her as the only child and grandchild. And now she was all that remained. She often wondered what became of the herd of over a hundred goats, consoling herself with the thought that they might survive in the wild.

She could escape tonight, she thought, and be far away before they missed her. Even if they tracked her down and killed her, that was preferable to life here. She was sure that that the Comanche loved their own way of life, but it was not hers. She could be down this wall in a half hour of cautious descent. If she slipped and fell to her death, so what?

But again, there were Noreen and Krista. She did not think she was deluding herself that she was their anchor and had given them hope of better days. It brought tears to her eyes to think of the girls raised as Comanche, and she had promised she would not leave them. She sighed and peered over the wall. Oh, Lord. A warrior stood there, naked but for a breechcloth, facing the wall with arms folded and gazing at the sky. Her blanket lay next to his feet, so he had to know she had been there, and not that much time had passed since she scaled the wall and went over the top. Had he seen her doing that? Still, he evidently had not raised an alarm.

He was chanting something softly, but she would not understand many of the words even if she heard them clearly. She could still descend the wall to Copper Canyon if she chose. No, she would not, could not. She reached up and clutched the ridge, braced a foot against a protruding stone and lifted her body over the top. She inched her way back down the wall and landed on the rocky surface not more than five paces from the warrior, a chunky man she recognized now as the shaman called Moon Watcher. She stepped nearer, bent over and grabbed her blanket and raced back to the tipi to join the girls.

Sleep was fitful that night as she wondered what she would face the next morning when Angry Wolf learned of her night journey. What was Moon Watcher doing there? Why didn't he accost her or say something to her? She could make no sense of it. She would learn more when Angry Wolf confronted her and delivered punishment.

Chapter 34

ANGRY WOLF AND Coyote Foot waited in the tipi for Moon Watcher's arrival. Angry Wolf found himself tense and agitated, and he did not understand why. Sometimes, he thought the man who called himself a shaman was a fool who simply had dreams. Everyone had dreams. He remembered when as a boy he had dreams that frightened him, and his father called them "nightmares." It occurred to him that Moon Watcher might just make up his visions. Still, why had his visions so often revealed the truth of what was to come?

Angry Wolf said, "Have you seen Moon Watcher this morning?"

Coyote Foot furrowed his brow and looked at him and then pointed at his mouth. Only then did Angry Wolf realize he had spoken English. He never spoke English among the People. Why would he do that? Was it an ill omen?

This time he spoke in the true tongue, Comanche. "Have you seen Moon Watcher this morning?"

Coyote Foot said, "No, I spoke with his woman. She said he did not return last night. She is not worried. This happens when an important vision comes to him."

This statement did nothing to calm Angry Wolf. On the contrary, it made him more apprehensive. Where was Moon Watcher?

The opening of the tipi entry flap answered his question. Moon Watcher stepped in covered only by his breechcloth. He appeared exhausted and haggard as if returning from a great battle. He sat down in front of the dying coals of the fire that had been burning to ward off the mountain's nighttime chill. Angry Wolf faced him from the opposite side of the firepit, a frown engraved on his face as he waited to hear Moon Watcher's words.

Finally, Moon Watcher spoke in strange singsong Comanche, so softly that Angry Wolf and Coyote Foot, who sat at his side, were forced to lean forward to hear his words. "The moon was full and bright until sunrise chased it away, and the moon spirit shared so much with me that we did not part till then. After that, I was so tired and weak, I fell to the ground and slept. When I awakened, I came here to tell you of my vision."

"Then tell us," Angry Wolf said, his patience being tested.

Moon Watcher appeared unfazed, almost as if he had not heard Angry Wolf's voice. "The Moon Spirit painted my vision on the canyon wall, and I could see it unfold as I chanted. A woman came over the wall, the low rocks on the west. She descended the wall gracefully like a spirit. I must think more on this, but I believe she was a spirit. Then she soared away toward the village and disappeared."

Angry Wolf said, "You don't know where she went?"

Moon Watcher seemed not to hear. "Soon, the vision returned to the wall, and I saw the woman again in the tipi where your Mexican wife and the two white children live. She went to each child and placed a hand on their cheeks before she faded away into the darkness. When she reappears, she is in your lodge staring at you, hatred burning in the flames that burst from her eyes. She turns away and disappears again."

"That is all?"

"No. The vision returns, and I see the Buffalo Soldiers and white men on the rim overlooking Copper Canyon. Later, they are at the Wolf's Mouth, and another woman appears, drifting down from the sky, and the men all drop to their knees and bow as her feet greet the earth in front of them. The Indian joins them now—I believe he is Kiowa."

"Does this woman speak?"

"Not in words that you and I can hear. But she stares at me from the vision, and I know that I am being warned that she is coming for the children. She and her band have no fear."

"Is this the woman I have called Warrior Woman?"

"I do not know. I have not seen your Warrior Woman, and the features on the visitors are blurred. I can only say they are coming, and that they must be confronted with great care."

Angry Wolf was skeptical about this so-called vision. He doubted these people were even coming to the Wolf's Mouth, but it still made him inexplicably nervous. "So, what do these people do? We outnumber them by too many. We have our hideaway that no enemy can broach."

Moon Watcher said, "I cannot say with certainty, but they are more dangerous than they appear. If you surrender the girls to them, I think they will go away. I will approach the Moon Spirit again tonight, and I must consider more the meaning of what I have seen. But first, I must eat and then sleep." He got to his feet and stepped through the tipi opening and appeared to fade away into the morning light.

Angry Wolf looked at Coyote Foot, who had remained silent. "Moon Watcher tells stories, and the People think this grants him special powers."

"Many of his stories have been true, although they are usually vaguer than this one, more difficult to confirm. He believes his Moon Spirit has delivered a message to him."

"That still does not make it true. We will know more when our scouts return."

Chapter 35

AS THEY NEARED the foothills that framed the Sierra Madre Mountain range, Con saw that they were moving very quickly into a very different landscape, one cloaked with a variety of trees, from oaks and alders to pines and spruces. Grasses of all sorts thrived on the hillsides, and the horses and mules would welcome the change. The vegetation told him that water should be abundant here.

Rover had advised they should ride southerly along the edge of the foothills for a day before they headed into the mountains. He promised to find a trail that others had used to ascend to the crest that took them to the rim of Copper Canyon. He saw Rover riding toward him now, his dust trail nothing compared to what his mount's hooves raised in the desert country. The searchers were moving at a snail's pace now that they were riding over rougher ground, and Con signaled his party to a halt.

Ginny reined in beside him. As Rover neared, she said, "He's riding like he's got news."

"Yeah, it's not noon yet. He wouldn't be back if he didn't have something important to report."

When Rover rode up, he didn't waste any time. "We're being watched again. I think they're the same two I followed for a spell several days back. I got in close this time. Young bucks without a lot of experience at this. I could've shot them dead, but I think the less gunfire the better right now. Besides, it bothered me to do that without warning for some reason. I fear living with Grit McKay has softened me some. I can do the job if you want, but I thought we should talk about this."

Con thought about the situation before he replied. Perhaps they could make use of these young warriors. "Do you think we could capture them?"

"It is possible, but not certain. A few of us could get close enough, but some believe death is better than to be taken alive. I suspect that is what Angry Wolf instructs them."

"I would like to try. Take me to them. I will have the others continue this trail. We won't be separated by much, because I assume the Comanche scouts will stay with our party."

"They might be wary when you drop out. They are likely watching us now. They have figured out that I'm scouting ahead but aren't aware that I doubled back."

"Well, let's you and I go ahead. Maybe you can point south every so often at first, so they assume you are going to show me something."

"Can't hurt."

Ginny said, "Con, is this really necessary?"

"There's a good chance we can learn from one of these men whether your sisters are actually in the village."

"You aren't going to torture them?"

"Do you care?"

"Well, I guess not," Ginny said, "if we get the answers we want."

"That probably wouldn't do any good anyhow. Just let me ask the right questions. Rover will need to interpret, of course. If we can take one alive, I think we can get the answer to that question. Regardless, I'd prefer to take both alive and deliver them to the village."

"Why?"

"I'm thinking it might help get us into the Wolf's Mouth."

"That's good if we can get out with my sisters."

Several hours later, after doubling back and leading their horses up a deer trail that took them beyond the foothills and into the lower mountain slopes, Rover signaled that they should tie the horses and then whispered. "We should move away from the horses, so they don't whinny and betray us when the Comanche come near. They, too, will be afoot. It allows for quiet which permits them to get nearer to our riders. They are foolish. They could learn all they need to know from much higher on the mountain slopes. Their higher view would even allow them to see farther and give them a head start on reporting to their leader. They think their willingness to go nearer to the enemy proves their bravery."

After securing their mounts, Con followed Rover through a maze of pine trees until they reached a stone outcropping that erupted from the mountain slope like the open palm of a giant hand that would hide them from any eyes below. Con spoke softly. "You've got something in mind. Tell me about it."

"We are well ahead of the scouts if they are moving at the pace of our riders. We should let them come to us now."

"That makes sense, but how do we get to them without a big ruckus and gunfire?"

"I can surprise them by just walking up to them and speaking to them in Comanche. I could certainly grab their attention for a spell, talk about the weather and such. They wouldn't know what to make of it."

"I could move in on them from behind while you have them distracted. When I'm in place, you could give them a chance to put down their weapons and surrender. If they aren't going to talk to you or put down the weapons, I'll just have to take them down with my Winchester and not worry about the gunfire racket. Of course, a lot of this depends on whether they are near enough for us to make that kind of move. If we stay low, this outcropping is the perfect place for us to wait. I don't think they can see a trace of us from below. We'll still need to keep an eye upslope in case they figured out they ought to be on higher ground. Why don't you keep an eye out below us, since that's where they'll most likely come, and I'll watch our backs?"

Rover nodded agreement.

"By the way," Con said, "when you're having your little social conversation, go ahead and tell them we're coming to bring the little white girls home. Just act like we know for sure the girls are there. See if you can coax one of them into admitting they've got the Harwood sisters. If they deny the girls are there, we have a new problem."

After an hour's wait, Con was starting to wonder if the warriors had changed course or even abandoned their watch over the strangers.

"I see them," Rover whispered, pointing northeasterly.

"I don't move as quietly as you. Looks to me like they'll end up close to a hundred feet below us. You'll have to keep them talking for a spell. I'll try to keep you in sight while I move down the slope and try to work in behind them."

Rover nodded and disappeared into the forest. Soon he emerged from the trees and stood where he would block the path the warrior scouts were currently taking. His rifle was cradled in his arms, barrel pointing toward the earth. There was a short wait until the warriors abruptly appeared from behind a rise. Rover stepped forward and called to them in Comanche. Con assumed it was a greeting of some sort. The warriors froze, but did not raise their own weapons.

Rover walked toward them now, speaking as he approached, and the two moved hesitantly in his direction. Rover obviously was claiming their full attention, and Con got up and moved downslope under cover of trees and brush. The Comanche warriors and Rover were talking louder now and more animated. Rover was probably goading their excitement to cover his partner's clumsy effort to slip in behind the two, Con thought.

When he was within nearly ten paces, one of the warriors swung around to face Con, dropped his rifle and raced toward him, war axe upraised. Con backed up a few steps and dodged when the axe came down, striking air where his head would have otherwise been and split like a melon. Before the warrior could turn and attack again, Con drove the butt of his rifle into the back of the man's head, and he bounced off a tree trunk and plummeted to the ground.

Con turned his attention to Rover, who was kneeling beside the other warrior who lay facedown on the earth, his hands pulled behind his back while Rover bound his wrists with rawhide strips. Rover rolled him over, revealing the young warrior's bleeding eye and upper cheek. Rover said, "This one's name translated to English is 'Hawk.' The other one is 'Runs Fast.' This fella tried to get his rifle up to shoot me. I yanked the warclub that was hitched to his waist and thumped him good. A lot faster."

"Can you spare a few of those rawhide strips hanging from your belt. I've got some, but they're in my saddlebags."

"Yep." He tossed two strips to Con. "We've got to find their horses. I don't think these two will cause any trouble for a spell. Our horses aren't far away. Do you want to watch these two? I'll bring our horses here, and then I'll take mine and go back and track theirs down. It might take a spell. They wouldn't have had to leave their critters anyplace if the fools had stayed to the high country, but they made our job easier."

"One question first. The girls. Did you learn anything?"

"Yeah. They're at the village. I did like you said. I just told them we were coming to bring the two little white girls back. Old Hawk laughed. He said Angry Wolf would never give them up. They're his now, Hawk told me. That's when he started getting loud and quarrelsome."

"His racket helped me get up here. I'm surprised one of them didn't hear me stumbling through the woods anyhow with the special hearing you Indians are supposed to have."

"Hell, we're not like dogs or wild animals. My hearing isn't any better than yours. We just learn to pay attention to what's around us. We see and hear things that your way of life didn't train you to listen for. As for me, I spent most of my life in the wild, and then when a half Anglo-half Mexican man took me in, I learned even more about such things. I think my dad, Grit McKay, knows more about hearing and seeing what's around you than any Indian."

Chapter 36

"BOSSMAN'S COMIN' THIS way." Ginny turned. It was Beanpole's distinctive, deep voice calling from a fair distance behind where he was trailing the others and leading a string of pack animals. Ginny spoke to Ezra who rode beside her. "They made it back."

Ezra winked. "Told you, girl. Y'all was worried about nothing. Between old Con and Rover, they can look after themselves. You sure started stewing about Con lately. I been wondering if you went and got yourself bit by that love skeeter."

"Grandpa, that's the silliest notion you've had yet."

Tige, who had assumed leadership of the column in Con's absence, signaled a halt and started reining in his mount.

Ginny said, "I'm going to swing back and see what's going on." She reined Artemis away and headed backtrail.

"Watch out for skeeters, girl," Ezra hollered after her.

As she rode, Ginny wondered what gave Ezra the notion she might have romantic feelings for Con. For the most part she kept her distance from Con when others were about. Of course, everyone knew they spread their bedrolls out side by side every night now, so she supposed it was not unreasonable that others were making assumptions about what was going on between them. She sighed. What did she care? She just wanted her sisters back, and Con would be moving on when that was accomplished. That thought made her more than a little uneasy.

She rode on past Beanpole to greet Con and Rover who were nearing now. When she saw that they were leading two horses with young warriors astride, she reined her mare in and waited.

Con smiled when he saw her and gave her a nod. When he reached her, he said, "Your sisters are both alive and in the Wolf's Mouth Canyon village."

"Thank God," she said, her voice a near whisper. She could not hold back. Tears began streaming down her face, and soon she was shaking with sobs.

Con nudged his buckskin ahead and moved in beside her, reaching out his hand and grasping hers. "We'll get this done, Ginny."

She looked up at him, wiped her tears on her shirt-sleeve, and said, "Yes, we will." Then she looked at the two grim-faced Comanche tied with rope to the horses behind Con and Rover, wrists cinched behind their backs. The side of one warrior's forehead was swollen, his eye sealed shut. Con's kerchief was wrapped around the other's head, obviously covering a wound of some sort. "What are we going to do with these men?"

"Return them to their village."

"Why? How?"

"We'll talk about this later. It will be dusk in a few hours. We need to find a place to set up camp for the night. Rover said that tomorrow we will start the journey up the mountainside. We should reach the Copper Canyon rim by nightfall."

"Will we be at the Wolf's Mouth then?"

"No. It will take another half day's ride along the rim before we get above the Wolf's Mouth, which is on the west side of Copper Canyon. We'll decide how we do this after we get to the rim and can get a view of what we're dealing with."

Ginny was both excited and afraid at the prospect of soon reuniting with her sisters. The optimist part of her was convinced that they would recover Noreen and Krista and be on their way home within a few days. The realist reminded her that they could all be dead within that time. The girls would not be surrendered easily by Angry Wolf, the one man she hated more than the now deceased Grizzly.

Evening found them in a clearing near a stream that tumbled over the rocks and down the mountainside. Rover had led the party above the foothills into the lower mountains before coming upon the place within the forest that ashes and tree stumps revealed had been a night's home to other travelers. They released the captives' bonds long enough for them to eat beans and hardtack. Being unfamiliar with spoons and forks, they scooped the soggy beans from tin plates with their fingers.

Beanpole and Irish led the two into the woods to relieve bladders and bowels, if necessary, then bound their wrists again and bound them to tree trunks. Following their meager supper, the searchers gathered around the fire for coffee to agree upon nighttime sentry shifts and to consider plans for the days ahead.

It was agreed that the former Buffalo Soldiers would take watch shifts that night and that the others would cover the next. Con started the discussion about strategy for recovery of the girls. "I'll listen to anything somebody's got to say about getting those girls out, and we might make changes in plans when we get an actual view of where we're headed. My first thought is that we should turn these warriors loose when we get to the rim and let them report to Angry Wolf with any messages we've got."

Tige said, "I'd sign on to that idea. Angry Wolf ain't going to make any trade for these fellers. Since they got caught, he'd likely say we could just keep them. At some point they're going to be more nuisance to watch than anything."

Ginny said, "Can we send a message that we want to ransom the girls for gold coin?"

Con said, "It seems to me we should start there."

"Let me ride into the Wolf's Mouth with Rover—he speaks Comanche. I know Angry Wolf speaks English, but I will need Rover to tell me what he might be saying to others."

Ezra spoke. "You ain't going without me, missy. I lived with Comanche for a spell. Never got the knack for speakin' their talk with all the grunts and such, but I understood a fair amount of what they said. Besides, you can't talk me out of going in with Ginny."

"But we do not take the gold with us," Rover said. "My father said that Angry Wolf can be bought for just as long as it takes to get what he wants. You can never, never trust him. Most Comanche chiefs are men of honor, but Angry Wolf has no notion of the meaning of the word."

Con said, "In other words, the exchange of money for the girls will need to be made on neutral ground outside the Wolf's Mouth."

"Yes," Rover said, "and Angry Wolf must be there within the sights of our rifles. We would be hopelessly outnumbered if he turned all the warriors of his band loose upon us. I'm more than uneasy about all of this. It's not like I am surprised at what we face, but this is getting serious now."

Tige said, "We're not necessarily outnumbered. I've got to get the lay of the land, but I've got a small Army packed in that Gatling gun if we can find the right place for it."

Con said, "I still don't like the idea of Ginny going in there. I can talk with Angry Wolf just as well, bargain and set the terms."

"No," Ginny said. "You mean well, but I want to see for myself that Noreen and Krista are there. And this is my responsibility. I've stepped back and let you run things for days now, and you were the right man to do that. But my time has arrived. I am doing this, and you are not stopping me. End of argument."

Con didn't like it, but he understood. Ginny had to do this. She had earned his respect, and he would not stand in her way. "Then we will back you as best we can."

Irish said, "There's nothing that says we can't get within sniping range of the place and be ready to start firing if they get forced to make a run for it."

Con said, "Absolutely, but my worry is they won't get a chance to make a run for it. I guess we can't do much more until we see just what we're facing."

That night, just before Con headed to the little cove at the forest's edge where he and Ginny had laid out their bedrolls, Ezra pulled Con aside. "What is it?" Con asked.

"Never worried or cared before about this, but I been thinking about what happens to my stuff when I become food for buzzards or worms. I ain't got much, but there's a fair amount of money in my saddlebags. Never been to a bank. Then I got my horses, Spot and Mort, and the tack. Just in case I don't make it back, I want you to see that Ginny gets it all, and if she don't get through this, you take it. If we all go down, I don't give a good shit who gets it. Comanches, probably."

Con said, "Well, Ezra, I don't expect to be giving it to anybody, but if the worst comes, you know that if I'm able, I'll do what you ask."

"Knowed that." He turned and hobbled away.

When he joined Ginny, she was sitting on top of her bedroll tugging her boots off. "Is Ezra alright?" she asked.

"Oh, yeah. He's just always got a bit of advice. Nothing important. You know how he is."

She giggled. "I sure do. I've been getting a lot of advice from him, especially the past few days."

"You have?" He was curious, but he wasn't biting since he had not shared Ezra's request of a few minutes earlier.

"Do you want to know what about?"

"It's none of my business."

"He said I need to quit wasting time and get my brand on you."

"What does that mean?" He dared not say what he hoped.

"I take it he thinks we should be together after this is all over."

"Oh, well I wouldn't argue against that."

"You wouldn't?"

"Nope. I rather like that idea."

"It's going to be cold up here in the mountains tonight. It's already getting on the chilly side."

"Yeah, I'd agree."

"You're not helping much."

"With what?"

"I was thinking I could get my brand on you tonight if we shared our bedrolls."

He was speechless for a moment. "We could do that."

They spread their bedrolls out together. Wanting to avoid the eyes of someone in the camp who might walk by, they disrobed under their blankets and soon lay naked in each other's arms.

"It's not fair," Ginny said.

"What isn't?"

"That I've never even seen you naked."

"You will someday, I promise." Their lips met in a lingering kiss, and he did not know how long he could wait. Her caressing fingers roamed, and her body pressed against his, telling him the waiting was not necessary.

Afterward, spooned up against her, he whispered in her ear. "You can tell Ezra that I'm branded."

"Can I take that as a proposal?"

"You can. I love you. Will you marry me, Ginny Harwood?"

"I love you, Congrave Callaway. I will."

"We'll finalize the deal as soon as we return to San Angelo."

She turned around, facing him again. "This calls for a branding celebration."

"It does, but slower and quieter this time."

Chapter 37

THE CLIMB UP the mountainside was on a narrow, frequently used trail that forced the riders into single file as it snaked along steep stone and shale passageways. The drops off the trail were not so sheer that a misstep would launch horse and rider a thousand feet into an abyss, but the mount would certainly die or suffer injuries that would require it be put down. The rider's fate would be uncertain, depending upon the ability to get free of the horse and ride the shale down the steep slope a hundred or so feet to the forested terrain below.

Ginny rode behind Con, who followed Rover. The mountains were majestic here and seemingly endless. Rover had told them that when they were three-quarters of the distance to the peak, the mountain range would be split by a chasm deep and wide as an ocean. She had never seen an ocean but assumed there was exaggeration in his choice of words. Regardless, the thought of the scene that awaited triggered butterflies in her stomach for it would signal that the confrontation with Angry Wolf was imminent.

She turned her eyes toward Con's back. She had felt the rippling muscles beneath that shirt last night, and her imagination stripped him naked. She feared tonight could be their last tonight together, and she would not waste it. She had not the least regret about their intimacy and her own aggressiveness. She had already learned that love was much more than such moments, but she had feared she might die without feeling again what she did last night. She prayed they would have many years of sharing together, but if not, she would not have passed through life without knowing how it could be between a man and a woman.

It had been a bit embarrassing, though, at sunrise when Tige and Grandpa had come to talk with Con about the day and found them snuggled in shared bedrolls. She had started to crawl out before she remembered she was stark naked and covered herself again. But they had got enough of a glimpse to eliminate any doubt about the status of the pair, and she decided it would be nice to drop any pretense now.

Con seemed unfazed by it all. Of course, such behavior was expected from males, where women might be labeled sluts by some. The visitors did not appear shocked, however, and Grandpa had even grinned and given her that impish wink of his. Later, when he was serving biscuits and gravy with the last of his bacon at breakfast, she held out her tin plate, and he nodded approvingly and said, "Branded, huh?"

She replied and smiled. "Yep. Branded." She smiled again in remembrance of the moment. How she loved that ornery old geezer. She hoped that if they made it through this, he would join them and make his home near theirs and be grandpa to Noreen and Krista, too—and any children she and Con might have. He was family.

Midafternoon the trail turned more westerly and led the party onto rocky flatlands, although mountains still towered above them. In a few minutes, Rover signaled a halt and dismounted. The others followed suit as they caught up. He said, "Follow me to the canyon's rim. Keep a good grip on the reins or lead ropes of the critters."

They followed until he stopped again. "Well, here she is folks: Copper Canyon."

They stepped more cautiously now, and Con edged in beside Ginny and took her free hand. Then she saw the canyon, a panoramic sight that left her breathless.

Perhaps Rover's description was not such an exaggeration. She could make out the river that threaded its way through the stone walls above. She saw no end to the canyon north or south, and to the west hidden in a haze of clouds or mist, she saw pieces of what she guessed was the far side's rim, but other places it seemed to be boundless like what she thought of an ocean to be.

Con said, "I've never seen anything like it: stone towers and formations of every sort, canyons within canyons, bluffs, huge stone shelves in the middle of a wall."

Ginny said, "And it's so quiet, like we're viewing a painting made by God."

"Well, I suppose in a way, one could say we are." He released her hand and wrapped his arm around her shoulder. "I could watch this for hours. I'll get my spyglass out later, and we can sight in on some things."

"Like the Wolf's Mouth?"

He sighed. "That, too. I guess that's the signal to get back to business." He released her, and they led their mounts back to Rover who was standing back from the others. Con also waved for Tige to join them.

"Got me that quick gander at this canyon once," Tige said. "North a good ways, though. Dang thing just goes on forever. Nothing like it no place, I'm betting."

Con said, "Rover, how far from here to the Wolf's Mouth?"

"Well, if we can ride another two or three hours yet today and get an early start in the morning, I'm guessing we could be at the rim overlooking that part of the canyon by mid-morning tomorrow. Then you've got to decide some things."

"Like what?"

"Well, it will take a good hour to get down to the canyon floor. You've got a trail narrower than the one we've spent the day on, and the drop is straight down. You won't be wanting to hurry. After you get to the bottom, allow a bit more than an hour to get you to the entrance to the Wolf's Mouth. Allow an extra hour to give you some leeway, so we're not going to be talking to Angry Wolf till the middle of the afternoon. Then it could take a lot of time to make a deal. Indians don't like to bargain fast, especially considering the way they've come out with the white man over the years."

Ginny said, "We could spend the night there if necessary."

Con said, "No, I want you out of there. Fast."

She didn't want to argue with him in front of the others. "We'll talk about it later."

Tige said, "We don't need to decide till we get there tomorrow morning. Be thinking about this, though. My Gatling ain't gonna do no good on the canyon rim, and it seems like the ransom exchange will be made somewhere down on the canyon floor. I'm wondering if maybe I ought to set my baby up to defend that trail when you leave, so they don't take a notion to come after us too soon."

Con said," You wouldn't have time to get the Gatling packed up and on the trail before they swarmed you."

"Well, if they don't show any signs of causing trouble, I'll have time. If not, it'll be like giving up a child, but I'll leave my baby behind minus a few parts they'd need to make her work."

"I don't know. We need to think more on how we're going to do this. It's hard to say for sure until we really see what we're up against when it comes to logistics of this whole thing. Now one other thing. I propose we release our captives now. They slow us down some, and I'd like to send a message for Angry Wolf with them. Any objections?"

Tige said, "Makes sense."

Neither Rover nor Ginny voiced an objection, and Con said, "Rover, tell the two warriors to tell Angry Wolf that we've got gold and will be coming to bargain for release of the girls, and that we will want to see the girls before we agree to terms. Say that three of our people will come to the Wolf's Mouth's entrance to bargain, that we come in peace and trust that will be respected."

Ginny went with Rover and Con to untie the bonds and release the warrior captives. The two looked perplexed by what was happening. When they were free, Rover, speaking Comanche, gave them the message for Angry Wolf. When he was finished, Ginny stepped forward and said, "One more thing to tell Angry Wolf."

"What is that?" Rover said.

She untucked her shirt and raised it, exposing her bare midriff. She pointed to the scar where the arrow had entered and turned around and revealed the raised, still red flesh where the point of the arrowhead had protruded. "Tell them that Angry Wolf loosed the arrow that made these wounds. Say that he called me a warrior woman that day and that I died, but my God sent two angels to return me to life so that I might recover my sisters."

She clearly had the young warriors' attention, and they nodded with wide eyes as Rover related her words. Within ten minutes they disappeared, riding their horses southerly along the canyon rim.

Dusk approached as the searchers rode slowly on a trail not far from the canyon's rim. Finally, Rover found a meadow edged by pine set back a good distance from the rim. After watering the critters at a stream not far away, the riders staked out the mounts and pack animals and settled for jerky and stale biscuits for supper, risking a small fire for brewing several pots of hot coffee.

Later, as the camp settled in for sleep, Con told Ginny, "I've got first watch, remember?"

"Yes, and I've got second."

"Well, you grab some shuteye, and I'll wake you. I think Ezra follows and then Rover."

"I won't be able to sleep. I thought we'd just share our watches."

"I do understand the sleeping problem, but you've got a lot to take on tomorrow."

"That's not my sleeping problem."

"Then what?"

She nudged him in the ribs. "Kiss me. Then you'll understand."

"Oh. I think I understand, but I'll kiss you anyway."

He took her in his arms and kissed her, holding her tightly against him. That tingling raced through her body, and Con left no doubt that he wanted her, too. But he stepped back and said, "I've got guard duty."

"You and your damned duties. You've got other responsibilities now."

"I'll gladly take care of the others later."

"Then we'll turn to another subject. We were going to discuss my visit to Angry Wolf's lair."

"Yes, but there's really nothing to discuss. You have already decided."

"Then you do realize the way it's going to be between us. Some marriage ceremonies provide for the wife to promise she will obey the husband. I won't make that promise, or if I do, I won't keep it."

"I figured as much."

"But you'll keep me anyhow?"

"Yep, I'm not going to let you break your promise to marry me, though. But please try to get some sleep. You need your rest for tomorrow."

"I'll try." Ten minutes later she was sleeping soundly.

Chapter 38

QUAIL WHISTLER HAD just departed his tipi when Angry Wolf heard Coyote Foot's voice outside. "Angry Wolf, we must talk," the sub-chief said. "Hawk and Runs Fast have returned."

Angry Wolf rolled out from under his blankets and grabbed the favored blue flannel shirt he had peeled from a dead settler a year earlier. There was a chill in the early morning air, and after buttoning the shirt, he wrapped one of the blankets about his legs and lower body before he replied. "Are Hawk and Runs Fast with you?"

"Yes. They have urgent news."

Angry Wolf sighed. The sun was not yet crawling over the mountaintops, so it must be important. "Bring them in." He added several more logs to the dying flames of the fire, seeking not only warmth but light that would permit him to see the faces of the young scouts so that he might judge them better.

When Coyote Foot brought the scouts in behind him, Angry Wolf waved for the visitors to sit with him at the fire. He noticed that the two were somewhat unsteady on their feet, and then in the firelight he saw Hawk's swollen cheek and cut about his closed eye. He deferred comment for the moment, gazing at them silently and enjoying their unease.

Finally, he spoke. "Tell me what you have learned."

Hawk, as usual, was the spokesman. "I am humbled to report that we were captured by those we were sent to watch. They knew we were watching, and they trapped us. We fought, but you can see that I was struck. Runs Fast was also taken down when struck on the back of his head with a rifle butt."

Runs Fast turned his head so his chief could see the bloated, blood-oozing gash on the back of his skull. Angry Wolf's eyes fastened on Hawk again. "You did not say what caused your wound."

"The man took my warclub."

"He hit you with your own warclub? I think it may be best for the two of you to care for the papooses and children till you can prove yourselves as warriors fit for battle."

"We had no fear. We were surprised. One of the men was Kiowa who spoke our tongue. He first claimed to be Comanche, and we allowed him to get too near. He acts as interpreter for these people, and we learned much while we were held, more than if we had not been captured."

"Tell me what you learned. It may lessen punishment for your foolishness."

"They are coming here, and the Kiowa appears to know how to find the Wolf's Mouth. I believe he has been here with others of our Comanche tribe. He also claims to be the son of a man known well by our people."

"What man are you speaking of?"

"A man called Grit McKay."

Angry Wolf looked at Coyote Foot, and the grim look on his face told him that the sub-chief was also familiar with the reputation of Grit McKay. "Do you know this Grit McKay?"

Coyote Foot said, "I saw him when I was with the Bug Eaters band. We thought no white man could find us in those Southwest Texas mountains, but he did. He came with the twin sister of the band's shaman, Medicine Fox, who had been the wife of the great warrior Many Scalps until he was killed. Medicine Fox had come to the band as a child and was raised Comanche. She had great medicine powers."

Angry Wolf said, "I have heard of this Medicine Fox, but she fled the people."

"Yes, but not before Grit McKay accepted the challenge of the great Striking Snake to fight with the blade till the death of one. I watched that fight. Grit McKay defeated Striking Snake and then insulted him by refusing to kill. The few Bug Eaters who remain still talk of this. Medicine Fox did not depart that night. She remained with the People until the Bug Eaters were defeated by the whites and being led to the reservation. It was then that Grit appeared from nowhere and took Medicine Fox and her daughter away into the night. He does not quit."

"But this Kiowa is not truly his son."

Coyote Foot shrugged. "As much so as the captives who grow to become our warriors. And there are many."

Angry Wolf turned back to the young warriors. "So far, you have told me little of value. There must be more."

Hawk said, "Yes. The Kiowa interpreted messages to us from a man who appears to be their chief and a woman who says you have met. The man said to tell you they are coming for the little girls, who are the woman's sisters. They have gold and want to bargain with you to sell them back. He said they come in peace and believe you will honor that."

"And the woman, what did she say?"

"She says you called her Warrior Woman."

Weakness swept through Angry Wolf's body. "What else did she say? That could not be all."

"That you shot an arrow through her body. She raised her shirt and showed us the wounds where an arrow went into her front side and then out her back. She could not have lived with such a wound."

"But you saw her and spoke to her."

"She died, and her God sent something called two angels who brought her back from the dead, so she could bring her sisters home."

Angry Wolf felt his heart racing. He looked at Runs Fast. "Did you hear what Hawk said? Is that what you heard?"

"Yes, my chief, and I saw those terrible scars where your arrow was lodged. Her God is powerful. We must be careful with this Warrior Woman."

Coyote Foot said, "Perhaps we should return these girls and let these invaders be gone. Moon Watcher has warned us."

"Do not be a fool, Coyote Foot. They are willing to pay ransom in gold. We will agree to bargain, but I must see this woman to believe. She may be an imposter, and these girls may be worth more somewhere else."

In truth, he wished the gold and the girls gone. He also wanted all the unwelcome visitors, especially Warrior Woman, dead. He could not allow all these people to know the location of the Wolf's Mouth. The safety of his band was at stake. This claim by Warrior Woman that she had returned from the dead was a lie. In his childhood, he had heard of this white man's God. He was said to have brought a son back from the dead. His father spoke of this and sometimes read from a Holy Bible. His mother repeatedly told him it was foolishness and taught him about the Comanche Great Spirit and other spirits that guided the People.

"When will these visitors arrive?" Angry Wolf asked.

Hawk said, "They did not say what they planned, but they could arrive today if they chose, sometime after the sun is highest in the sky."

"I must think on this. Coyote Foot, you stay." He nodded at the young warriors who were staring at him with fearful eyes. "You two may go. Your information has redeemed your stupidity. There will be no punishment."

Their relief was visible, and Hawk and Runs Fast got quickly to their feet and slipped away into the darkness.

"What are we going to do about our visitors?" Coyote Foot asked.

"I have not decided. I want to see this Warrior Woman first, but they cannot leave Copper Canyon alive. None of them. That includes the girls. We must be rid of them. You will arrange for extra guards at the entrance. Notify me immediately when this enemy appears and hold them until I give instructions. Under no circumstances will I go out to meet them. They will be escorted to me at the time and place I choose."

Chapter 39

ROVER HANDED CON the spyglass that he had been using for studying the enormous depths of Copper Canyon. He said, "Focus first on the river, move south and you will see a giant cottonwood tree on the west bank. From there, raise the telescope where the canyon narrows. You will see that wall disappear, but there is a higher wall a mile or two to the west. In between is flatland with grass and water where Comanche live."

Con said, "And how do they get to this place?"

"You cannot see the entrance or trail from here, but there is a path along the wall like the one below us that leads to the canyon floor. Across the river, another such path weaves along the wall to a crack that opens near the top that admits horses and riders through the Wolf's Mouth and onto the plateau hidden by the surrounding walls. There is no other opening or way out without scaling the inner side of that wall where it is low and leaping off to your death below. A few might try to climb down that wall, but insanity would be necessary."

"I see horses grazing in the canyon."

"Oh, yes. Their herds flourish there. Some required for immediate needs graze within Wolf's Mouth Canyon, too."

Con passed the spyglass on to Ginny. "Take a look and pass it to Tige. Let everyone see what we're up against."

"When will we do this?" Rover said.

Con said, "It's high noon. We'll round up something we can eat without a fire and then we will move ahead."

Rover said, "They will disarm us as soon as we enter Wolf's Mouth Canyon. I'm thinking we should leave our guns just outside the entry. They'll have sentries in the rocks, and they'll see us, but it's a long distance from their posts to climb off the wall and then come through the ten-foot wall opening out of their hideaway. I'd feel better leaving the weapons than having Angry Wolf's warriors take them from us."

"Yeah, that makes sense." He stepped over to Tige who was talking to Ginny. "What about the Gatling? Do you still want to take it to the bottom of the canyon?"

Tige said, "Yep. I can't see enough to know what I've got for set up there, but I'll figure it out. I'll want Irish to help me with it. Takes another man to feed the cartridges to my Babe."

"I'm going with Ginny and the others as far as the opening to the Wolf's Mouth, and I'll be waiting there to provide cover in case they need it."

Ginny said, "Con, that's not necessary."

"We don't know what's necessary, so we're going to spread our guns out some. Tige, I'm thinking we should set Woody and Beanpole in the rocks above wherever you set up the Gatling. They can give you cover as well as the rest of us in case we've got to hightail it. Originally, I thought I'd leave all the spare mounts and mules staked out back from the canyon rim, but if we're trying to move fast, we'll be easy pickings trying to head back up that wall like a herd of snails."

"I've been worried some about that. What are you suggesting?"

"That we take all the critters down to the canyon floor, and if we've got a band of Comanche on our trail, we head north along the river." He turned back to Rover. "Need to talk, Rover." When the Kiowa joined them, Con said. "How far north have you been in this canyon?"

"A lot of miles along the east rim, but not far at the bottom. You're thinking about heading back that way?"

"We might need to. Can you get us out of here another way?"

"Sooner or later, probably later. There will be a good number of trails, some fit only for deer or mountain goats, but I'd find something. We'd want to stay to the east side as much as possible. Remember, from a lot of places you can't even see the west side, and with all the twists and turns and small canyons, if you're not careful it's like one of those maze drawings to get out of."

"Eventually, we'd come to one of those mining towns, right?"

"We'd hope to be out of here and on our way home before that happened. We're talking about at least several weeks to do that. Of course, the Comanche wouldn't chase us that far. They aren't wanting trouble with folks down this way, the kind that might bring Mexican soldiers looking for them. They keep kind of an uneasy truce."

Con said, "All the critters and gear go down with us."

Chapter 40

GINNY FOUND HERSELF trembling as the searchers descended into Copper Canyon. She was uncertain whether it was anxiety about finally entering the Wolf's Mouth or the single-file journey on the narrow trail down the canyon's sheer wall where a misstep or stumble ended life for rider and horse. She thought she would rather be shot out of her saddle than plummet like a wounded bird through the air on a long journey to the canyon floor.

Rover, as usual, led the riders, now followed by Ezra. She trailed Grandpa, and Con, leading his white mule Chester, remained within talking distance behind her, not that it mattered much because the almost hour's journey was made in dead silence. She suspected there were others who did not enjoy their ride so much either.

When everyone arrived on the canyon floor, Ginny cast her eyes about, thinking she felt like a tiny field mouse within the immensity of the towering canyon walls and the vast space surrounding them. Tige was already searching out a position for the Gatling and apparently found it as he and Irish commenced relieving the pack mule of its burden. Woody and Beanpole, after staking out their horses and the spares, were walking along the canyon wall's base seeking perches they might occupy later.

Rover said, "We can ride our horses across the river and until we get to the Wolf's Mouth wall. Then we'll have to stake them out and walk up the trail. We don't want the critters trapped in the village."

Ginny said, "How deep is the river?"

"It won't reach your stirrups this time of year. A month or two back, it would have been over the banks with melting snow from the mountains."

An hour later, Angry Wolf's visitors had crossed the river and were nearing the base of the outer wall of Wolf's Mouth Canyon. Ginny and Con rode side by side as they approached. Con said, "I still don't like sending you into that canyon without me."

"Damn it, Con, we've been through this. You're running this outfit, and you've got to be where you can give orders to Tige and his bunch. Somebody's got to be ready in case things go sour, and we're forced to make a quick escape. If I could speak Comanche, I'd go in there alone."

"You'd have to take Ezra. The last few days, you've hardly been out of his sight."

"Grandpa doesn't feel right about all this, and that scares me some."

"He just loves you, Ginny. You are the only family he's had since he lost his wife and children so many years ago."

"I'm proud to have him claim me as family. My sisters will join that family—and you, as my husband. We won't let him be alone again."

"Unless that's what he chooses."

They dismounted near the trail's beginning and staked the mounts out in the lush grass. They would be content here, Ginny thought. They all hiked up the trail that took over a half hour since they were slowed by Ezra's limp and shortness of breath. Twice, she had seen warriors peering down at them from high in the rocks. The appearance of the strangers would certainly be no surprise.

They stepped onto a stone shelf where the path expanded to over twice its usual width. "This is the opening to the Wolf's Mouth," Rover said, pointing to a jagged opening in the recessed wall that looked like it might be a bear's den. "We will walk through what you might call the wolf's throat. It won't take but a minute or two, and there will be a sliver of sunlight creep in from the top that will provide dim light. Our visit has been announced. Don't be surprised if there is a large greeting party. I doubt if there is any danger—yet."

Ginny said, "I guess it's time to let go of our guns."

"Don't like it," Ezra said. "I feel plumb naked without them. I'd sure like to sneak my Peacemaker in there, but I know them Comanches wouldn't take that kindly and would have it out of my hands faster than a fart."

Con said, "I'll have your guns ready as soon as you get spat out of the Wolf's Mouth." He stepped over to Ginny and took her in his arms, brushing his lips against her ear and whispering, "I love you, Ginny. Promise you'll get back to me."

Her lips found his, and they shared a kiss that turned the heads of their companions away. "I promise." She hoped this was one she could keep.

The three headed into the mouth and through the wolf's throat. As Rover had promised, there was ample room and sufficient light to go effortlessly through the passageway. When they stepped out onto the flatland that stretched as far as she could see, they were met by a crowd of Comanche, mostly warriors but a sprinkling of women and even a few children. They were not greeted by smiles, however. Frowns were set on their faces, eyes glaring with contempt and hate. She had a feeling that it only took a word from the right person, and these people would overwhelm the visitors, strike and beat them into the earth and then dismember what remained of their bodies What had they walked into?

One of the taller warriors stepped forward from the group. From his calm and almost regal bearing, she knew he was a leader, but this man was not Angry Wolf. She would never forget the war chief's face. First, he turned and spoke to the gathering behind him. She could not understand a word, but from the tone of his voice, she assumed he was speaking sternly. The mass began to break up, and singly and in small groups walked slowly away, leaving behind only a dozen or so armed warriors scattered about but watching for signs from the leader. All were armed with shiny rifles, either recently stolen or delivered by Comancheros, she supposed.

The leader faced them now and spoke in Comanche. She looked at Rover. Continuing to meet the leader's eyes, he said, "This man's Comanche name translates to Coyote Foot. You will see a coyote's foot dangling from a leather thong on his neck. He claims he is one of the great warriors and leaders of his people, responsible directly to Angry Wolf. He asks why we come here."

“But he knows.”

“Yes, but we must play his game.”

“Well, just tell him we come to bargain for release of my sisters and wish to speak to Angry Wolf.”

Rover began speaking in the Comanche tongue, and Coyote Foot looked bored and disinterested. When Rover finished, the Comanche replied, turned and walked away.

Ginny said, “What did he say? Where is he going?”

“He says he will try to convince Angry Wolf to see us. This is part of the game we are playing. Angry Wolf will see us out of curiosity if nothing else.”

Ezra said, “I don’t like this game a dang bit. We’re up against a stacked deck anyhow, and I don’t like the feeling I’m getting. I just wish we could grab those little gals and run.”

Ginny said, “I don’t know how we’d run, Grandpa, with these warriors standing around just waiting for an excuse to take us down and collect our scalps.”

“Didn’t say we could, just wished.”

It was nearly an hour before Coyote Foot returned. He spoke again at some length. Ginny thought he must be impressed with the sound of his own voice.

Rover said, “We are to follow him. He will take us to Angry Wolf.”

They followed Coyote Foot across the near end of the plateau, the warriors splitting up and walking in lines some ten paces distant on each side. She could not believe the expanse that the village covered and the tipis and mud huts that dotted the landscape. Many of the lodges were in clusters, and she wondered if those represented family units of some sort.

Finally, they came to a cluster of four tipis, and Coyote Foot signaled the warriors to stay back, and they scattered but did not depart the area. When Ginny and her companions stepped into the tipi cluster, Coyote Foot separated and went to a tipi at the far end that was painted with many symbols, including the image of a wolf's head. Out of the corner of her eye she saw that Rover barely noticed the tipi. His eyes were fastened on those of a young Indian woman who was gazing back at him. She was off to one side of the tipi farthest away from what was obviously the chief's tipi. She was moving her hands and fingers in strange motions. Sign language? Rover would nod and look around before responding. She now had no doubt a conversation was taking place.

Then she noticed some cloth that was slung over the young woman's shoulder. Oh, my God. It was Krista's dress, the one she was wearing the day she was taken. Ginny was shaken for a moment, but she collected herself quickly when the flap was pulled back from the tipi, and Coyote Foot waved them forward.

They stepped into the tipi, and suddenly she was face to face with Angry Wolf, who sat on a buffalo robe in the center of the tipi. She would have recognized him without the scar that furrowed its way through the flesh about his eye and down his cheek. She had somehow memorized every feature on the Comanche's fierce face, and her hate blossomed anew.

He was glaring at her, and she could see that the hate was mutual, but she wondered if it was her imagination that she also discovered a hint of fear in his eyes. He said something in Comanche to Coyote Foot, who in turn spoke to Rover.

"We are to sit on the blanket in front of the chief," Rover said.

The three sat down with Ginny in the middle. She faced Angry Wolf directly now, separated by no more than six feet. His eyes bored into hers, and she suspected he was trying to force her own gaze away. To hell with him. If he wanted a stare down, she would give it to him. They exchanged glare for glare before he spoke, again in Comanche to Coyote Foot. Rover did not wait for the sub-chief to relay the message. Good, Ginny thought. This was getting silly. If Angry Wolf was not going to speak

English, at least the son-of-a-bitch could speak directly to Rover.

Rover said, "He wants you to stand up and lift your shirt so that he might see the scars from your wounds."

"Why not? But that's all the sick bastard is going to see." The chief jerked his head back and his eyes widened for a moment at the insult.

Good. She wasn't going to get anywhere with this man by trying to play nice. She stood, lifted her shirt just high enough to see the wounds, then turned and let him view the backside. She sat down and said, "Now let's get down to business. You speak English. I am here to bargain for my sisters. Let's quit pretending you cannot speak directly with me."

"Chiefs do not speak to enemy women." At least he was speaking English now.

"I think you made that up. You are afraid of my powers." Her statement was a gamble, but what did she have to lose?

"Ha. Why should I fear your powers?"

"Because you killed me, and my God sent angels to restore my life. He sent me to bring my sisters home. If you defy me, you defy Him, and many in your village will suffer and die."

"You speak foolishness, and you are not treating me with the respect due a chief."

"Respect? For someone who tortures and kills women and children and steals some away from their homes? For a man who attacks those who have never sought to harm him? Piss on your respect."

Ezra nudged her gently, apparently suggesting she should calm herself. Angry Wolf was taken aback at her assault. Obviously, he expected her to exhibit fear in his presence. Well, she was afraid, but she had decided that to reveal it would get her nowhere with this ruthless killer.

After a prolonged silence, Angry Wolf said, "What makes you think we hold these girls you call sisters?"

At first, she thought to mention the admissions of the captured scouts, but then she decided to continue playing the God card. "Because my God told me they are here, and He does not lie."

"Then why does he just not take these girls from us and return them to you?"

"He has sent me to do that for him along with His angels and others He selected to carry out this mission. I am told that your gods also act through their believers."

"But you are willing to bargain? Why would you need to do this if your God has such power?"

"Because He is a God of peace and mercy. He does not wish to hurt or kill others if it is unnecessary."

"I was told that you have gold. How much gold will you pay?"

"Do you understand the money used by my people?"

"I do. I often talk money with the Comancheros."

Ginny said, "I will pay a ransom of five hundred dollars in American gold coins for each of my sisters. One thousand dollars total."

"Ha. You think I am a fool. The Mexican whorehouses will pay more than that."

"How much do you want?"

"Two thousand for each. Four thousand total."

With what Grandpa and Con said they would make available, she could raise almost six thousand dollars in gold coins, mostly in the twenty-dollar double eagles, but she wanted to pay this from her funds which would amount to a bit over thirty-five hundred dollars. "I do not have that much money."

"Have your God make you more."

She ignored his remark but conceded he had scored a point. "I will double my previous offer. Two thousand dollars."

"Three thousand dollars, and I will consider the bargain made."

"Very well. Three thousand dollars."

"But I must see this gold first."

"You will see it when the exchange is made. I will deliver the gold to you when you surrender my sisters to me. And not in this village. It will be outside the Wolf's Mouth within range of the guns of my people and within range of yours. I will deliver the money, and you will personally bring me the girls."

"I do not like this."

"Why not? Simultaneous exchange. It is the fair way to do it. The exchange can be made tomorrow, but I would like to see my sisters before I leave today."

"No. I cannot see the money, so you cannot see your sisters until the exchange is made. I must think on this overnight. There are others I must speak with. You and your angels or whatever you call these men will stay in our village tonight. A tipi is already set aside for you. Coyote Foot will take you there. Our women will bring you food and water. We will meet in the morning, and I will give you my decision. If I agree, we shall agree upon how the exchange will be carried out."

"And if you don't agree?"

He shrugged.

Chapter 41

ROVER HAD A bad feeling as they ate slices of venison and corn mash with their fingers. It was nearly dusk, but they had not yet had an opportunity to discuss the bargaining session with Angry Wolf. They were in the tipi now but apparently would be denied a fire. A blanket had been provided for each, however. The tipi was set off from the others, and Rover suspected it was one of those set aside for a woman's retreat when she experienced her menses. Many bands had such practices.

"Well," Ginny said, "what do you think about our meeting with Angry Wolf? Do you think my brashness will cause a problem?"

Rover said, "No. If you had done otherwise, it likely would have been the end for all of us. You left him uncertain. He is worried about your possible power. He doesn't quite believe in it, but he fears the result if he should be wrong. You are seen as a threat, but he is afraid of the possible consequences of doing you harm."

Ezra said, "Can't trust anything he says anyhow. Nobody's safe till we get out of here with them little gals and get ourselves back in Texas. Maybe not even then. I'd like to see that no-good kilt before we're on our way."

Ginny said, "Rover, were you signing with a young woman near the tipis?"

"Yeah. She was very adept at our Indian sign language."

"And, of course, you are, too."

"In all modesty, I must say so. Roaming to the different bands and tribes as I once did, it was very useful."

"Well, what was she saying?"

"First, to beware, but we know that. She is Angry Wolf's third wife, and she has been caring for your sisters. She is not Comanche, which I suspected. I think she is likely of Spanish descent. She is also a captive."

"But why did she start a conversation with you? It had to be risky."

"She says it is urgent that she speak with me. Your sisters are no longer in her lodge, but they are in the village, and she knows where. She also wants to go with us."

"I would like to help her, but I don't know how we can. Angry Wolf would not let us bargain for his wife. Anyway, how would you ever talk to her?"

"There is a big tree, I think a pine from the form she made with her fingers. I am to walk along the west canyon wall until I find it. If she is not there, she will be very late."

"What if it is a trap?"

"I think not."

"She was a pretty thing, not more than sixteen I would guess."

"I noticed."

"I'll bet you did. Just don't let your eyes cloud your brain. You're going to try to meet her, aren't you?"

"Yes."

"There will be at least one guard watching our tipi, maybe two."

"I can slip under the tipi wall in back. It might help, though, if you would go out some distance and water the earth at that time."

"You want me to piss in front of those warriors?"

"There is no avoiding it anyway unless you have a way of emptying your bladder that other people do not."

"Alright, but I would have no way of knowing when you return."

"I will think of something."

It was after midnight when Ginny provided her distraction and Rover slipped away. Shirtless and already wearing moccasins, with a kerchief wrapped around his head, he hoped he would attract no attention if he happened to be seen. All was quiet on the plateau, and most in the village were sleeping by now.

Walking along the canyon wall, he quickly found the tree. He saw no sign of the young woman until she stepped away from the tree trunk. She obviously was not a woman sheltered from outdoor life. Of course, that would be true of most western woman.

She came up to him and said, "Thank heaven, you came. I wasn't completely certain we understood each other. I just arrived. I had to be certain I would not be summoned to Angry Wolf's tipi. Thankfully, he is too busy tonight to command the appearance of any of his wives."

"My name is Angus McKay, but most call me Rover. My blood is Kiowa. My heart is Scottish. It is very complicated. That story is for another time maybe."

"I am Ana Vasquez. I am Tejano. Texan since my birth. My Mexican grandfather stood by Texas during the revolution that obtained our independence from Mexico. My father and mother were murdered by Angry Wolf. I am his unwilling wife and am called Hissing Cat among his people. I will kill him given the chance, and he fears this. He will probably sell me to a whorehouse soon, but I will escape from there if I do not escape from this place first. But you came for Noreen and Krista."

"Yes. What can you tell me?"

"First you must know that Angry Wolf is planning to kill all of you. I crept near his tipi and heard him talking to the warriors and the shaman, Moon Walker. You have met Coyote Foot. He has no mind of his own. He favors whatever Angry Wolf wants. Two other warriors in the tipi support whatever Coyote Foot does. That is how they gain power, just like some of our American politicians."

"You just heard this tonight?"

"No. That is why I signed to you. I have heard them talk like this ever since they learned you all were coming to the Wolf's Mouth. Only Moon Walker opposes. His dreams warn that this could be dangerous for the band. He believes Angry Wolf should accept the ransom, release the girls and let you go in peace. Angry Wolf says they will collect more than the gold offered, and all your horses as well, when you are dead. The girls will die, also, because they carry the warrior woman's blood. I heard that tonight, and this is what I feared."

"Somehow we've got to find the girls and leave."

"I know where the girls are at, and I will bring them to you. Will you take me with you? That is not a condition for my help, but my death is certain if I free the girls. They are held by a hateful woman, and I will be forced to kill her."

"You can do this?"

"I have a skinning knife with me that has been hidden away in my tipi. The blade was originally intended for Angry Wolf."

It occurred to Rover that he was encountering the two most cold-blooded women he had ever met on this journey, and this one, hardly more than a girl, was like a sorceress, captivating him and gently surrounding him with her magic. He was her slave. He had never, never felt this way about a female, and in a way, it frightened him.

"You are quiet," she said, her voice just above a whisper.

"Just thinking. Everything is happening so quickly."

"I know where you are staying. There is a tree line that stretches for some distance near there that will help me move the girls without our being seen. My only concern is that there could be a guard near the woman's tipi."

There was no time to consult with his companions. A decision must be made now. "If you loan me your knife, I will go with you and take care of any guard. I will return the knife and leave the woman to you. I would frighten the girls if they awakened and saw me in the tipi." He did not add that the thought of cutting a woman's throat was abhorrent to him.

"Then we will go now. Come with me. We are lovers taking a walk in the moonlight." She slipped the knife hilt into his hand, and he shoved it behind his belt. Ana then took his hand and led him away, moving quickly. Ten minutes later, they approached the tipi, and Rover spied the guard some distance from the tipi, a rifle cradled in his arms and a cartridge belt resting on his shoulder and crossing his chest and back.

Ana said, "Keep walking toward him. I know you speak Comanche. Speak loudly when he sees us and tell me I am beautiful, that you love being with me—anything romantic. He may recognize me, but in the darkness, we will get near, and you must rush him before he can raise his rifle."

Rover found he did not have an original thought when he was speaking to this girl-woman who was obviously wise beyond her years, and he simply repeated the essence of the script she had given him. The guard was looking at them and started to move the rifle into firing position, but Rover was already on him, driving the blade into his gut and ripping it upward. The warrior grunted and collapsed.

Then a woman's voice speaking Comanche asked, "What is the matter? Is there a problem?"

A stocky woman stepped out of the tipi, but Ana had already raced to the opening and pounced on her like a mountain cat, her hands closing around the woman's throat. The woman started choking and toppled over with Ana on top of her with fingers grasping and squeezing like a vise. The Comanche woman's legs and arms flailed, struggling to break free from this wild creature, and then they were still. But Ana did not release her hold.

Finally, she rolled off the woman and stood. "She's dead. Now I will get the girls." She disappeared into the tipi.

Rover waited outside, his eyes searching to see if anyone had heard the disturbance. Fortunately, unlike many Indian villages, the lodges were spread out here, the clustered tipis generally representing family units. He walked over to the dead warrior's body and relieved him of his cartridge belt and a sheathed knife before plucking the new Winchester from off the ground. By that time, Ana had awakened and calmed the girls. From the muffled voices coming from the tipi, he could tell that Noreen and Krista were thrilled to see her.

Ana peered through the tipi opening and stepped out, a frightened girl clutching each hand. He stepped closer now, uncertain what to say.

Ana rescued him. "Girls, this is Rover. He has come with your sister, Ginny, to help her take you home."

The taller girl with long, blonde hair that seemed to gleam even in the moonlight brightened. "Ginny? But she's dead. Is she taking us to heaven?"

Rover said, "Ginny is very much alive, and you will see her very soon. But now we must go quickly and quietly. Ana, you can lead us to the tree line you spoke of. I want you to take the girls directly to the tipi. Ignore whatever the guard says." He handed her the skinning knife, first wiping the blade on his britches to clean off the blood caked there. "Just in case. I have no doubt that you can use it if you are forced to, and I have my own knife now."

"I assume you intend to deal with the guard."

"Oh, yeah. He will have his eyes on you when I come up from behind and cut his throat."

"I'll pick up his weapons before I join you, and we can add to our arsenal."

"We may need them."

Ana led them to the tipi site without incident, and while she and the Harwood girls headed for the tipi, he circled around and came up behind the guard who was stationed some twenty paces beyond the lodge. The guard was focused on ordering the intruders to stop when the knife blade sliced into his neck and instantly silenced him.

When Rover joined the others in the tipi, he found Ginny on her knees with an arm wrapped around each girl, the three joining in a chorus of happy sobbing. Ana stood off to the side, a smile on her face and a few silent tears streaming down her cheeks. She looked at him and nodded approvingly when he placed another Winchester and knife on the blanket. He basked in that little nod, mystified as to why this young woman's approval meant so much to him.

Chapter 42

EZRA STUMPF HAD lost one family years earlier, and when Ginny introduced him to Noreen and Krista, and they both hugged him, his heart nearly melted from the love he had not felt in all those intervening years. He truly felt he had family again, and he vowed that he would allow nothing to happen to this one.

They sat in the tipi trying to plot a strategy. Ana said, "We cannot wait long. If someone finds the bodies, the entire village will be alerted, and the hunt will start."

Ginny said, "Can we get to the entrance without being seen?"

"Probably not. We can only hope we can get far enough to outrun them. And then, we must race fast enough down the trail to outrun the rifle shots that will be coming our way. You said you have one man outside the entrance to the canyon?"

"Yes, I hope he is still there."

"That was a dangerous undertaking on his part. It's possible they have taken him out by now."

"I think we would have heard gunshots if someone tried. He would not surrender easily," Ginny said.

Ana said, "We need a diversion that will draw attention away from the canyon's mouth for a spell."

Ezra reached over and picked up the rifle Rover had dropped on the blanket and began examining it. "Magazine's full of cartridges. Should be at least a dozen. It's a 1873 model Winchester. Nothing but the best for these devils. Just lever one into the chamber and squeeze the trigger. It ain't got the distance of my old Sharps, but it spits the lead out mighty fast."

Ginny said, "You've got something in mind, Grandpa."

"I get to be the diversion."

"I don't like what I'm hearing. Tell me what you are proposing."

"I ain't proposing nothing, Granddaughter. I'm doin' it." He got to his feet. "With my gimpy leg, I'll do nothing but slow you down. Maybe get us all kilt. I ain't going to let my family die here."

"Please, Grandpa, don't do anything foolish."

"I get to decide what's foolish and what ain't, Sweetheart. You get ready to run. When you hear gunfire, shoot out of here like jackrabbits. I'll come along later, I promise. A good luck hug would be nice, though."

He was surprised when all three sisters surrounded him and nearly drowned him with hugs and kisses. Even the pretty Mexican gal stepped forward with an embrace that was as close to a bear hug as he had ever gotten from a female.

Rover stepped outside with him and shook his hand with a firm grip. "You're going wolf hunting, aren't you?"

"Damn right. You just get all them girls out of here safe. You hear? Safe."

"I hear, and I understand. I'll never forget you, Ezra Stumpf."

With his rifle clutched in his hand, Ezra hobbled away on a beeline toward his destination.

Chapter 43

BACK IN THE tipi, Ana took charge. "At the first gunshot, you should head for the east canyon wall. Run as fast as you can and then follow the wall north. It will take you to the throat of the Wolf's Mouth. Because of rockslides, there is more cover along that wall, and for the same reason, tipis and lodges aren't nearby. You likely won't run into trouble till you get sighted by guards near the mouth."

Ginny said. "Just a minute. You sound like you aren't going."

"I am, but I've got to see what Ezra is up to. I at least know my way around the plateau. I may be able to help him out of here. I'm hoping we both meet up with you before the night is finished. Your job is to get our girls out of here."

Rover said, "You do know where Ezra was headed?"

'No, do you?"

"He was going to visit Angry Wolf."

"Oh, Lord. I wish I had another Winchester."

"Take mine," Rover said.

"You're going to defend these girls with your damned knife?" She wheeled and rushed outside, knowing she could not handle emotional good-byes. Besides, she was determined not to die in this hellhole they called the Wolf's Mouth, but if that was the way things were meant to be, she would rather die here than live here.

She hurried after Ezra, fearing she would be too late to dissuade him. They could just fire the rifle a half dozen times some distance away to draw attention and then make a run for it. She had made it her business to learn all the nooks and crannies in this evil place. They had a chance. As she approached the tipi cluster where she had lived for nearly a year, she heard a gunshot and then another. She slowed her pace and surveyed the scene.

Ezra was dragging one leg now as he staggered toward Angry Wolf's tipi. The flap opened and the war chief stepped out, apparently to see what the racket was all about. He faced Ezra not more than ten feet in front of him. Ezra's rifle, held waist high, fired, knocking Angry Wolf backwards against the outer tipi wall. It fired at least two more times. She could not tell for certain if there were more shots from his rifle, because the sounds of rifles cracking filled the air as lead rained on poor Ezra.

She turned and raced away, running faster than she ever dreamt she could. Angry Wolf was dead. She could not believe it. And the price had been Ezra's life.

It took her almost a half hour to find the others who were cautiously moving along the craggy walls as she suggested. She dreaded answering the questions she would face. Winded when she caught up with them, she bent over to catch her breath.

Ginny did not allow her to rest. "Ezra?" she said.

"I'm sorry. Truly sorry."

Ginny was silent for a moment before speaking. "It will take some time for me to really believe this."

"Angry Wolf is dead, also. Ezra killed him. I saw it."

Ginny said, "He knew that was the only way his grandchildren would ever be safe."

Rover said, "As word spreads, there will be even more chaos, and thoughts of revenge will appear first. We must keep moving. Our only hope is to make it to the entrance before the stampede comes."

Chapter 44

WHEN CON HEARD the gunfire from inside Wolf's Mouth Canyon, especially in the middle of the night, he knew that the bargaining was ended. His optimism had already expired an hour earlier when two warriors, obviously on the hunt, crept through the wolf's throat and onto the wide ledge outside the mouth where he had remained positioned.

They confirmed he was their quarry when the first man through charged him for a kill with knife upraised. Con dodged the first slash but had taken a cut to his upper left arm on the second thrust as he was driving a fist into the warrior's gut. He slammed the man's jaw with another punch before pushing him over the edge and into Copper Canyon below.

The other fool was struggling with levering a cartridge into his rifle's chamber when Con grabbed his arm and gave him the same treatment. He had figured it was best for other Comanche sentries not to see fellow tribesmen stacked on the ledge below. That was likely irrelevant now, but at least the path was clear. He picked up the rifles his two companions had left behind and carried them through the tunnel which was nearly pitch-black without the small light the sun's rays had provided. That was not all bad if he ended up defending the place, since he and his companions would make poor targets.

He was certain the gunshots from the village meant trouble. For all he knew his friends, including his betrothed, could be dead. He shuddered at the thought and tried to wipe it from his mind as soldiers were sometimes forced to do. He set the rifles down at the end of the tunnel-like entrance and waited.

Looking out on the plateau in the moonlight, he could see shadowy figures running back and forth in confusion. He could hear women wailing, babies crying, and men yelling and screaming frantically. Then he saw movement along the east canyon wall. He watched, and shadowy figures neared. Rifles fired from sentry perches on the walls above, confirming the identity of the people running in his direction along the wall.

Con stepped out, took the time to aim carefully at a Comanche positioned on an outcropping above the canyon floor and squeezed the trigger. His Winchester cracked and the warrior plummeted to the earth before he could take another shot. His own shot had attracted attention and drawn fire his way, but that was fine by Con. He had cover, but his comrades had nothing.

He fired wildly now, mostly for distraction. Another sentry fell from the wall, but he suspected the shot came from one of his friends. He could make them out now. The children were with them and a stranger. A woman. But Ezra was missing. Of course, he could not have maintained the pace of the others and might yet appear. Yet, he could not imagine Ginny abandoning him.

When they neared the opening. Con stepped out and fired as rapidly as he could. He saw that Rover carried a rifle but yelled, "Guns are inside, loaded with a cartridge already in the chamber." Soon Ginny was at his side, rifle at the ready.

She said, "I gave Ana Ezra's rifle. She says she can shoot."

"Ana? Ezra?"

"I'll explain later. Ezra's gone, but he killed Angry Wolf first. You need to know that."

Again, he had to shrug off his emotions. He looked over his shoulder and saw Rover was moving Ana and the two children through the throat, and he was confident they would immediately head down the trail to the horses. They just needed time, or the Comanche would start picking them off the trail. Sunrise was already coming on, and the cover provided by darkness would soon disappear. They had to get out of here and across the river soon or the Comanche would overwhelm them.

"Go," he said. "Help your sisters. I'll cover you as long as possible." He fired a few token shots again to let the gathering crowd know it did not have a free exit through the canyon's mouth.

"No. Listen to me, Mister. Where you go, I will go; where you stay, I will stay. I think it says something like that in the Bible. Anyhow, that's how it's going to be with us from now on. If you don't leave with me, I'm sticking with you like glue."

Con sighed, "Well, damn it then; let's get the hell out of here." He got up and nudged her ahead of him as they started back through the tunnel.

"You don't need to cuss."

"You're one to talk. You cuss more than I do."

"Then maybe we'll both have to clean things up if the girls are going to be around."

They stepped out onto the shelf outside the opening and headed down the trail. The others had a good lead and were nearly halfway down the wall, Con judged. Rover was carrying Krista, and Ana held Noreen's hand as they wound their way down the trail. The sound of gunfire came from above, and he grunted when a slug tore into the back of his upper thigh and sent a surge of pain down his left leg. He swung around and returned fire, but the assailant dodged back into the opening.

"Are you hit?" Ginny asked.

"Not bad. Nothing serious. Keep moving."

Gunfire came again and rocks chipped off the stone wall beside them. Again, when he returned fire, the shooters disappeared. He was hurting now and could feel blood trickling down his leg. The arm of his shirt was already blood-soaked from the knife wound.

Tossing a look over his shoulder, he saw now that Comanche warriors were pouring out of the mouth of the canyon, and several were on the trail following them. To his relief, Rover and the others were almost to the canyon floor. He decided to turn and face the pursuers, take a few with him and buy some time for Ginny. Suddenly, gunfire erupted from the canyon floor below. At least two Comanche tumbled from the trail and dropped over the edge of the wall.

Another wounded warrior was blocking the trail in front of the others temporarily. As the gunfire from below continued, some warriors stopped and began to back up. Con continued down the trail when he saw that Ginny had slowed her pace to allow him to catch up. Dang woman was hanging on like glue just like she said. Looking out over the canyon floor, he saw the source of the gunfire. Beanpole and Woody had moved down from the west wall of Copper Canyon, crossed the river and taken cover behind some rocks. They might just discourage the Comanche long enough to allow the pursued to reach their horses and escape temporarily to the west wall where they would all be united again to make a stand. Tige had doubtless recognized the potential dilemma when he heard gunfire coming from Wolf's Mouth Canyon.

As Con and Ginny neared the canyon floor, he saw that Ana was astride Ezra's gelding with Noreen holding on tight behind her, and Rover was lifting Krista with him as he swung into the saddle. In moments, they were racing west across the river toward Tige's stone fortress.

As Con and Ginny hit the canyon floor, Ginny turned and looked at him. "Oh, my Lord. You're a bloody mess. You need some help."

"Well, we don't have time to stop and doctor wounds right now, Ginny. Let's move. After we've got the horses, we've got to swing by and pick up Beanpole and Woody or they'll be swarmed before they can get back. You take Beanpole. He's the heaviest. I'll get Woody."

The trail was packed now with warriors from the Wolf's Mouth, pushing others to move down the path so they could slaughter the invaders. Shortly, under a rain of lead, the riders were crossing the river. Woody, hanging onto Con's waist, moaned. "I'm hit, Con."

"Where at?"

"Middle of my back. I ain't doing so good. My arms are weak all of a sudden. Don't know if I can hang on."

"Just a few minutes, and we'll be there." With one hand, Con grabbed Woody's wrist as he felt the man's fingers slipping away. They reached the stone barricade the Buffalo Soldiers had put together during their absence and no sooner had Con reined in Quanah than Woody slid off the buckskin and onto the rocky ground. Con dismounted pulled his rifle from its scabbard and slapped his gelding's rump, knowing he wouldn't wander far.

He knelt beside Woody who was eerily still and pressed his fingers to the former soldier's neck and then his wrist, searching frantically for some sign of life. "He's dead," Con hollered to Tige who was positioned at the Gatling with Irish.

Tige yelled back. "The Comanches are coming like an army of ants. You got to get up here."

A wave of dizziness swept over him, and he was only vaguely aware of Ginny screaming at him.

Con got to his feet, suddenly feeling weak, and staggered behind the stone barrier. Only then did he see the Comanche splashing through the river. They could take some down with the rifles now, but he had agreed Tige would give the orders here.

Ginny squeezed in beside him. "I've got the girls lying flat behind some boulders, and Ana is staying with them with her rifle at the ready. I think they prefer her really. Now what about you?"

"I'm fine, but I hate to wait till they're on top of us to fire."

"You're not fine, and Tige knows what he's doing."

The Comanche were coming fast now, and finally Tige yelled, "Fire at will."

Side by side, Ginny and Con propped their rifles on stones and began to fire and lever cartridges into the chambers, but then the Gatling started its rhythmic hammering as Tige maneuvered the gun, and Irish fed the cartridges into the weapon. The Comanche warriors were dropping now, and those who were able began to back away toward the river.

The Gatling continued its clatter as more attackers fell, and the remaining warriors turned around and ran in full retreat. Con judged that as many as twenty dead or wounded warriors were strewn about the rocky flat between the defenders and the river, not counting those who had fallen in the village and during the chase down the trail from Wolf's Mouth Canyon. But two of their own good and brave men had fallen. Ezra and Woody had died for a cause that neither had been forced to sign on for. It bothered him, especially, that if Woody had not been riding behind him, the bullet that took his friend might well have struck his own back.

The dizziness returned, and he leaned back against the boulder, closing his eyes as drowsiness threatened to carry him to sleep. He opened his eyes, however, when he felt something tugging at his shirt. Ginny was bending over him and had already unbuttoned the shirt and was pulling it away from his arms and shoulders. Tige was coming now to assist with a blanket and the medical bag that had been with Chester's load.

Ginny was taking his knife and cutting a strip from his shirt now and tying a tourniquet on his upper arm. He closed his eyes again, unconcerned as to whether it might be his last time. The sun was overhead when he awakened, informing him he had slept for most of the morning despite the nightmares inflicting pain to his wounds. He turned his head when he felt the familiar hand squeeze his own, and his eyes met Ginny's.

She smiled. "About time. You've got work to do around here, bossman."

"You've been here all this time?"

"You've already forgotten what I said up there in the Wolf's Throat?"

"Well, no. But I didn't take it literally."

"Good, because I don't either, but somebody needed to be with you, and I didn't have anything better to do."

He felt the breeze caressing his legs and looked down. "Where's my britches? Damn, I'm near naked except for my undershorts, and my ass hurts like hell."

"My, we do need to clean up our language. The girls aren't far away. Your bloodied undershorts I tossed in the woods for coyotes to suck on. I found a pair with your things that hadn't been worn more than four or five times. I thought of getting you into a pair of mine, but I was out of spares till I launder."

"You changed my drawers for me?"

"I did, and I helped Tige get the slug out of your rear end. You have a very nice ass, incidentally. You might have a little scar, but who am I to criticize. I'm sorry you got wounded, but it gave me a chance to check the merchandise in the daylight. I'll still marry you."

"You're torturing me. Could we separate long enough for you to find me a shirt and britches? You had to see the extras if you were snooping through my things."

"I'll do that. I see Tige coming this way. I'm guessing he wants to talk to you."

Tige knelt beside him. "You're looking better than the last time I seen you, Con."

"I'm feeling better for dang sure. Could you help me scoot my back up against the rock. I don't take to being flat on my back. And thanks for patching me up."

"Well, I don't know what the lady said, but she took the slug from your butt. It's actually your upper thigh, and that's what I'm calling it, but she's sticking with ass-wound. When Ginny was getting the slug out, she told me she was branding you, whatever that meant. I took a few stitches in your arm. We'll need to be changing the dressings on the trail, but I'm afeared riding horseback ain't going to be no fun. Might have to pad things up somehow."

"Do you think we can pull out of here soon? This doesn't seem like a good place to vacation."

"That's what I come to talk about. We've been doctoring the wounded warriors best we could. Now, somebody's crossing the river with four warriors holding a travois betwixt their critters. The feller in front is carrying a white flag. I'm supposing he wants to talk."

"Why don't you get Rover and go out and have a chat? If what they're asking sounds reasonable to you, agree to it."

"Not likely they're wanting to fight no more. If we can work things out, I say we stay overnight and head out in the morning."

"I'm thinking the same thing."

"We'll need to get Woody buried somewhere this afternoon."

Shortly after Tige left to retrieve Rover, Ginny returned and helped him dress even though he insisted he could do it himself. "You're not so shy under the blankets," she said. She had been winning too many of the verbal skirmishes lately. He decided he would be more careful about taking the bait. Her mood had brightened noticeably since the recovery of Noreen and Krista, which was understandable.

Ana and the girls joined them while they watched the parley between the apparent Comanche leader and Tige and Rover. Ana said, "That's Moon Watcher, the shaman. He wanted to exchange the girls for gold and allow you to go in peace. He warned that terrible things would happen if the Comanche band did otherwise. Of course, his warning should have been heeded."

"What do you think will happen to the band now?"

"There is no other leader to unite them. They will split into smaller bands. Many will return to the reservation. Moon Watcher may lead those. I do not see him as a war leader. He will see that there is no future in that."

Con wondered about the travois when the warriors placed it on the ground and rode away with Moon Watcher. It couldn't be, could it?

When Tige and Rover returned, they came directly to Con, and Tige dismounted. "It's over," Tige said. "No more fighting. We can remain as long as we need. The Comanche will be coming soon to remove their dead and wounded."

"The travois?"

He cast a glance at Ginny. "Ezra Stumpf's body is wrapped in a buffalo robe."

Con expected Ginny to burst out in sobs, but once again she surprised him.

"We should bury Grandpa and Woody side by side, here in this beautiful canyon. I will place a marker in his honor in the family cemetery and always carry him in my heart. His life was in the untamed wilderness. His soul would love roaming here, and this place will never be tamed."

Chapter 45

AS THE RIDERS neared the Pecos River, it struck Ginny that they would be in San Angelo in a few days, and she and Con had hardly talked about their future. In fact, after they departed Mexico and crossed the Rio Grande, he had turned strangely silent. She wondered if he was having second thoughts about their marriage and their future together. She would never hold him to his promise. The last thing she needed was a reluctant husband.

She suspected that her mother's life had been like that, only Mama had been the reluctant one, a woman imprisoned by a commitment to a man who did not appreciate her and did not treat her with love and respect. Ginny and Con had enjoyed only occasional intimacy on the journey back when she sneaked away from her sisters in the middle of the night to rendezvous with Con who waited with a blanket at some secluded place where they might share an hour, no more than two. If it was not going to work out between them, they would part at San Angelo. It was time to talk.

That afternoon, when they took a rest on the trail, she approached Ana. They had become close friends since departing Copper Canyon, and she had confided her plans to marry Con with her.

"Ana, I must spend some time with Con before we reach San Angelo. Would you put your bedroll next to the girls tonight? Just tell them I need to be alone for a while. I will try to be back by sunrise."

Ana giggled, "Of course, I can do that. You do know, of course, that you are not fooling anyone. Everybody can see how you and Con feel about each other and I doubt they think you are just shaking hands when you slip away at night. I don't think the girls will be the least worried by your absence. They know you came for them, and you are not going to run off."

Ginny could feel her face flushing and just rolled her eyes. "I guess I won't worry about sunrise."

"One more thing. I have told you that I will be going with Rover to the Diamond M after San Angelo. After that, he will take me to see what is left of my parents' farm and any goats that may have survived all this time. There is no romance between us—not yet—on my part, anyhow, but he insists on helping me. He is a good friend. Only time will tell if there is more. It will be difficult to explain to the girls, but I will keep my promise to see them again someday soon. I just need a few months to decide where I go from here. Before we part in San Angelo, we must share how we can reach each other by mail, so we can find each other someday."

"Just remember, there will be a home for you at Harwood Place, or wherever the girls and I might be, if you are ever looking for one."

Next, she asked Con to find a spot where they might have a private night together when they camped for the night. It pleased her to see the twinkle in his eyes when she made the request, but he seemed suspicious when she told him they needed some serious talking time.

Later, after supper that night, Ginny made no pretense that she and Con were just friends. She did not lay out her bedroll. It was not yet sundown when she picked it up and walked over to Con who was finishing his turn at clean-up. "I assume you found a private place," she said, as others sitting around the fire looked at her.

"Uh, yeah."

"Well, let's go."

He was obviously taken aback, and she loved it. He grabbed his bedroll, and she strolled with him as they went to a hollow in a sandstone bluff some fifty yards from camp.

Ginny said, "Well, we certainly have a private place."

"That's what you asked for. And the floor's all sand. Should be soft."

They combined their separate bedrolls into one and sat down on top. Con said, "If I know Ginny Harwood, she will want to do the talking before the fun stuff."

"Talking to me isn't fun?"

"Sometimes. Not always."

"First, I need to know if you still want to marry me."

He took her hand. "Yes, Ginny, I still want to marry you, and if you have changed your mind, you're sure making a mess. Tige is going to be my best man, and he knows a chaplain at Fort Concho who will do the vows in the middle of the night if need be for a ten-dollar gold piece. We're planning on the day after we get back—in the Fort Concho chapel. He says Juana would be thrilled to host a small reception at their house. Well, I suspect he'll catch the devil about such short notice, but I'm betting Juana comes through."

"You've been making arrangements without consulting me?"

"Well, do you want to take over? I'll step aside."

"No. I don't want to deal with it."

"And Ana will stay in San Angelo with the girls for three days while we find a hotel and honeymoon and see whatever sights there are to see around town. I think she would like to stand up with you, if you ask her. I didn't think I should go that far."

"Ana didn't say you talked to her."

"It was all supposed to be a surprise, and I didn't want to risk giving you a way out."

"But you have been so quiet lately."

"I do that when I'm thinking. For instance, we've never talked about where we're going after San Angelo."

"I'm sorry. It's been selfish of me. I've always assumed I was going to rebuild the ranch and maybe the trading post. I haven't even asked what you wanted."

"I want to be wherever you are. I just want to make a life and stay put someplace. Why not old Harwood Place? Maybe I can learn to be a merchant, and you can run the cattle business. I'm not a bad cowhand either. We can do a lot of things. We'll build our own empire right there along the Canadian River, buy more land, even establish a town, maybe. Whatever we do, we'll be partners."

She leaned over and kissed his cheek. "You are a prize, Con Callaway."

"One thing that's been on my mind involves a visit I made to the lawyer in San Angelo before we left." He told her about his supposed inheritance and the fact that she might have a claim to the property regardless.

He also explained the terms of his will and the fact that he would have deeded the land to her even if they had not married. "We'll visit the lawyer and do whatever it takes to see that we both own the place with a good title and ask about any other legal arrangements we should make while we're in town."

"I don't know what to say. You really have had things on your mind."

"Yeah, and I've never mentioned to you that you own Ezra's critters, Spot and Mort, and whatever else of his we've been dragging with us. I know there is money in those saddlebags of his. I figured it was your place to go through that."

"My head's spinning. We've talked more than I can handle for one night. Why don't we get to the fun stuff?"

About the Author

Ron Schwab is the author of several popular Western series, including *The Blood Hounds, Lockwood, The Coyote Saga*, and *The Lockes*. His novels *Grit* and *Old Dogs* were both awarded the Western Fictioneers Peacemaker Award for Best Western Novel, and *Cut Nose* was a finalist for the Western Writers of America Best Western Historical Novel.

Ron and his wife, Bev, divide their time between their home in Fairbury, Nebraska and their cabin in the Kansas Flint Hills.

For more information about Ron Schwab and his books, you may visit the author's website at www.RonSchwabBooks.com.